TREES
OF
STONE

Thirteen Days of Midnight
Eight Rivers of Shadow
Seven Trees of Stone

TREES OF STONE

LEO HUNT

CANDLEWICK PRESS

First U.S. paperback edition 2019

Library of Congress Catalog Card Number 2017947004
ISBN 978-0-7636-9173-8 (hardcover)
ISBN 978-1-5362-0373-8 (paperback)

18 19 20 21 22 23 BVG 10 9 8 7 6 5 4 3 2 1

Printed in Berryville, VA, U.S.A.

This book was typeset in Palatino.

Candlewick Press
99 Dover Street
Somerville, Massachusetts 02144

visit us at www.candlewick.com

For Flossie

(old year's day)

The end begins on a cold December morning. We're walking through Dunbarrow Park, hands buried in our coat pockets, our breath billowing in clouds. Elza has her scarf over her face like a bank robber. The sky is a delicate unbroken blue, the sun harsh and white and low. The newscasters said this was the coldest winter in fifty years, a crisp, breathless cold, where stepping out of your front door feels like jumping into a frozen bath. The grass and path and park benches are ice coated, crystallized; the bare branches of the trees glitter with frost like someone sprinkled them with sugar. The Brackrun River has been frozen for weeks. We're in the post-Christmas days, when everyone's house is full of leftovers and presents. Cake for lunch, shimmering ornaments still hanging from every hook. The lazy limbo as the year winds itself down.

Given the temperature out here, I'd have taken the bus up to my house, but Elza liked the light for photos, so here we are. I have to admit, now that we've worked up some body heat from walking, it is really beautiful. The frosted earth shimmers where the new sun hits it, like the light is turning solid. There's no wind and nobody else around, no sound but our footsteps and breath. We could be the last two living souls. We stroll down toward the river, past the bandstand, and as we round the corner, Elza catches my arm.

"Look," she says softly.

There's a swan standing on the path: elegant white neck and head, tipped with a flaring orange bill; rubbery black feet that look like something you'd buy in a joke shop, a mismatch with its regal body. It's almost dazzling white in the morning sun. Without fear the swan watches us approaching and lets us get close enough that I could reach out and touch it.

Elza kneels down and unscrews the lens cap from her camera, raises the viewfinder to her right eye. The bird obliges her with a pose, neck curving like a ship's prow, and once Elza has taken a few shots, it ruffles its wings and stalks off toward the river.

"Let's follow it," Elza says, taking my left hand. The empty finger of my glove bends back at a weird angle. I'm starting not to notice so much, but it can look pretty odd sometimes. The swan doesn't move that fast and we amble after it, and I'm thinking maybe we'll walk over the bridge and get up to my house through town, take the long route since the day's turning out so beautiful, but when we get to the bank of the river, we both stop dead.

For a moment my thought is that it has snowed but the snow only fell on the river, except of course that makes no sense. Then again, what's actually happened to the river makes no sense either, because it's covered in swans.

The frozen river is heaving with the birds. They don't squabble or squawk; they just move slowly, aimlessly, pushing against one another, a crowd that has forgotten what they're supposed to be crowding around. They're so densely packed, we can't see the river's surface. There must be hundreds, thousands of them. It looks like an art exhibit.

"What on earth?" Elza whispers.

"I have no idea," I say. "It's like a flash mob or something."

The first swan, our swan, is looking back at us from the side of the river. Slowly, the bird makes it way down the muddy bank and joins the rest of them, walking on the ice.

"This is so weird," Elza says, and she takes her camera out again and starts snapping. The birds don't pay us any attention. I walk slowly alongside the river, toward the footbridge. They're totally silent, sticking only to the ice, never venturing back up onto the banks. They don't seem to be walking in any specific direction, and if there's a purpose to their movements, it's too subtle for me to see it. I reach the bridge and wait there for Elza, who's moving even slower than I am, viewfinder glued to her eye.

"These are going to come out amazing," she says when she catches up to me. "You couldn't ask for a better scene than this. People will think I faked it."

"How many swans do you usually see in one place?" I ask her.

"I don't know," she says. "Two? Three?"

As we watch, another pair of big white birds comes flying in low, from the direction of the town. They land on the opposite side of the river, fold their wings, and make their way down to mingle with their fellows.

"They must be coming from all over," I say.

"Yeah," Elza says, "but why? Have you ever heard of anything like this before? I mean, I know some birds migrate en masse, but swans . . . I don't think so. And why would they all come here? I'll have to ask my dad."

Elza's father is an avid bird-watcher and will know all there is to know about the migration habits of swans.

"This is nuts," I say. "There have to be, like . . . I don't know how many. How far does it go on for? Have they covered the whole river?"

"They can't have. The Brackrun goes for miles and miles."

We decide to find the limits of the swan crowd, and cross the bridge and set out again along the river, this time on the side nearer the town square. We walk for about ten minutes, and the frozen river is still thick with white birds. We can see more arriving every minute, groups of swans flying in from all directions to join the horde. After we walk under the traffic bridge to Wormwood Drive, the birds start to thin out; a ten-minute walk past that and the swans have dwindled down to just a few outliers. They seem to be concentrated within the town limits of Dunbarrow.

We walk back to the traffic bridge in silence and head for the stairs that lead from the low-lying riverside path to the sidewalk. There are some people standing on the bridge, also looking at the swans. They're taking photos with their phones. It occurs to me that this will probably make the news. We climb the stairs to the traffic bridge and find ourselves face-to-face with my old friends.

I didn't recognize them from the riverbank because they've got their hoods up, but I should've known it was them. Before my life changed, I used to be on the rugby team at Dunbarrow High, go to all the right parties, have the right friends. I haven't seen much of them since me and Elza left Dunbarrow High and decided to do our A Levels in Brackford, where nobody knew us. But here they are: Kirk Danknott, Mark Ellsmith, and Mark's girlfriend, Holiday Simmon, who I used to have the biggest crush on.

All of that seems like another life to me now, before Elza and the Host, before my dad and the Book of Eight, before the Shepherd and Ash and Mr. Berkley. Kirk and Mark are wearing tracksuits, bright neon sneakers. They notice us and smile with amused contempt. Kirk looks about the same; Mark's hair is longer, and he seems to be growing a beard. His nose has reset from when the Shepherd broke it. Holiday is wearing pale jeans and a tan parka, glasses with heavy frames. She at least gives us a genuine smile.

"Luke, Elza," Holiday says, "good to see you."

"Yeah." I shrug. The last time I spoke to Holiday was . . . I can't remember when. Was it when I gave her back the *Best of Hannah Montana* DVD we stole from her room in the spring? (Long story.) I think it must've been then. The last time I saw her was after our final exam, in the summer. Everyone signing one another's school shirts. I think me and Elza just snuck off somewhere by ourselves.

"Hey, bird-watchers," Elza says.

Kirk snorts.

"It's so weird," Holiday says, gesturing to the river crammed with swans. "Have you ever seen anything like this?"

Obviously nobody has. Mark has his arm curled protectively around Holiday's waist.

"*They* probably did it," Kirk says. "The spooky kids."

"We did what, Kirk?" Elza asks him. "Invited a bunch of swans to Dunbarrow? How do you think we did that? Some kind of swan mailing list?"

Kirk scowls at this.

Kirk stumbled across us summoning a demon last Easter, which didn't end too well for him. Ash, a teenage necromancer with a unique fashion sense and a sideline in altering people's memories, erased his recollections of the event, but I think something from that evening stuck all the same.

"Why would we have anything to do with this?" Elza presses.

"Because you're messed up in the head," Kirk says. He spits on the ground by her boots. "Voodoo child."

"Elza—" I begin, but Holiday's already pulling Mark away from us.

"Nice to see you again," she says brightly. "Come on, Kirk."

Holiday's defusing techniques aren't subtle, but they seem to work well enough.

"Yeah, leave it, man," Mark says. "She's not worth it."

Kirk glares at us, and then he leans in toward me and says in a low voice, "You wanna go? You know where to find me."

"OK," I say. "If I want a fight, I'll head right over. Thanks. Good to know."

Kirk spits on the ground in front of my shoes as well. After this, he turns away and follows Holiday and Mark. We're left on the cold bridge, swans milling aimlessly below. My old friends' backs recede away into the distance. I squeeze Elza's hand. She's shaking with anger.

"How can he just—You let him—"

"He didn't spit *on* us," I say. "That's a start, right?"

"That idiot drives me insane," she says. "I don't know how you were ever friends."

"I don't know, Elza. He's not always like that. He can be a good guy . . ."

Elza snorts. "God, that got me so wound up! I really want to smoke."

She unwraps a stick of spearmint gum and starts chewing it ferociously.

"How long's it been now?"

"One month, two weeks, five days, nine hours. Not sure how many minutes—I'm trying not to count them."

"You're doing well," I tell her.

She winds her hair around her finger. "I feel good," she says. "When I walked from the bus station to my house, I barely felt out of breath. That's new to me."

My ex-friends have vanished around the corner. We're alone again. Another swan swoops down and lands in the mud by the side of the frozen river.

"How are you doing with the book I lent you?" Elza asks, looping her arm with mine. We start to walk again, leaving the river behind.

"All right. They shouldn't trust those pigs, if you ask me. Especially Napoleon."

She laughs. "You have no idea."

The winter sunlight is just as beautiful on the frosted plants as it was before, but as we walk up the hill toward my house, I'm struck with a strange dread. Something about the swans has gotten to me, even as we joke and talk about other things. I feel like we're slipping between the cracks again, moving from the world that makes sense into the other world that lies just beneath it. The sun shines on us, but I can't feel its warmth.

At the top of the hill, where my road starts, I see something white lying in the path, and I know what it is before we're even close enough to make out its shape.

The swan is curled on the frosted ground, graceful even in death. I stop to look more closely at the body. I can't see any clear injuries, but there's a small flush of crimson next to the swan's head.

"Do you think something's happening?" Elza asks me.

"What do you mean?" I ask, even though I know what she means.

"Something . . . I don't know. Magic, I suppose," Elza says. "I can feel something. Like a sound you can't really hear, but you can feel it shaking your bones. You know?"

"Yeah," I say. "I can feel it too."

There's a fragility to the day, a sense that the ground we're walking on is ice that's starting to break. There's something bad in the air you can taste, like smoke. The frost crystals that appeared so beautiful earlier now seem gaudy and brittle.

"Maybe it's nothing," Elza says. "It got hit by a car, probably. They're just birds."

I look at the dead swan's head, the glassy open eye, black and bottomless.

"Yeah," I say. "Maybe it's nothing."

My name is Luke Manchett, and I'm seventeen years old. I have nine fingers, nine magic rings, and one ancient book of unspeakable secrets, and eleven GCSE exams that I passed at grade C or higher. I've been going to Brackford College since September, taking math, psychology, physics, and sociology. In my spare time I've been trying to find ways to escape the debt that I owe to one of the most powerful and evil spirits in the afterlife. My girlfriend, Elza Moss, goes to Brackford as well and is descended from Lilith (first witch, semi-mythic). I used to have a pretty normal life, not that you'd believe that now.

I unlock the front door of my house and brace myself

for a giant dog to fling himself at me. Nothing happens. He's been dead for months now, and I still can't stop imagining that Ham's going to show up again. The hallway feels empty without him. I pull off my shoes and wait for Elza to untie her army boots. I'm still thinking about the swans, wondering what they mean. It could just be that we're freaking out over something that has nothing to do with us. That's one of the problems with magic—it makes you think like a lunatic, trying to see patterns in things that might not contain any. Sometimes I'll think I saw a sigil mark in the clouds, a magic circle forming in the ripples on a pond. Sometimes I know I'm imagining it, and other times I know that I'm seeing what's really there.

Bea rushes full tilt in from the laundry room and starts barking.

"Hey, it's just us," I say. "Bea, c'mon."

Bea barks louder, retreating backward into the living room. It's not that Bea and me don't get along, exactly. But she's only lived here a couple of months, and I don't think we're that sure about each other yet. We got her from a rescue group, and she's an angry dog.

"How are you, love?" Mum asks from the living room, above Bea's racket.

"All right! Elza's here," I reply.

"Oh, wonderful. Darren was about to start cooking."

Great.

"I thought we were going to his place later?" I ask, coming into the living room.

"Just dropped by," Darren says. "How's things, mate?"

"Yeah, great. Mate," I say.

"Cool, cool," Darren says. He's spread-eagled on our sofa, with Mum's head resting on his shoulder. "We're just having a mellow morning. Gonna get some lentils going in a bit."

"Can't wait," I reply.

Mum met Darren Hart in the summer at some kind of conference on meditation. He literally lives in the woods, in what I can only describe as a compound of wooden huts and tents. He has a single dreadlock that goes halfway down his back, and he makes his money from selling large-scale sculptures that he carves with a chain saw. He's really into circus tricks.

"Hi, Persephone. Hi, Darren," Elza says, resting her hand against my back.

"All right, Elza," Darren says. Mum smiles sleepily. Bea is standing on the sofa beside Mum, hackles still raised, ready to start barking at a moment's notice if I make any sudden moves. She's like Mum's bodyguard, I swear. I think Bea is at least half border collie, but it's difficult to be sure. She's small and sleek, black furred except for some white specks around her nose, and one white foot, like she's wearing a single athletic sock. Mum gently strokes

Bea's shoulders with her free hand. I know it's unfair, but I can't help missing how calm Ham was by comparison, how easy to get along with.

"All ready for tonight?" Darren asks when neither of us says anything.

"Absolutely," I reply.

"It's gonna be great," he says. "Fire pit, veggie burgers, got the slackline set up."

"Luke can't stop talking about it," Elza says.

This is true, in much the same way condemned men can't stop talking about their upcoming executions. Darren's eyes light up.

"Wow, amazing, man," he says. "I'm stoked on you dudes coming up to my place."

As often happens, me and Elza have now run out of things to say to Darren. We've been in the same room maybe two minutes. He and Mum smile at us.

"We're going, uh, upstairs," I say, gesturing toward my bedroom, as if they might be confused about where it was.

"All right, love," Mum says. "We'll call you when lunch is ready."

Me and Elza make our way to my room, which, unlike me, hasn't changed much over the past few years. There are still clothes on the floor, a beanbag chair, my TV, school-work on the desk. There's the same photos Elza took taped to my closet door, the same cereal bowls with dried milk in the bottom of them. I sit down on the beanbag.

"I'm stoked on you dudes coming up to my place," I say in my Darren voice.

"You're really mean to him," Elza says with a smile.

"I can see you're trying not to laugh."

"I didn't say it wasn't funny. But you are mean. He tries."

"He tries extremely hard."

"He's just nervous around you," Elza says. "He really likes Persephone. He wants it to work out."

"I know, Elza. I just . . . like, how would you feel if your dad left and then Darren moved in? Like, you come downstairs one day, and Darren's sitting there instead, going like, *Oh, dudes, can't wait to get some lentils going*? Looking at his weird little dreadlock rattail thing every day?"

"Well, I wouldn't be thrilled," Elza says, sitting down next to me. "I can't deny that. But your dad didn't just disappear yesterday, Luke. He's been gone more than ten years."

"Yeah," I say. It's hardly like they were a happy ten years for Mum either. She was a mess. I know I should be glad she's met someone again. It's just when I see her sitting there watching TV with Darren, and Bea curled up next to both of them, I feel like there's less room on the sofa for me. And I'm glad she met someone, but Darren . . .

"He's just such a weird loser," I say after a while. "Remember that, like, half-hour monologue on how water has a memory? Like, it remembers what you put in it? And then you asked him if water has a memory of being dinosaur piss, and he didn't know what to say?"

"Yeah, that's homeopathy," Elza says. "Your mum's into that stuff, too, though."

"I know. It's just not annoying when she talks about it."

"He does have a lot of strange ideas."

The thing is, Elza's not wrong about Mum having weird ideas. She's into crystal healing, books about ancient astronauts, Reiki, and ear candling, to give just a few examples. My dad, my real dad, had some strange ideas, too. He had a TV show where he exorcised haunted houses. The thing about my dad was that his weird ideas, unlike Darren's, were true. There really are ghosts, and Dad kept eight of them as his servants. When he died, I inherited them, along with his book of magic and his sigil ring. That was more than a year ago now, last Halloween. The ghosts nearly broke free, and I had to make a deal with the Devil to stop them.

"So where were we?" Elza asks, pulling out her books.

"I don't know," I say. "Who cares?"

"Luke."

"I'm joking! Ha-ha. Funny. Of course, I care. What's on the menu this week?"

"Well, we've got *Satan: A Semiotic History.* And *Performative Gender in Dante's 'Inferno.'* "

"Elza . . ." I look at the library books. Their plastic laminated jackets are pristine. She's clearly the only person who's ever borrowed them.

"I'm running out of stuff in the Dunbarrow Library," she admits.

"Do you really think these are going to help us?" I flip through *Satan: A Semiotic History.* I can't understand a single sentence in any one of the seven hundred pages. Over the past eight months, we've been trawling through everything ever written about the Devil. We've done *Paradise Lost, Faust,* the *Inferno.* Elza even read most of the Bible. We've suffered through weird websites and blogs about modern Satanism, which Elza says isn't really proper Devil-worship at all, and it's closer to Objectivism (whatever that means). Unsurprisingly, none of it matches up remotely with the Devil I know. He isn't red, he doesn't have horns, doesn't speak in verse, and I don't think he was ever an angel. The lurid, sailor-tattoo Devil you're thinking of has nothing on Mr. Berkley. He looks like a tanned, handsome lawyer, with a smile that's a little bit too white. And then, once, I think I saw what was underneath that mask. It was bottomless darkness.

"I suppose we could start on the university library next," Elza's saying, flipping through *Performative Gender* with a scowl. "Brackford might have something we haven't—"

"We've got the book we need," I say, for the hundredth time.

Elza's scowl deepens.

"You know exactly what I think of *that*," she says.

The book I'm talking about is in a metal toolbox, buried under old clothes at the back of my closet. It's the Book of Eight, the powerful magic book I inherited from my dad. It contains the spells you need to bind the dead, open the gateways into their world, and lots more. I've only used it twice, and each time it ate into my mind, replacing my normal thoughts with whatever's written inside the Book. The first time I read it, I was immobile for three whole days, and I can't remember anything about where that time went. Elza thought I might be dying. Ever since then, she's understandably not keen for me to read the Book again.

"You know I don't want to look at it either," I say. "But we don't have many options."

"Luke, come on. How many times have we gone through this? Berkley gave you the Book of Eight himself. He's given it to you three times now. Why would he give you the thing that tells us what his weakness is?"

"He wouldn't," I say. I know that. Elza's right. I still want to look in the Book, though, if just to check. To make sure. Sometimes I take it out and think about opening it, at night, when nobody else is around. I'll sit there with the Book of Eight held in my lap, imagine putting my sigil ring on, opening the Book up, letting the words flow into me. Sometimes I think about what Ash told me, that my mind was part of the Book now, and the Book itself is a lake of stars and darkness. If someone cut into my head with a knife, I wonder what they'd find. Whether night sky would be looking back at them where my brain used to be. When I close my eyes sometimes, I almost feel like I can taste the stars.

"Luke."

"What?" I say. I had my eyes shut without realizing it. Elza looks worried.

"You just drifted off," she says. "Are you feeling all right?"

"Yeah," I say, flashing what I hope is a convincing smile. The truth is I don't feel that great. I keep thinking about the dead swan. I keep thinking something terrible is happening, but we just can't see what it is.

The last afternoon of the year passes uneventfully. We eat Darren's lentil stew, which I have to admit is pretty good. Even Elza can't read the books she borrowed for more than a few minutes without getting a headache. They seem like the kind of books that were written by the author only for themselves. In the end we give up and watch a movie.

At eight we get into Mum's yellow car and drive off to Darren's place, leaving Bea shut in the laundry room. Ham used to batter the door with his body if he thought I was trying to leave home without him, but Bea just settles down without a second thought, tucking her legs under herself and folding her ears over her eyes.

As the car moves down the hill, away from Wormwood Drive, I find myself straining in my seat, trying to see if I can catch a glimpse of the frozen river through the trees. I want to see if the swans are still there. Elza's looking, too. I can't see any birds, and when we cross the bridge over the frozen river, there's not even a sign of a single white feather. They've vanished. I can't tell if that makes me feel more nervous, or less.

We drive through the center of Dunbarrow, the town square already filling up with people ready to celebrate New Year's Eve. All the Christmas decorations are still up, strings of red lanterns, enormous gaudy coils of golden wreaths hanging from every lamppost. We drive through the outskirts of town, past close-packed redbrick houses, past the garage next to the motorway, done up for the festive season with a truly frightening inflatable Santa who looms over their roof, swaying in the wind. We pass under the motorway and go north, heading for the wild moors and forests where Darren lives. The streetlights become less frequent, then stop entirely. For a while we drive through farmland, hemmed in by hedges, then the road winds higher, up into the hills, and the fields are replaced by bleak moors, stony ridges, lonely trees. Dunbarrow and Brackford are just a smear of orange light on the horizon behind us. The sky is clear, with a wide, fat moon, a splattering of stars. I can see the comet everyone on the news has been getting so excited about, a greenish-blue streak in the sky. I point it out to Elza.

"Oh, yeah," she says, looking past the trees. "I was just reading about it yesterday. That's a rare one, you know. It's got this massive orbit: they worked out that it comes by the sun every eight hundred years. The last time anyone saw this comet with their naked eyes was medieval times."

"Beautiful stuff, man," Darren says. "It's such a privilege to witness something like that. Did I ever tell you how I saw the eclipse this summer in Thailand? I'll never forget that. Was out there with my little sister Margaux—man, we were so wasted, had a bit to drink, some good smoke—" Darren breaks off here and glances at Mum, with a bit of an *Aren't I daring?* expression, like any of us are going to be surprised he smokes weed. "Anyway, the sun went dark, and Margaux said it was, like, the most spiritual experience of her life. That eclipse. She's really stoked to meet you guys."

"Your sister's here?" Mum asks. "I thought she was traveling."

"Yeah, she's crashing at my place for a few days. I thought I told you, babe? It's cool. One more for the party, right?"

"Of course." Mum smiles. "It'll be lovely to meet her."

"So shall we get some jungle going on?" Darren asks, reaching for the CD player. Elza takes a deep breath.

Great, so now we're spending New Year's Eve with Darren and his younger sister, who I'm imagining is exactly as annoying as Darren.

The car travels on. Our headlights illuminate stone walls, overgrown hedges, a group of sheep huddled against a wire fence, their eyes reflecting the glare from our headlights like tiny green mirrors. For a moment I think their faces look like masks somehow, or maybe lanterns with pale fire burning inside them, and then we drive past them and the sheep are gone, and once again I'm left wondering what I was thinking. Maybe I really am just cracking up, finally. After everything I've been through, it might've been a long time coming. In the dark I reach over and take Elza's hand, and without asking why she squeezes it.

We come to Darren's place almost by surprise, rounding a corner and suddenly seeing soft orange firelight shining through dark trees. The car bumps up a rutted track, obviously carved out by vehicles a lot more practical and hardy than Mum's little yellow car. We pass through a wooden gate, and we're in Darren's yard.

I haven't been here before, but Mum's told me all about it. Darren's off the grid, lives without a telephone, electricity, or gas. The glow we could see through the trees is a bonfire burning in a big rounded pit off to the side of the buildings. Darren's main house is an old cottage, maybe a farmhouse from a long time ago, big gray stones coated in ivy. I can see candles burning through the windows. There are sheds, a garage with a big rusty truck standing up on blocks, a tree trunk that Darren's halfway through carving into something with his chain saw.

"Well, here we are, dudes," he says with a grin.

"Wow, yeah," I say.

We get out of the car. Without any electric light, the darkness seems thicker than it ever does in Dunbarrow. The fire illuminates the side of the house and the yard where we're parked, but the shadows are heavy and long, and a black double of me stretches from my feet all the way to the edge of the barn, where the light fades. Elza crushes herself against me.

"So cold," she whispers.

"There's no heat inside either," I whisper back. "We're not part of the capitalist system out here. So get used to that. Forget about material comforts."

"Surrender your flesh," Elza whispers, grinning. *"Join ussss . . ."*

"What do you think the chances of this being a cult induction are?" I ask her.

"Extremely high," Elza whispers. "If he wheels out a big wicker man, that's when we run."

"So where is your sister?" Mum asks Darren.

"Oh, yeah. She built the fire—doesn't seem to be watching it, though!" he says, like it hadn't occurred to him before now. "Could've burned the whole place down, ha-ha!"

"Maybe she's inside?" Elza suggests. "There's smoke from the chimney, too."

"Yeah, maybe, man, maybe," Darren says. "All right, let's go check."

He leads us across the yard and into his house. The door frame is low, the walls heavy and thick. It's very warm in here, and I feel a prickle of sweat break out on my forehead. Guess I was wrong about the no-heating part. The place is hung with rugs, swaths of Indian fabric, and there are candles jammed into jars and bottles, lighting everything with a buttery radiance. The heat's coming from a real log fire in the fireplace, with a woman, who I assume is Margaux, sitting in front of it.

She looks up at us as we stumble in, and for a moment

it seems like she doesn't recognize anybody, like she's not sure what to do, and then a smile breaks out on her face.

"Sis," Darren says, "this is Persephone and her kid, Luke. And this is his girlfriend, Elza. So glad you guys could all be here tonight!"

"Margaux, it's lovely to meet you," Mum says. "Darren's told me so much about you."

"Me, too," Margaux replies. Like her brother, she's got the skin of someone who spends a lot of time outdoors in the sun, a deep bronzed glow that you can tell is real and didn't come from a tanning salon. Her hair's long and red, spilling over her shoulders and down into her lap. She's younger than Mum or Darren, but older than us, maybe thirty. She's wrapped in a blanket, with a pack of cards on the floor in front of her. Playing solitaire or something, I suppose. It's not like Darren has a TV up here.

"So there's a bonfire outside," Darren says. "Thought you were going to watch it."

"I'm cold," Margaux says, giving him a wide smile. "Northumbria's a shock after Malaysia."

"You've got thin blood, Sis," Darren says. "Look, I better make sure it's burning right. Coming out, babe?"

For a moment I don't know who he's talking to, then I realize he meant Mum. Wow. He's got his hand right on her bum. Just lying there for anyone to see. They're like lovesick teenagers. They slip back out into the cold, leaving me and Elza with Margaux. Nobody says anything for a moment. The fire spits, spraying sparks up into the chimney. She must be absolutely roasting under that blanket.

"I really like your hair," Elza says at last.

"Oh, thanks," Margaux says. "I love yours too, Elza. It's very new wave. Would you two like a drink?"

"Sure," I say. Margaux gets up and wanders over to the side table, where a few bottles are. She's wearing brown overalls, a purple sweater with holes at the elbow. Her hair's insanely long, like down to her waist, bloody crimson in the firelight.

"Rapunzel," Elza whispers to me.

Margaux Hart pours us out some wine into tea mugs and shuffles back over. Her eyes are green, I see, as she hands us the mugs. The wine is warm and sweet. Margaux settles back down in front of the fire. We sit on one of Darren's lumpy sofas, Elza's leg pressed against mine. Margaux watches as we both drink.

"Are you playing cards?" I ask.

"Oh," Margaux says, "I'm not really playing. I was asking for advice."

"Tarot, right?" Elza says.

"Yeah," Margaux replies. "Do you read the cards as well?"

"My gran used to," Elza says. "I still have her set at home somewhere, I think. I haven't looked at them for a while."

"Why do you have them?" I ask.

"They tell the future," Margaux says carelessly. "Other things, too. They can tell you stuff about yourself that you don't know. Answer questions. Tell you the truth."

She gestures with her hand, which is tattooed, spirals of blue ink spilling from the back of the hand down to each knuckle, an ornate pattern. Maybe she got that done in Asia.

I look closer at the cards in front of her. They're larger than normal playing cards, lined with gold trim, and each one has a picture on it—colorful illustrations of peasants and knights and angels and stars.

"I was just asking them about a bloke," Margaux says, smiling in a mock-embarrassed way. "Didn't tell me anything I don't know already. You can give them a whirl if you want."

"I dunno," I say. I know all about this fortune-telling stuff, tea leaf reading and whatever. I don't believe in it. As someone who's seen and done real magic, I don't have a lot of patience for tarot cards. Real magic comes from the dark places inside you, and it hurts people. It doesn't give you advice.

"Why not?" Elza says, at the same moment.

"Really?" I say.

"Men often don't have time for the cards," Margaux says. "It's something where you need a woman's intuition,

I feel. Do you have a particular question or problem, Elza?"

"Yeah, I do have a problem, actually. I want to know what we should do about Mr. Berkley."

"Are you sure we should be asking that?" I hiss.

"Why not?" Elza says. "He's just our neighbor," she explains to Margaux. "He's having this fight with Dad about building a new, uh, extension on his house. It's really stressing me out."

Margaux gathers the cards up and starts shuffling them.

"I'm really not sure about this," I whisper again.

"What harm would it do?" Elza whispers back. "Books aren't getting us anywhere. We need something to go on."

"So I'm thinking a five-card spread," Margaux says as she shuffles. "That's simple enough, good for giving you an idea for a direct course of action about this Berkley."

"Sure," Elza says. I take a sip of wine. Elza's never met Mr. Berkley in person. I'm not saying she doesn't take him seriously, but . . . I just wonder if he's watching us. He might be able to see us right now. He might have heard her say his name.

Margaux lays the first card down, taps it with a tattooed finger. It has a yellow background, and the picture shows a man in a white-and-red robe, with an infinity sign scrawled above his head. My skin starts to prickle. There are red roses around him, and he's holding a white rod in his right hand. I know this is just some dumb pack of cards, but the infinity sign makes me think of the Book of Eight, Dad's magical book with an infinite number of pages.

"This is one of the major arcana," Margaux explains. "The Magician."

"The Magician," I repeat. I look at the little figure and think again of my dad and his rings, think of the Shepherd, with his sigils tattooed on his palms. I think of Ashana Ahlgren, her white hair and gray eyes. I think of myself, sitting here by the fire with a mug of wine. The Magician.

"So normally this first card gives you the general theme of a reading," Margaux says. "The Magician's a good card. Skill, action, willpower. So this reading might be giving you a course of action to sort out your problem with Mr. Berkley."

"Sounds good," Elza says.

"The second card of the five will determine past events that are affecting this current problem," Margaux tells us. She licks her finger and flips over the second tarot card. Despite the heat of the living room, I feel deathly cold. I can see the card before she flips it over, know what picture will be there on the other side.

The background to this card is black. There are three figures on it: two small ones that are human, and one that isn't. The two small figures are naked people, a man and woman with red hair, chained to a post by collars around their necks. The third figure is enormous, perched on the post the humans are chained to, a red monster with furry legs and bat wings and the face of an angry bull, with big drooping gray horns. He's holding his right hand up to the sky, and in his left hand is a flaming torch, pointed toward the ground.

"The Devil," Margaux says. She doesn't seem afraid.

"Is that bad?" Elza asks, keeping her voice steady. Maybe this is what she expected to see.

"Sometimes," Margaux replies, running a finger over the card. "Nothing in the tarot is inherently 'bad,' though. Everything has multiple interpretations. The Devil can mean addiction, sensuality, materialism. It can also mean power reclaimed, a personal change, breaking free of bonds."

"So the Devil's affecting our current problem," I say. "Didn't know that."

"Well," Margaux continues, "maybe not the actual Devil. Like I said, the cards are more metaphorical. Anyway, let's try the third card, and look at the future of this issue."

She closes her eyes and places the third tarot card down, to the right of the other two.

I blink.

Is this really happening?

"It's the Devil again," Elza says quietly.

There are two Devil cards now, black backgrounds and hulking red devils, one to each side of the Magician card. I can hear a ringing in my ears.

"Oh," Margaux says. "Well."

"How many Devil cards are there?" I ask.

"There's only one of each major arcana," Elza tells me.

"Mix-up," Margaux says. "I might have shuffled two decks together."

"Does that mean the reading's wrong?" I ask.

"I think we have to read what the cards want to tell us," she says, "even if we don't understand it fully." She puts the fourth card down above the other three.

It's another Devil.

My stomach churns. There's something different about this card. The Devil on it looks darker, thinner, less like a silly drawing and more like a monster. On the first two cards he was frowning, but on this card it looks like there's the beginnings of a smile on his face. A big white grin. Nobody moves. I feel strange and sleepy, and although I'm very afraid, I don't want to move a muscle.

Margaux frowns. "Well, that's very strange," she remarks drowsily, and lays out the final card.

It's the Devil again, four Devils in a circle around the Magician card. This Devil is black, so black you can't see him against the darkness of the card's background. All you can see are blue eyes, a white mouth. The people chained to the post don't have red hair anymore. The woman has black hair, and the man has brown. It's me and Elza. I'm sure of it.

Margaux is staring down at the cards without a word. She starts to turn the rest of her stack over, one by one, and each one has the same picture, me and Elza tied to a post by our necks, with a hellish smile in the darkness above us. I'm cold and hot at the same time, sweating, Elza's hand is gripping mine so hard, it feels like her nails might be drawing blood. The floor is carpeted with Devil cards, what seems like hundreds of them.

"How can this—" Margaux says, and then there's a bang behind us.

Elza shrieks. I whirl around, heart pounding, fully expecting to see *him* standing there, Mr. Berkley, the Devil in the flesh, expecting to see his wolf-gray suit, his eyes like poisoned blue stars—

Darren stares back at me. "Uh, are you all right?" he asks us.

"Fine," I say. "We're fine."

"The door just gave me a shock," Elza says weakly.

"Yeah, it does bang a bit," Darren says. "Uh. Well, fire's going nicely. How about you come out? I've got some veggie burgers sizzling. You really ought to try one, Luke—you'd never know they're not really meat, I swear, mate."

I look back down at the floor of the living room, where Margaux is still sitting. The cards have normal pictures again: knights and lovers and people chopping firewood. There's only one Devil card, the first one Margaux chose. Whatever strange, horrible spell was forming here, Darren seems to have broken it.

I think this could be the first time I've been glad to see him.

Margaux doesn't speak to us much after that. She sits on the opposite side of the bonfire, still wrapped in her blanket. Darren's talking enough for all of us, waving his beer around to make a point, sitting with Mum and a battery-powered radio next to them. It's not exactly warm out here, but the fire is so high and fierce that I can't say I'm too cold either. I have a veggie burger with some lettuce and pickle. You can definitely tell it's not meat. My stomach's churning, maybe nerves after that horrible tarot reading, so I leave about half of it on the plate.

What exactly happened to us in there? We asked the cards about the Devil, and they gave us the Devil. Could Berkley feel us asking about him? Do tarot cards actually tap into the spirit world, in some way I don't understand? Whatever it was, I don't think we're any closer to discovering something that would help us. The bad sensation I had this morning is back with a vengeance. I feel queasy, like the world's spinning too fast. Darren's music is giving me a headache.

Mum's laughing at something Darren said. She's happy at least. Elza is thoughtfully chewing on her burger, staring into the fire. The sky overhead is clear, and I can see the comet, a glimmering streak in the blackness.

Darren bumps my shoulder with his fist, making me jump.

"All right, Luke?" he asks loudly.

"Sure," I say.

"You look mopey, dude," he says.

"I'm fine," I say.

"You should give the slackline a go," Darren says.

"I'm OK right here," I say. My head throbs. Just take the hint. I'm not in the party mood. I keep feeling like I'm going to look up from the ground and see Berkley standing at the edge of the clearing. Why did we ask the cards about him? That was stupid. Why were those swans gathering on the river today? What's going on?

"Come on," Darren says, nudging me. "I'll show you how, mate. It's easier than you think."

"Look just—no! All right? Leave me alone!"

That came out way louder than I thought it would. Darren's face visibly falls.

"Yeah," he says. "That's cool."

He turns around and heads off to his cottage. The door closes behind him with a quiet click. I think I really hurt his feelings. This is so awkward. Nobody says anything. The fire crackles.

"I don't know what's gotten into you tonight," Mum snaps at me. She gets up, brushing dirt off her trousers, and stomps away into the darkness. Margaux and Elza look at me.

"I've got a headache," I say.

"Go and say sorry," Elza hisses, elbowing my ribs.

"All right, all right," I say. I get to my feet. The world lurches. I feel awful, like I've drunk way too much. My mouth tastes of the red wine. I follow Mum into Darren's yard. She's standing by her car, leaning against the hood for support.

"Are you OK?" I ask.

I come closer. Mum doesn't turn around.

"I'm sorry," I say. Blood pounds in my head.

"I don't know why you have to be like this, Luke," Mum says.

"I said I was sorry."

"I see how you look at him," she continues. "You never want to talk to him."

"I just feel ill! I'm sorry!"

"It's not just tonight, Luke," Mum says. "You can never get out of there fast enough."

I pinch the bridge of my nose. This is the last thing I want to talk about right now.

"He's not my boyfriend," I say. "I don't have to like him."

"I feel like you don't try at all, love."

"Look, I just don't feel well . . ." The world lurches again. Mum ignores this. She seems unsteady as well.

"I know you miss your dad," Mum says. "I miss him, too. It's hard, not having him around. I know he loved you."

"Can we just, like . . . not?"

I remember Dad's form emerging out of the fog of Deadside. Remember that conversation I had with him and Berkley, promising to take on Dad's debt if Berkley let him go free. Sometimes I wonder what I was thinking.

"He loved both of us . . ." Mum says, and I can see she's crying. Dad tore my unborn brother's spirit out of her and used it to bind a demon into his service. I don't know what you'd call that, but it's not love. I feel like I'm going to be sick.

"He never loved us," I mumble.

"What did you say, Luke?"

"I said, he didn't love us! If he did, he wouldn't have—"

"You didn't know him," Mum says.

"I know him well enough! He left me with an awful mess! That's what I know!"

Mum doesn't say anything for a moment.

"He left you with me," she replies, quietly.

"No! I meant—"

I don't know how to finish that sentence. I meant he left me with a Host of angry spirits, let Mr. Berkley come gliding into my life like a shark that's smelled blood, left me with the orphaned daughters of his old ally coming after me, but Mum doesn't know about any of that.

She bursts into tears. I try to touch her shoulder, but she shrugs me off.

"Mum, please . . ."

She's trying to talk, but the tears are distorting her words. She pushes me away and sets off down the track, away from Darren's house.

"Mum! C'mon!"

She stumbles away into the night. Strange lights are flashing in the corners of my eyes. Green, blue, green. I'm going to be sick. This is such a mess. Worst New Year's Eve ever.

Darren's standing by the door to his cottage when I turn around. His face is blurry.

"Are you all right, mate?" he asks me.

"Mum, she—"

"It's all right," Darren says. He doesn't sound too upset with me. "Luke, just go get some rest, yeah? I'll talk to Persephone. I think she's had a bit too much to drink."

He sets off down the rutted track after Mum, calling her name. I feel like worms are eating my insides. My stomach boils. I can taste sweet wine. Ugh. I only had one mug . . .

I stumble back around the house, toward the fire.

It seems to be flaring much higher than when I left. Elza is still sitting beside it, but the fire is climbing up into the sky, like a tower of flame. Margaux is gone.

My ears are ringing. What's going on?

"Elza," I say, but my words are slurred. "Elza, Mum's—"

Elza doesn't turn around, and as I walk across the grass toward her, I fall, the world lurching beneath me. I hit the cold ground hard. I can't seem to move my legs properly. I manage to turn onto my side and I throw up, spewing out the red wine. Green and blue light surges in my eyes. I taste bile.

Something's really wrong. I need help.

"Elza!" I shout, but I'm not sure I'm making a sound at all.

Someone or something is standing beside me. It leans down to look at me more closely.

The figure is draped in a black robe and wears a black-and-golden mask, the head of an owl. Monstrous hands with long, clawed fingers protrude from the sleeves.

I try to scream and can't.

The masked creature raises me in its cold arms and carries me like a baby, away from the bonfire, into the woods.

I'm walking in the forest. Elza is beside me. The bird-woman walks before us, arms raised in welcome. The owl-man follows behind.

There's rippling light in the sky, green and blue, like someone dropped wonderful paint into water. I can see stars there aren't names for. I can feel the ground breathing beneath my feet. The forest is about to speak. Pine trees shiver like a plucked string. We're going to break the bones of the world.

The light walks with us. Its voice rings in my ears.

"The twice-born and the Speaker's pawn."

I can see the gateway, three locks ready to crumble.

The shadows walk beside us too, and I know they're here for the feast.

(the storm)

My jaw hurts like someone took a drill to it, waves of pain throbbing through my teeth and skull and neck. What's happening? Where am I? I'm so cold. I'm not wearing my coat, just a sweatshirt and jeans. I'm already shivering. This is very bad. How did I get here? Last thing I remember was at Darren's house. Mum turned and ran away, down the track, and Darren went to get her. I was going back to the fire, feeling sick, looking for Elza . . .

Wherever I am, I'm not there. I can't see any sign of firelight. All I can see around me are dark trees, brambles, a hard-frosted forest floor. I feel out of breath, like I was running, but I can't think why that would be. My ears are ringing faintly. Someone breaks a branch behind me, and I whirl around.

"Hello?" I say, and my voice sounds terribly small in the enormous cold forest. Why did I say anything? For all I know, this is the person I've been running from. I keep feeling like I should be able to remember, but I just can't. It's like waking up, except I was already awake. Who's out there?

I hear a rustling and a hiss of breath.

"I know you're there," I say again.

"Luke?"

"Elza!"

I push back toward her voice. She's leaning against a tree, dark hair piled wildly above her head. She's breathing heavily.

"What's happening?" she asks. "My teeth . . ."

"I don't know!" I say, coming closer. I wrap my arms around her. She's shivering. "Mine hurt, too," I tell her.

"Why are we out here?" Elza says.

"I have no idea. Last thing I remember is Mum . . . I made her cry and she ran away. Then I went back to the bonfire and . . . don't know what I saw."

"Me, too. I was sitting by the fire, and then blank. I keep trying to remember what happened, and I can't!"

The trees rustle in the wind. I see a rabbit, running as fast as it can, cross the forest floor in front of us and disappear again into shadow. I'm shivering really badly now. It's a crushing, tightening cold, like chains wrapped around me. Elza at least has her peacoat. I don't know what happened to my jacket.

"We need to get inside," I say.

"We could be anywhere, Luke," Elza says.

"It's England. You're never that far from a house."

"We should try and get out of the woods," Elza says. "Do you think we're up on the moors? We drove through a bunch of forests to get to Darren's house."

"Probably," I say. "Why would we be out there, though?"

"I'm really worried," Elza says. "Something happened, Luke. This isn't right. God, my teeth hurt so much. Whatever bad thing we've been worried about . . ."

Another rabbit breaks cover, running past us in the darkness.

"You think it already happened?" I ask.

"Yes," she says quietly. "I do. But I can't remember what it was! Like a nightmare you just woke up from . . ."

Gray mist is flowing around our feet, like dry ice, flowing from the direction the rabbits were fleeing. It ripples silently. How did I not see it before? How did I . . . oh.

"Elza . . ." I begin. "We might be dead."

"What?"

"Ghosts never remember how they died. Also . . . look down."

"It's just mist."

"No," I say. "That's Deadside fog."

"Luke . . ."

"It is," I say. "I've seen it before, remember. I know that fog."

But my teeth ache so badly. I feel so cold. Dead people can't feel true pain, can't shiver.

"It's just ground mist," Elza says, but I can tell she's not certain.

"I wish it was. But listen, do you feel cold?"

"Do I . . . Are you joking? We're going to freeze to death out here, if we aren't already ghosts."

"Then we're alive," I say. "Dead people don't get cold. I remember that much. Deadside isn't hot or cold. We still have bodies."

Elza frowns, thinking this over. She pinches herself.

"That really hurts," she says. "I think I'm still here."

I run my tongue over my back teeth and wince. I've spent a fair amount of time as a spirit, more than Elza has. It doesn't feel like this. I don't think we're dead. But that is Deadside mist.

There's a silent flash of frozen blue light, illuminating the sky and the bare trees around us. I see that the forest floor is alive with animals, squirrels and rabbits, and I can see the slender shapes of deer in the far trees. All of them are running away from the source of the light and mist.

We look at each other.

"I think we should go the opposite way from whatever that is," Elza says, and we set off at a sprint. The forest is tangled and dense, and I nearly fall a few times, Elza huffing behind me. Branches slap my face and rake my hands. We pass hedgehogs and a rabbit with a limp and are overtaken by a red fox that flashes past me so fast, I almost think I imagined it. After a few minutes of blind, panicked running, we break out of the forest and I get the biggest shock yet.

We're standing on the edge of a large flat field, currently alive with fleeing wildlife. Beyond this field I can see a complex of square sullen buildings, a tall white pair of rugby goals. Dunbarrow High, our old school. How are we here? I thought we were out in the wilderness. We're back in Dunbarrow?

"Elza," I begin, but she grabs my arm.

"Look," she says in a small voice, and I turn around.

"What?"

There's something happening behind us, in the forest where we came from. It's like a volcanic eruption, a cloud of light, cold patterns of blue and green snaking up from the tree line. There's a cloud of spreading fog, too, illuminated from within by the snaking patterns of light. Elza's face is lit a gruesome green. It seems like there should be a sound, but there's nothing to hear, just our breath and our footsteps. The fog flows silently around us. And above it all, gleaming in the sky, I can see the comet, a stitch of blue-green thread.

Turning back toward the school, I can see the fog has reached the buildings, lapping against the walls and doors like a rising tide. The air around us is becoming milky, translucent. It's so cold.

"Isn't that where the Devil's Footsteps are?" Elza asks me, pointing to where the light is erupting from.

"Yes," I say.

I think we were there. . . . Something happened, but what? I can't remember. All I remember is the sky, shimmering green light . . . shadows and stars. Something like a dream, a heap of broken images.

"I can taste magic," Elza says. "Big magic. Can't you?"

"My ears are ringing," I say.

"We should get far away from here," Elza says. "I think we should get indoors. Shelter."

I don't argue. Apart from anything, I'm going to freeze to death if we stand here any longer. My jaw pulses like it's full of magma. I almost want to scream. You get to thinking that discomfort means not being able to reach the TV remote without standing up. Discomfort actually turns out to mean coatless in January with a red-hot needle of pain stuck into your gums.

We run, mist swirling around us, bracelets jangling on Elza's wrist. Is this something to do with Berkley? I remember the tarot cards as Margaux turned them over, remember the Devil's grinning face in the blackness. I remember the

Magician card, an infinity sign emblazoned above his head. This is my fault somehow, I'm sure of it.

Last time we ran down this bank, we were chasing Alice Waltham, with my dad's demon controlling her body. The time before that, we were climbing up it, with Ham in tow, hoping to sacrifice a gerbil to the Devil. It's strange to look back on that night as the good old days.

For no reason, I think of the dead swan, blood in the frost by its white head.

Wait, is that a different swan?

I'm thinking of one lying on moss, not on the road. I'm picturing a different dead swan.

When?

Something happened and it keeps jumping out of reach.

Did I already pay the Devil? Is this what I paid him?

What was it that I gave?

The soccer field's underfoot now, the ground firmer and more even. I'm still cold, but running's building up heat in my chest. There's light dancing overhead, strange lightning bolts of green and blue, but they don't flash like lightning normally does, instead crawling across the sky at a lazy pace, almost like vines growing. I can't see any stars. The mist is slowly thickening, condensing.

We arrive on the playground itself with a suddenness that startles me. Elza's boots are clacking against concrete.

The buildings of the school are just vague shapes, the world a haze.

I hear a noise behind us and grab at Elza's wrist. She startles, but I pull her down, behind the low wall that runs along the side of the science block. We're crouching in some shrubs, and for a moment I feel stupid, but then I hear some heavy clopping tread on the concrete school yard and a metallic jangling sound, like chains scraping against each other. It sounds like horses approaching, maybe chained to a cart or pack.

"Do you hear that?" I whisper.

Elza nods.

We're low to the ground, peering over the wall. I can definitely hear hoofbeats, some large animal moving very close to us. The playground is thick with gray fog now, billowing lifeless clouds. A silent flash of green light illuminates the yard for a moment, and I jump.

There's a pair of riders making their way across the school yard. I see humanoid shapes astride large, powerful-looking horses. I can't see the riders clearly, but it looks like they're wearing masks, oversize bird heads like plague doctors from medieval times. This is frightening, of course, but that's not the thing that scares me most.

I only get a single glance in the green-lit mist before the light fades, but the horses seem to have human heads.

o o o

We stay hidden for as long as I can bear the cold, the mist shimmering with blue and green glare from the sky overhead. The riders have vanished and don't seem to have been aware we were watching them. It looked as if they were heading for the center of Dunbarrow. I wonder why they were here, how they connect with everything that's been happening tonight. They must've come from the other side of the gateway, Deadside; that's the only place you'd get horses with the heads of men.

There's no more sounds in the fog; no wind, no voices, nothing at all. It feels like being underwater, the bottom of a freezing toxic ocean. My jaw still hurts, like I've got a wisdom tooth coming through. Elza's hand is clamped to mine, and we lie as close as we can to each other, shivering beneath a bush.

"We need to get indoors," she whispers. "You'll die of cold if we don't."

"Yeah," I say. I'm shivering like a struck glass.

"What were those things?" Elza says to herself. "Were they after us?"

"I've seen—" I shudder, almost biting my tongue. "I've seen things like that before. Deadside. Black horses with human faces. They're spirits."

"They came from the Devil's Footsteps," she says.

"I think something came through. From the other side. Something bad. And we can't remember what. Or why."

"We need to move," Elza says. "We have to keep going. Get somewhere safe. Then we can figure out what's going on."

"Where?"

"My house is closer to the school," Elza replies. "We should go there first. Get warm, get off the streets. Before those riders, whatever they are, come back."

Another surge of blue light in the sky above us.

"I've got a really bad feeling about this," I say. "What happened to Mum and Darren and Margaux? Where did they go? Last I saw, Mum was heading away from Darren's place. He said he'd go and get her, then—"

She squeezes my hand harder.

"One thing at a time," Elza whispers. "We can find them. I know it. But first let's get up to Towen Crescent. It's not far."

We stand and move, jogging through the mist, hoping not to run slap-bang into the horse creatures or their riders in the dimness. If anything it seems colder now, the flashes of light in the sky less frequent. There's no electric light anywhere to be seen, and our phones are dead, their touch screens mute black rectangles. Even my digital watch has stopped, at exactly midnight. Whatever happened, it must've been the exact moment the old year became the new. I still don't know as much as I ought to about magic, but I know days and times are significant. Halloween is one moment when the boundaries between Liveside and Deadside are weak, but there must be other times as well. Is the gap between the years one of them? What about the swans we saw this morning? The comet? It all must mean something.

We cross the staff parking lot, go down and out toward the school gates. They're locked and we have to climb over them, the cold metal biting into my hands. The road outside is deserted. None of the street lamps are on, and there are no lights in any windows. There's just milky mist and silence.

"Where is everyone?" I whisper.

"I don't know," Elza whispers back. "Maybe it's the Rapture."

I'm not sure if she's joking.

It's amazing how different this street looks. I walked up and down it twice a day for the entire time I came to school here in Dunbarrow. It was this exact street where I spoke to Elza the first time, more than a year ago. Visibility is only a few feet in front of us. I can't see the spire of St. Jude's or the clock tower by Dunbarrow Square or any of the normal landmarks.

Another surge of green light in the sky, turning everything around us gauzy emerald for a brief moment. Elza stops me.

"Did you see that?" she asks.

"See what?"

"There was someone ahead of us."

I can't see anyone. I can see maybe two cars in front of us. I think we're coming up to the junction by the pub, with the bus station right ahead of us, but I have no idea. Was it just another person? Was it something from Deadside?

"Well, let's take it carefully," I say.

We move forward. There's a man standing with his back to us in the street. He's just a silhouette in the fog. I can't see what he's doing. Our best bet might just be to walk quietly past. I don't feel good about it, but I don't know what else to do.

We press ourselves against the farthest fence, inching our way past the figure. My heart's going like a drum. The man seems to have his hands over his face, but I can't really tell. My teeth are yammering with pain, clicking together as my jaw chatters. We need to get inside. I really will die if we stay out here much longer. The sky and mist light up blue, but not the hearty blue of a summer sky; the fog turns unearthly pale blue, the color of a swimming pool lit with submerged lights at night. In the same moment as that flash, the man looks up and sees us.

"Luke? Elza?"

I recognize the voice, but I can't place it.

"Yeah?" I say, my voice squeaking. Elza's hand is gripping my elbow, trying to pull me away. She wants to run.

"Hey. It's good to see you guys. I'm so glad you're here."

"Who is that?" Elza asks.

"It's . . ." The figure takes a shuddering breath. "Can you feel that?"

"Feel what?" I ask.

"It's here," he says, moving toward us. "It's finally here. It's . . . oh, man."

I think I recognize his posture as he moves.

"Andy?" I ask.

Andy's one of the town ghosts, part of a group of lads who died and hang around Dunbarrow, not wanting to move on into Deadside. He's a pretty decent guy. He doesn't usually talk like this. He sounds drunk, but I don't see how that's possible. Blue light flickers in the sky again. He takes another step toward us.

It definitely is Andy. He's wearing his normal jeans, polo shirt, white sneakers.

"Can you feel it?" he asks us again.

"Feel what?" I reply. "Are you all right, mate?"

"Fine," he says, laughing. "I feel great. It's great."

He steps closer again, and I recoil.

His eyes are luminous, gently pulsing with the same

greenish-blue light as the sky and mist. Andy's head seems to be lit from the inside, like a lantern.

"Are you really . . . OK? You're, uh, glowing," I say, shielding Elza from the ghost, both of us slowly backing away from him.

"You really don't feel it?" he asks. "It's a special night. It's calling everyone."

"What is?" I ask him. This is not good.

He sighs deeply.

"I don't know," Andy says. "But it feels amazing."

"All right, man," I say, slowly backing away, "good to hear. We're just heading back home. Give us a shout tomorrow, yeah?"

"There's not going to be a tomorrow," Andy says happily. "This is all there is."

"All right," I say, our backing away becoming faster and faster, "good to know. Take care of yourself, mate. Have a good one."

We both turn and bolt at the same time, running full tilt along the road, breath steaming in our mouths, Elza's boots racketing on the road. We take a hard right, hurtling down the road, parked cars like sleeping animals in the fog. I can hear Andy shouting something after us, but I can't make it out. He doesn't follow us. After a few minutes of running, I get scared of what might be in front of us and slow down, panting.

"No tomorrow . . ." Elza gasps. "What is he talking about? Why are his eyes glowing like that? It's like something was taking him over . . ."

The fog flickers green again, a sickly jade. I can hear something faintly, like people talking in a faraway room, coming from where I think the center of Dunbarrow might be.

"He seemed totally out of it," I say. "Do you think something happened to the town ghosts?"

"Maybe," Elza says. "His eyes were like the light up in the sky. Is something spreading through that light?"

"I don't know," I say. "We'll keep walking, OK? We'll get to your house. It's not far."

Something comes drifting down in front of my nose, pale and out of focus, and settles on the road in front of me. It's a snowflake. A big, fat snowflake, like something from a Christmas card. Another comes spiraling down to join it. You have to be joking.

"Is that . . ." Elza begins.

"Yeah," I say. "As if the weather wasn't strange enough."

"Snow in winter isn't that strange," Elza says.

"Whatever. You know what I mean."

We keep walking, uphill now. The flakes quickly turn into a genuine storm, thickening the foggy air even further. Elza's hair is heavy with them, tiny hair ornaments. I'm shivering like crazy, hitting my forearms and chest with my hands to try and whack some warmth back into my body. My teeth are chattering, which makes my gums start aching again.

I hear a crunch behind me and turn around to see Elza kicking the back window out of a car.

"What are you doing?"

"There's a parka in here," she says. "Backseat."

The car window gives out after another blow from her combat boot, shattering into glittering squares of glass that are quickly lost in the blizzard. Elza reaches in and pulls out a parka with a fur-lined hood. She thrusts it at me.

"Put this on. You're going to die otherwise."

I take the jacket, heavy, with a weird smell to it, musty beer and cigarettes. I put it on. It's too big for me, with sleeves that cover my entire hands, but given how cold I am, that doesn't seem like a bad thing. I zip the coat all the way up and pull the hood over my head. I'm still shivering but at least the wind isn't slipping in between my ribs like a dagger anymore.

"Sorry," Elza says, "I should've thought of that way earlier."

"Nah," I say. "My fault. I didn't say anything."

"Next time you're about to freeze to death," Elza says, "do mention it, all right? Now let's get moving. I'm still worried about you."

She kisses me, a precious touch of warmth in the cold, and we forge on into the storm.

We're nearly at Towen Crescent, just at the turnoff from the main road, when we hear voices out in the fog. The snow is still pelting down, the ground blanketed in white, all sounds muffled and strange. Walking uphill in the parka has warmed me up, although my fingers and toes still feel numb and frozen. My sneakers are soaking wet now, coated with fresh snow.

The voices are muffled and distant, but they sound human at least. We still haven't seen another person, an electric light, or a moving car anywhere in Dunbarrow. Since we were in the woods, I haven't even seen any animals besides the horse creatures.

"Do you hear that?" I ask.

"Hear what?"

"There's someone coming," I say.

Without another word, we duck behind a parked car.

The voices are nearer, although I still can't make them out properly. There's some strange sound, too, like metallic clanking, the same noise we heard back in the school yard. Is it those riders again? We're so close to Towen Crescent, Elza's house. Maybe we should just run up there.

My gums still hurt; less intensely now, but it's a sour

ache, more noticeable now that we just have to crouch here and wait.

Then the owners of the voices appear out of the mist and I forget all about my teeth.

They're two hulking creatures, dim forms in the dimness, and they stalk down the road in tandem, bickering with each other. Their bodies are horse-shaped, but their heads and voices are definitely human. This must be the same pair of monsters we saw by the high school. Where are their riders? Elza's warm hand grasps mine, and we crouch behind the car, barely daring to breathe.

"—to take only the unmarked," one's saying, "that is what she tells us. I did never hear the like, Dumachus, I surely did not. This be lunacy. We are promised a feast, and then told only the scraps are to be had. It is a feast of nothingness, Dumachus, that is what it is. A feast of lies."

"That it be," the other horse-man replies. I think they're men; their voices sound male at least. There's a rhythmic metallic clanking noise as they walk.

"Years she holds us to wait, and for what? To bear them on our backs, as though we were common mules, Dumachus, mules, and then to wander in the cold, bereft of sport and food, to wander this township searching for those wayward few she has not marked, like we were mongrel hunting hounds. I wish to eat, Dumachus, my old friend, I am sorely tested. My stomach sings for a meal. It has been so long since we have supped together."

"That it has," the other monster says.

They're closer now. Another green flash illuminates the road, and I see these creatures clearly. They have the bodies of cart horses and the heads of old, long-haired men. These horse-men are much like the horrible herd I saw drinking by the banks of the Cocytus, but larger and stronger-looking, and clad in dull battered armor, war gear made for horses. This is the source of the metallic noise: plates of steel moving against one another as the monsters walk. I wonder who armored them; without hands, they certainly couldn't have strapped the plates onto their bodies themselves. Perhaps it was the riders that we saw.

The horse monsters are close enough now that I can make out the details of their faces; pinched and cruel-looking, with tangled manes of gray hair. Their heads are proportional to the size of their bodies, and they're much larger than any human's, powerful and thick-necked. One of the creatures has a stringy mustache drooping from his upper lip; it's this spirit that does most of the talking.

"Hold ho!" this talkative one says suddenly. "Hold ho, Dumachus!"

"What be it, Titus?" the other horse monster asks, coming to a halt alongside his companion. They're barely a car's length from where we're hiding. The sky flares blue, and the creatures are silhouetted against it, like statues sunk in the depths of a nightmare ocean.

"I believe I smell something," Titus says cheerfully. "We may yet feast tonight, old friend!"

Elza's hand grasps mine tightly. Do we run? They'll catch us, I'm certain. One look at their muscular bodies tells you that. We're frozen in place. They don't know exactly where we are. We have to stay put as long as we can.

"I believe I smell it, too," Dumachus says thoughtfully. "I believe that I do."

The armored monsters are poised, front legs raised. Their horrible old-men heads are pointed into the wind.

"Flesh," Titus sings softly, "flesh is what I smell. Flesh and spirit both. It is close, old friend."

"Where be it hidden?" Dumachus whines.

I hold my breath. Snow settles on my face and hair.

The horse monsters move with lightning speed, leaping at a car parked on the other side of the street. They ram the vehicle so hard it tips over, exposing the wheels and undercarriage to the blizzard. Something erupts yowling from underneath it, maybe a fox or a dog, and takes off into the snow.

"There it be!" screams Titus. "There it be! Only a mouthful, but food all the same! After the rascal, Dumachus! After him!"

The spirits shriek with delight and gallop off after

the animal, armor plates clattering, hooves pounding the snowy road. They vanish into the dimness within moments, their cries echoing strangely.

I let out a loud breath.

"What the f . . ." Elza whispers.

"So now you've met some residents of Deadside. Let's go. If we get to your house's hazel charms, they can't touch us."

I don't know that for sure—the hazel charms guard against ghosts, and I'm not sure these horse monsters count. They might be some kind of demon or another type of spirit I don't have a name for. Regardless, we're surely safer inside a house than we are crouched out here in the road.

We break cover and run across the road, up the hill that leads to Elza's house. The cars are totally covered now, strange lumps of snow with the suggestion of metal beneath the whiteness. We pass a telephone pole, and the drifts are so deep, I can't see the bottom of it, while fog hides the top. Snowflakes whirl in mocking spirals before my eyes. I barely recognize this street. Our home is being erased. Dunbarrow is becoming something alien and hostile, a place that frightens me. And what happened to all the people? This is so awful that I can hardly get my head around it. All I can think about is one foot, then the other, my toes throbbing with cold in my sneakers. Elza's hand is clamped to mine, less from affection than from a genuine worry that we might lose each other in the bleakness.

Finally we reach the end of Elza's road, and I'm certain of that because we can see her house, almost highlighted in the murky storm, and it takes me a moment to realize what's so strange about this view. The mist isn't flowing into Elza's garden, instead breaking around it, like the house is encased in a glass bubble. It must be the charms, the magical defenses she hung around her house and mine to keep uninvited spirits away. They're keeping this fog away as well. We've found a safe place.

She smiles at me for the first time since we came awake in the forest, and we hurry forward, both with the same urge, to get into the house and bolt the door, finally get warm. Then, once we're safe, maybe we can work out what's going on here, how we can —

There's a high, shrill scream behind us. I whirl around but can't see anything. Nothing but whiteness, snow, shifting fog. The cry comes again.

"Titus!"

I hear it clearer now. They're coming back. They picked up our trail somehow.

"Run!" I shout to Elza, and we take off, snow spraying around our legs. My breath rasps.

"Yes, my brother in arms, I hear it, too! The patter of feet!"

The horse monsters' voices are louder already. I glance back over my shoulder, but I still can't see anything. Snow, mist, empty front yards.

"They flee!" I hear one yell, with fierce joy. "Make haste, Dumachus!"

There's a thundering gallop of hooves behind us now, the harsh sound of armor plates clashing. They're so fast.

Elza's house is just ahead. I can see the empty milk bottles by the garden wall.

I can read the number on her gate.

I imagine their monstrous old-men faces leering at me in the fog, their mouths opening wide like mantraps—

Their hoofbeats are cannon blasts now.

We're at Elza's front wall. She hurls herself over it, not bothering with the gate.

"Have at him, Dumachus! Have at him!"

I jump as well, vaulting the low brick wall.

I'm expecting to fall into the snowy garden, but I don't. Something grabs my back, jolting me, my legs hitting the wall, I'm being dragged back—

"Luke!" Elza screams.

"What—"

Elza grabs my arms and pulls as hard as she can. There's a ripping noise and the pulling at my back vanishes. I collapse onto Elza, tumbling into her yard, face-first into a snowdrift. I scramble up, trying to get closer to the door, not understanding what happened.

The horse creatures are both at her garden wall. They're barely a foot from me. It seems like if they lunged across the wall, they could bite us, but they don't. We're protected by the hazel charms Elza hung around her yard. The spirits are even more hideous now that I can look at them up close, without thick fog between us. Their heads have gray mottled skin, wrinkled and unspeakably ancient, with long graying hair that merges into a mane on their necks. Snow settles on their armored shoulders and bare heads. One of them has a scrap of khaki fabric held in its mouth. It must be the back of my parka, I realize. He bit at me in mid-air, grabbed hold of my big jacket instead of my back. The other horse creature—Titus, I think this one is—looks at the two of us with a mixture of lust and loathing, running a fat gray tongue over his lips.

"That was ill struck, Dumachus," he remarks. "A fine folly these two have led us on."

"Donoff mggbh," Dumachus replies through a mouthful of parka.

"You see the hazel-wood wards upon their abode," Titus continues. "Another deception. She told us the old ways were forgotten now. They would be helpless, she said."

"Who told you we were helpless?" I ask.

"Luke," Elza says, "what are you—"

"Who told you that?" I ask again.

"You speak to us," Titus replies. He sounds surprised.

"Yeah," I say. "We can talk. Who brought you here?"

"Be you a sorcerer?" Titus asks me.

"I'm a necromancer," I say.

"A necromancer," Dumachus replies, finally managing to spit out the scrap of fabric. It looks like getting stuff unstuck from your teeth is difficult when you don't have hands.

"Bah!" Titus barks at me. "Slaveholder! Enthraller! I'll have none of your tricks, sorcerer! The gate is open, and the Winter Star waxes in the heavens! Tonight is our night, and it is a feast for the dead, not the living! Do not think we fear your sigil!"

"What are you?" I ask them. "Why are you here? What do you mean, the Winter Star?"

"No, we shall not parley with you, necromancer. This is our feast, our hunt. We are sworn Knights of the Tree. Cower behind your wards, and do not dare interfere. If we see you again, it will go ill for you."

Titus turns without another word and trots away into the fog. Dumachus stands by the wall a little longer, looking me up and down. I like his face even less than Titus's, sunken and hungry-looking. His teeth are sharp and inward-facing, like a shark's.

"I smell your blood through your skin, boy," Dumachus

(63)

says softly. "I'll quench my thirst before this long night is through. Mark my words."

He turns, armor clanking, and fades into the storm, following Titus. I let out a heavy breath.

"Luke," Elza says shakily, "what were they saying? How were you talking to them?"

"What do you mean?"

"You were speaking another language. It wasn't English."

"I thought . . . I don't know. I have no idea how that happened. I thought you could understand them, too."

"What did they say to you?"

"Their names are Titus and Dumachus. They said it was their hunt and that they're Knights of the Tree. They said that the Winter Star was waxing, whatever that means. Oh yeah, and they really want to eat us."

"Yes," Elza says heavily, "I kind of gathered that much."

Snow settles in her hair as we stand there looking out into the fog. The house opposite is invisible. We could be the only people left in the world.

The thought occurs, as the sky flickers green again, tinting the fog and snow a sickly jade, that maybe we are.

It's a bit warmer in Elza's house, but not as warm as I hoped it would be. In fact, there's a howling draft blowing into the hallway, which turns out to be coming from the kitchen, where the window on the back door has been broken and the door itself unlocked. There are shards of glass scattered all over the kitchen floor.

"Oh, you have got to be joking," Elza says. "Who did this? What is going on?"

"Where are your parents?" I ask.

"They went to a midnight concert in Brackford. . . . Did someone rob us? It can't be a ghost. They can't get in here."

I quickly look behind us, into the dark hallway. Nothing. The wind whistles in through the hole in the door.

"Do you think they're still here?" I whisper.

"Maybe," she says grimly. "I don't like this at all, Luke. We should've been more careful coming in. We made so much noise . . ."

I hear a soft bump upstairs, like somebody shut a door a little too hard. It seems like we're not as safe here as we hoped.

Someone—something—is definitely still inside the house.

I motion to Elza, and she opens the cutlery drawer and pulls out two knives. She passes me one without a word, and we step silently into the hallway. My mouth tastes sour and my heart thumps. I slide the door to the living room open, but there's nobody inside, just the dark bulk of the Moss family's Christmas tree, sofas, a television. The laundry room is similarly empty, and the downstairs bathroom as well. Which leaves upstairs.

We tread as quietly as we can, but the staircase is creaky and unbearably loud. Another green flash lights the upstairs landing through the windows, painting Elza's worried face in gruesome highlights and shadows. I point to her bedroom door, which we definitely left open this morning. It's closed.

We stand on each side, knives clenched in our hands, and then Elza turns the handle as silently as she can and pushes the door open.

"Whoa," she whispers. "Look."

Elza's room is dark and it's hard to make out details, but it's clearly been ransacked. Someone's been through here in a big hurry, pulling stuff out of drawers, tearing the covers off her bed, even ripping some of the photos and posters down off her walls. There are books scattered all over the floor.

"Why would someone do that?" I whisper back. "What are they after?"

"When we find them, we'll find out," she replies.

I move past her, back onto the dark landing, and softly make my way down to the spare bedroom, the room I slept in when everything was going wrong for me all those months ago, just before Halloween. I push the door open and move inside. The blinds are drawn, and the room is almost pitch-dark. I'm about to turn around, when someone roughly grabs me. My heart nearly stops, and before I can say or do anything, I feel the cold edge of a blade at my neck.

Shit. They were standing behind the door.

"Drop the knife," a voice hisses in my ear. "Do it."

I drop the kitchen knife onto the floor. Elza hears the noise.

"Luke?" she calls.

"Tell her to drop it, too," the man says. He's got a deep voice, a local accent. "Tell her to sit on the ground and don't do nothing. Tell her now."

"Elza," I call, feeling the blade caress my throat as my vocal cords move, "I found them."

(firelight)

I'm sitting on the sofa in Elza's front room. She's sitting next to me. We're not tied up, but there's a definite sense we shouldn't get up or make sudden movements. Two men in dark sportswear and ski masks are standing in the middle of the room. One's holding a sword; the other has a cricket bat. They seem very agitated, which doesn't put me at ease.

"Why are you wearing Big Chris's coat?" the guy with the sword asks me.

"What?"

"That's Chris Stokey's coat," he says, gesturing at my parka. "Big Chris, man."

"We stole it from his car," Elza says calmly.

"Don't lie to me, man," the masked guy says. "Don't screw with us. What have you done to him?"

"Nothing," I say. "It was on the backseat of a car. I was going to freeze, so we took it."

"This isn't important," the guy with the bat says. "Keep it together, mate."

"Yeah, yeah," the other one agrees. "All right. What's happening to the sky?"

"We don't know," Elza says.

"I'm asking Luke!" snaps the guy with the sword, and at that moment I'm sure who's under the ski mask.

"Where did you get a sword, Kirk?" I ask.

"We ask the questions," he growls.

"I've known you since we were eight, man," I say. "I know your voice. Mark's, too."

"I said there was no point in the masks," the guy with the bat—Mark—groans.

"Whatever, man," Kirk replies huffily. "At least I'm having some ideas, you know? Putting some stuff out there. It was worth a try."

"This is itchy as hell," Mark says. "I'm taking it off."

He peels off his ski mask with one hand, keeping an even grip on the cricket bat with the other. What are they afraid of? Is it me and Elza? Why did they break into her house? The fog flickers green, and I see Kirk's eyes glittering in the eyeholes of his mask. The green light shines down the length of his sword, which seems to be a Japanese design, like something a samurai would use. I know there's a proper name for it. Kirk's obsessed with martial arts movies, always used to talk about them.

Mark drops the mask on the other sofa. "We've still got questions for you," he says.

"What do you want to know? Why did you come here?" I ask. The hot pain in my jaw flares up again, and I wince.

"You know something," Kirk says. "You're not like the rest of us. You know something about this."

"Like the rest of who?" Elza asks.

"The rest of Dunbarrow!" Kirk yells. "You *know*!"

"We really, really don't," I say, as gently as I can. Kirk has always talked tough, but I've never seen him as an especially dangerous person. He has some nasty friends, but I don't think deep down he's ever really wanted to hurt people. Tonight, though, I'm not so sure. I feel like whatever's happening here may have rewritten all the rules about what people will and won't do.

"Turned midnight, man," Mark says to me, "they all went weird. Everyone, except us. Dunno why."

"What do you mean by 'weird'?" Elza asks him.

"Weird," Mark says. "Not right. All laughing and stuff. Talking crazy. And the light starts going up in the sky over the forest, and everyone was singing and cheering . . ."

"Where was this?" I ask.

"Dunbarrow Square. We were all waiting for the New Year. Night out, all the crew. Then—"

"They went funny," Kirk says. "Everyone, not just our mates. Little kids and grannies and granddads, too.

Everyone came out of their houses. They were building a, like, bonfire. Some worship-type thing. We got out of there. Then this fog came down, all the power went out . . ."

"So we came looking for you," Mark says.

"Why us?" Elza asks.

There's a moment of silence. Snow swirls outside the window. I can't see their faces, just their shapes, slumped and worried.

"You're different," Kirk says. "Both of you. You're not like us."

"What do you mean?" I ask.

"C'mon, man," Kirk says. "Something happened to you. I've known you for years, then one day you go all weird. You don't talk to me, you start hanging around with her, then Holiday says your dad died or something? You don't tell me nothing about that."

"You didn't ask me," I say.

"All right, so I never know how to talk about that stuff. Feelings or whatever. But look, man, there was that Halloween party, and you and Elza show up, and you're weird all night, and then we all wake up in the morning and nobody can remember what happened, and there's a cat cut open on the lawn—"

"—plus you've gone missing," Mark says to Elza. "Only person who wasn't there in the morning."

"Yeah. Exactly," Kirk agrees, jabbing a finger at her.

"So how's that look? Then we're in the park and you eat a crow—a whole crow, mate—and you say something to Mark that makes him go dead white, but he still can't remember what it was. You go nuts on us. I'm scared of you. And it keeps going, right? You're in math that time when the new girl came in—and, like, people think there was no new girl. Holiday still says I'm making that up— and she comes in, and you go into a demon trance and start drawing pentagrams all over the board. Plus you've got nine fingers now, and people said there was an accident but, like, an accident with *what*? What kind of accident can you have where one day you've got ten fingers and then nine the next, and nobody ever saw a bandage on that hand? People notice these things, man. Am I wrong, or am I right?"

"You are right," I admit.

"So anyway," Kirk finishes with a deep breath, "as soon as everything starts happening, we think how we need to find you dead quick. Find out what you know about it."

"Why come up here, though?" Elza asks him. "How do you know where I live?"

"I told them," comes a voice from the hallway. I turn my head, careful not to make sudden movements. Two girls are standing there. Is that Holiday Simmon? It must be. I can't tell who the other girl is; it's too dark. They're in parkas with fur-lined hoods, jeans, boots. Neither of them seems to be armed.

"Where were you?" Elza asks. "Were you in my room?"

"We hid under your parents' bed when we heard the front door open. We didn't know if it was safe," Holiday says. "But it sounds like you're just talking."

"Dunno," Kirk growls, "still might have to get rough with them."

"We'll explain as much as we can," Elza says. "You don't have to beat it out of us. But we don't know what's happening in Dunbarrow tonight."

There's a silent flash outside, illuminating the room. All of us look out at the snow, the mist, briefly tinted blue.

"It might take a while," Elza says. "Is it all right if I light a fire? Help us warm up. I'm worried about Luke. We walked all the way here from the high school in the snow."

Kirk seems agitated. "No sudden moves," he tells her.

"What do you think I'm going to do to you?" Elza asks him. "If I were going to turn you into a frog, I'd have done it the second I saw a man with a sword in my hallway. I can't hurt you."

I have a pretty vivid memory of Elza head-butting Kirk so hard his lip split, so I understand his wariness, but I don't bring this up. I imagine it's a sore spot for him.

Kirk walks Elza to the door. I stay where I am, hands

clasped on my lap. I feel stupid, never even thinking about what me and Elza must seem like to people who don't know us as fully as we know ourselves. I sort of thought I'd gotten away with it, somehow, but I don't know why. Holiday and her friend take seats opposite me, with Mark still standing between us. I can't see anyone's face properly in the dim room. Snow is still falling fast, and I start to wonder when it'll stop. This has already gotten worse than a normal Northumbrian winter, as vicious as those can be. We're far beyond dangerous-driving weather and into husky-team-and-a-sled weather. Nothing of Elza's yard is recognizable anymore. I'm worried the snow will start piling up at the windows, smothering the doors, burying us in this house.

Elza comes back with fire-lighters and an armful of wood. She kneels in front of the grate and sparks a flame, a wash of orange light playing over her face. Her shadow looms on the wall. It's the first natural light I've seen for a long time, I realize, and her face looks beautiful in it. Mark stands behind her. Kirk's leaning against the wall, by the door. They're still guarding us; they're just not as on edge as they were before we started talking. I wonder if they really meant to hurt us. Kirk held the sword to my neck, but would he really have killed me?

The fire starts burning properly. Now that there's real light in the room, I can see my old friends more clearly.

Like I noticed this morning, Mark's hair is longer now, just like mine, I guess. I stopped buzzing it so short, because Elza didn't like that look too much, and it didn't seem so important what the other guys thought. Kirk looks the same, maybe a bit heavier, like he's been bulking at the gym. Holiday's still blond, still perfect, the kind of face that was made for TV. The girl next to her is her old friend Alice Waltham, I see now. I didn't recognize her because she's had a haircut; her hair's dyed dark red now, cropped way shorter. She doesn't look like a version of Holiday anymore.

Elza's still kneeling, watching the fire.

Holiday pushes hair out of her eyes. "I'm sorry for busting in, Elza," she says quietly. "Sorry about your room, too. We were just looking for answers. We didn't know what else to do."

"That's all right," Elza replies. "We did the same to your house a while back. Desperate times, desperate measures."

Another surge of blue light outside, this one sustained, a chain of blue flashes, like lightning without the thunder. Nobody says anything. My head's spinning, so much to think about: the storm and the mist; Titus and Dumachus; what exactly me and Elza were running from in the forest. *The gate is open, and the Winter Star waxes in the heavens.* What is it that we can't remember? Where are Mum and Darren and Margaux? Is this something to do with them?

What about Berkley? Where does he fit into this? What did those spirits mean when they said they were the Knights of the Tree? What tree? What exactly is happening in Dunbarrow tonight?

Alice is staring at my left hand with undisguised disgust. People don't normally make a big deal about the finger, I've found; they just act like they can't see it's missing. I've come to feel more awkward about it than I imagined I would at the time I bargained it away, but I don't feel like hiding my hand. I keep it out on my lap. Let her look at it.

"So what's going on?" Kirk asks us again.

I take a deep breath.

"It's pretty complicated," I say.

"Try us," Mark replies.

Elza walks slowly across the room, watched closely by Kirk, and sits down next to me again. Her hand rests on my thigh. Everyone's looking at me. The firelight casts the room in black and gold.

"OK," I begin, "so you know how none of you ever met my dad? Well, one day, about two weeks before Halloween . . ."

Without clocks or daylight, I can't tell how long I talk for. It might be an hour, maybe two. I tell my old friends the truth about my dad, about his Host, the ghosts he bound into eternal service. I tell them about the Book of Eight, about Dad's sigil ring, about the desperate race before Halloween to banish the Shepherd and the rest of the Host into Deadside. I tell them what really happened at Holiday's party. I tell them how I went to the Devil's Footsteps and called on the actual Devil, how I talked with him and Dad on some gray forgotten shore. I don't tell them about my unborn brother, the Innocent; I think some things are better kept private. Elza takes over sometimes, filling in parts about her own life, talking about how she could always see ghosts.

I tell them about Ash and Ilana and the Widow, about the Fury and the nonpareil and Elza's first death. I tell Kirk and Alice how they caught me and Elza with Ash up at the Devil's Footsteps, about the Fury possessing her and Mr. Hallow. I tell them how I brought the Shepherd back into the living world, bound him to my sigil ring, and set off into Deadside after Ash. I tell Mark how the Shepherd tried to kill him, and I saved his life. I tell them about sailing the Cocytus, about the Riverkeeper that took my finger with its teeth. I tell them about my fight with Ash, about the Shrouded Lake, and about waking up in a tent with Ham dead beside me.

Finally we tell them what happened to us tonight, all the parts we can remember anyway, from Darren's house and Margaux's tarot cards through to our meeting with the Knights. And then I stop.

Nobody says a word. The fire's died down while we were talking, from a roaring gold to simmering red. The room is blood light and shadows.

"That's the craziest thing I've ever heard," Kirk says with a whistle. "You really expect me to buy all that?"

"Bollocks" is all Alice says. "Liar."

Mark runs a finger over his nose, feeling where the break mended. He says nothing.

"It is pretty difficult to believe," Holiday remarks.

"It's really true," Elza says.

"Your dad had, like, ghost servants," Kirk says.

"Eight of them," I reply.

"I said they were cracked," Alice says.

"I dunno," Mark says, "there might be something to it. I remember being in that tent."

"Do you?" I ask him.

"Yeah," he says, "you and some long-haired girl were there. You were talking to me, but I couldn't move. I only remembered it now."

"It's called implanted memory," Alice says. "Like, hypnotic suggestion? You only remember it because he talked about it. They had it on TV one time."

"Can you prove this stuff?" Kirk asks me and Elza.

"Look out the window!" Elza snaps back.

"Yeah, there's fog and weird light in the sky. Don't mean ghosts exist," Kirk says, not unreasonably.

"So these ghosts came to my house?" Holiday asks me.

"They did," I say. "I'm sorry. I tried to stop them from hurting people, but I didn't know how."

"And this Ash person stayed with me?"

"You don't remember anything about her?" I ask Holiday. "I know she affected your memories, but I wasn't sure how well it worked."

"What did she look like?"

"Small. White hair. Always wore white."

Holiday shakes her head. "I'd definitely remember someone like that."

We never thought to take any photos of Ash, that I can remember. I should've gotten some pictures of her with Holiday.

"You guys were best mates for, like, a week. Are there no selfies? Nothing online at all?"

Holiday holds up her phone, a mute black slab. There's no way to check.

"I remember Ash, man," Kirk says. "I kept saying! None of you listened!"

"They're making it *up*," Alice whines.

Elza fixes her with a look.

"OK," Elza says, "fine. We're making it up. Off you go, then. Go home, Alice. I don't want you in my house. I've never liked you."

Alice doesn't reply.

"Seriously, you're welcome to wander back off into the town. Since there's nothing going on."

"It doesn't make sense," Alice says to Holiday.

"Nothing that happened in town made sense," Holiday replies, still looking at me. "We all saw it. We all saw the fog."

"That's true," Kirk says.

"I mean, all those people going crazy, now this light in the sky . . . something's happening," Holiday continues. "We can all see that. And we all decided, didn't we, that Luke and Elza would know something about it."

There's a general silence. Nobody disagrees.

"And now they're telling us as much as they can about what's happening," Holiday says, still looking at me, as if she's waiting for me to correct her, "and we don't want to hear any of it."

"They didn't tell us what happened," Alice says. "Not tonight."

"Do you believe any of what I said?" I ask her.

"I dunno. How can I? It's crazy."

I wish there were some simple trick I could do to prove it to them. Pull a rabbit out of a hat. Turn water into wine.

But I can't, and my "magic stuff"—the Book of Eight and sigil ring—is in my house, on the other side of Dunbarrow. All I can do is talk.

"I can say what I think is happening," I tell them.

"All right," Holiday says.

"Normally, there's Deadside, where the dead are, and Liveside, where we all are," I continue. "They're separated. There are gates between the two worlds, but usually they're shut. Not just anyone can pass through. I think tonight . . . it might be different. I think the gate has opened the whole way. I think Deadside is spilling through to Liveside, to here, like water through a hole in a dam."

"What makes you think that?" Holiday asks.

"The fog and the light are coming from the gateway. The Devil's Footsteps. Me and Elza don't remember what happened, but we were running away from the gateway when we came back into ourselves. And those monsters we saw, the Knights of the Tree . . . they're from Deadside. They've crossed over, somehow, and they're here in Dunbarrow."

"Right," Alice cuts in, "the talking horses."

"I saw something," Kirk says to her. "Out in the snow. When we were coming across the fields. I saw something like that."

"What?" Alice whispers.

"I didn't wanna scare the rest of you," Kirk says. "But I

saw, like, a horse wearing a mask, or something. It was far away. I didn't see it properly."

"So if what you said is true . . . how do we stop it?" Mark asks loudly.

"I don't know," I reply.

There's another flash of green light outside. The snow-drifts on the window ledge have to be at least six inches deep now. Elza stands up and moves over to the fire. She kneels, throws a couple more logs in there, pushes at the ashes with the poker. Hundreds of sparks fly up the chimney. As the flames take hold of the fresh wood, the room lightens from deep red to a more hopeful honey color.

"So what happened to you?" Elza asks them. "We've said our part."

"We were in the square," Holiday says, "waiting for the New Year. The countdown, you know. Everyone was drunk. And just as it turned midnight, everything changed. The people changed."

"Changed how?" Elza asks.

"Just . . ." Holiday swallows. "They were different. They went crazy, started smashing up the shops. The man next to me was speaking this language I'd never heard in my life. They were all singing, and someone started lighting fires. I was really scared."

"Clock didn't strike neither," Kirk says. "Was stuck

just at midnight. Everyone's phone went dead then too, I reckon. But we didn't check that until later."

"Was that when the light started?" I ask him. "The sky, I mean."

"Yeah . . . I think so? We had a lot on our minds."

"But no fog?" Elza asks them. "We're trying to get a timeline here. Me and Luke, like we said, we're missing something. Maybe even a lot. We're missing the time between midnight and us running away from the stone circle. We don't know how long that was."

"Couldn't keep track," Mark says, frowning. He sits down on the arm of the other sofa, cricket bat against his legs. He doesn't seem to think we're a threat anymore. That's a start, I guess.

"We never saw no fog until after Luke's . . . after your house, I mean," Kirk says.

"What did you do at my place?" I ask them.

"We were going to break in," Kirk says, "but that dog was going crazy in there. Didn't fancy it."

It takes me a moment to realize he's talking about Ham. I remember then that they don't know Ham died. They heard Bea barking inside our house and must have thought she was Ham.

"She's new, actually," I say. "Ham's gone."

Still, good job, Bea. I haven't thought about her at all

since this started. I hope she's all right over there. We need to go to my house for a number of reasons, but this just added one more.

"Sorry. So, anyway. There was nobody there but the dog, far as we could see. Wasn't about to open that door. Looked around, through the windows, couldn't see nothing. So we thought we'd try here."

"And the fog appeared as you were walking over here?" Elza asks, sitting back down next to me. They all nod in agreement.

"We first saw the fog when we were running away," I tell them. "It was thickening up by the time we reached the school. So you must've been on your way over here then. So how much time did we lose?"

Mark shrugs. "No way to know. It must've been a couple hours, though."

That's longer than I thought. What happened to us in those missing hours? Whatever it was, it's crucial to what's going on here tonight.

Kirk finally sits down, with his back to the fire. He lays the sword on the carpet. We seem to have won them over, at least for now. I look at the faces around the room: Elza, tired and worried-looking. Alice's face is closed off, expressionless. Holiday is scared, I think, fiddling with the zippers on her jacket, staring down at the carpet. Mark and Kirk are scared, too, but hiding it behind stern frowns and stiff backs. I'm warming up, at least. I don't think the spirits can get in here. We're safe for the moment, but we've no idea what's happening down in the town itself. It sounds like everyone in Dunbarrow is affected by the gate opening, except for us. Can anyone get into Dunbarrow from somewhere outside, like Brackford? I think with snow like this, we have to assume they can't. We're on our own.

I'm standing in Elza's bathroom, holding a candle, trying to get a look at my back teeth in the shaving mirror. The others are still down in the front room; the house feels like an ice-box when you're away from the roaring fire. The bathroom window has frosted glass, and it's difficult to see out of it on the clearest of days; tonight it might as well be another wall. The wind is a high, desolate note and sneaks into the room through a crack in the window frame, causing my candle's flame to twitch and dance. The shadows move with the flame, ebbing and flowing like the tides. I think about Deadside, creeping into the living world through a crack. My face is lit from below in candlelight, my hair pushed back from my forehead. I look myself in the eye. Is this my fault? Did I do something, break the balance of the worlds? Was this because of the debt I owe Berkley?

I don't know. The knowledge must be there, but there's no way of getting it.

I pull my mouth open as wide as I can, the candle resting on the edge of the sink. It's terrible light, and I can't get a clear look at my back teeth, but I can definitely see something that wasn't there before, a dark protrusion where my bottom right wisdom tooth would have come through. The lump itself isn't tender, doesn't really hurt to touch, but I can feel it with my fingers, cold and hard, some kind of invading mass. What does this have to do with what's happening tonight? Why have I grown an extra tooth?

Someone knocks softly on the door.

"Just a moment," I say.

"It's me," Elza says, "can I come in?"

I unlock the door. She's holding another candle, smiling thinly. She's changed her clothes: loose black sweater and jeans.

I lock the door behind us again.

Elza sits on the edge of the bathtub.

"I gave them some chips and stuff," she says. "I don't think they'd eaten for a while. Do you think they're still drunk?"

"Yeah, maybe. They'll sober up soon, though. . . . They're the last people I expected to see tonight," I say.

"I know. It makes sense, I suppose. I never really thought about how we must look to other people. It just didn't bother me."

"Why do you think they weren't affected by . . . whatever this is?"

"I've been thinking about that," Elza says. "The only thing I can come up with is they all drank from Ash's cup. The one that erased your memories? I mean, that might be it."

"Could be."

"Can you see what's inside your mouth?" she asks.

"I don't know what it is. It's not a tooth."

"What about mine?" Elza opens her mouth, and I hold the candle as close to her face as I dare without the flame hurting her. I can see something dark and toothlike at the back of her mouth, sticking out of her bottom left gum. It could be a stone, although I don't see how that's possible. I tell Elza this.

"Right," she says, "we both have rocks stuck in our jaws. Why? What on earth were we doing up there?"

"You don't remember anything at all?" I ask.

"No. And there's no Internet, so we can't start there. We're lost."

The windowpane lights up sickly green. I put my arm around her.

"There is something," I say softly.

She doesn't reply.

"The Book of Eight," I say. "It's in my bedroom. We need the Book."

"No—" she begins.

"What else can we do? This is a disaster, Elza. This is terrible. Whatever's happening, it's not just you and me this time. It's everyone in Dunbarrow."

"I know," she says, "I just . . . Is there no other way?"

"I can't think of one," I say.

She doesn't reply.

"So we need to get back to my house," I say. "I don't know if they'll be up for that. I don't know if I am, honestly. I don't want to go back out there."

"Well," Elza says, "whatever we do, we can't just sit here."

We can agree on that, at least. The light from our candles gleams on the taps, the showerhead, the frosted glass of the window. The bath mat is still damp from the showers we took this morning, before we went to the park to take photos. I try to focus on these things, keep my mind from going in circles. We need to get to Wormwood Drive. That much is clear. Exactly how we'll manage that, and when, I don't know. One thing I hadn't realized until we were sitting here together is how exhausted I am. I'm having trouble keeping my eyes open. It seems absurd to sleep at a time like this, but that's what I want to do.

"Let's ask the others," I say. "They'll have their own ideas."

The others are sitting downstairs, still in the living

room. Alice and Holiday are sharing a bag of chips. Mark's eating a chocolate bar. Kirk has a can of beer and is taking a deep drink. There's a platter of cold lamb leg on the floor, half covered by aluminum foil. Cheese rolls, mini sausages, cake in a tin. Old party food from the Moss family Christmas.

I sit back down on the sofa, Elza next to me.

"So we need to decide what our next move is," I say.

Nobody disagrees. I continue.

"I think we need to get to my house."

"Why?" Mark asks me.

"That's where my—our—magic stuff is."

"Your spell book?" Holiday asks.

"The Book of Eight. I think if there's any chance of us stopping whatever's happening, we need the Book."

"Do you know that for sure?" Kirk asks me.

"No. But there's no other way to get information that might help us."

"We'll need to travel across Dunbarrow to get there," Elza says. "I think the weather puts driving out of the question, if any of the cars out there will even start. We'll be walking."

"We?" Alice says. "Who's 'we'? Since when is anyone giving me orders?"

Elza takes a deep breath.

"Alice—" Holiday says, "if we just—"

"No," Alice says. "You listen to *me* for once, Holiday, yeah? We ought to get the hell out of Dunbarrow. That's what we should do."

Nobody says anything.

"Seriously," she says, "whatever's happening here, and I honestly don't care what that is, we need to leave. Let's go. Leave them. It's their fault. We can follow the road up to the motorway."

"And then what's your plan?" Elza asks her.

"Shut *up*," Alice retorts.

"No, really, Alice, I'm curious. What then?"

"We walk to Brackford," she says.

"That's fifteen miles along the main road," Elza replies. "In a blizzard. That's your plan? Not to mention we don't even know if we can leave Dunbarrow. We have no idea how far this fog stretches."

"Alice," I say gently, "if we are being swallowed up by Deadside somehow, Brackford might not even be there anymore. I don't know what we'd find, but—"

"Shut up!" she screams at me. "SHUT UP! They're *lying*! How can you just sit here and listen to this? We're not being swallowed by Deadside, because Deadside doesn't exist, because they're lying! How can Brackford be gone? Cities don't disappear!"

"I don't like this either—" I begin.

"*I said shut up!* Holiday, you don't believe this, do you?"

Holiday doesn't move.

"Alice," Kirk says, "you gotta calm down a bit—"

Alice starts to say something else, but no words come out, just a scrambled roar of anger and fear. She gets up and runs out of the room. I hear the bathroom door slam shut.

"Great." Elza sighs.

"Will she be OK?" I ask Holiday.

"I don't know," she replies. "She hasn't been dealing with this very well."

"How about you?" I ask her. She smiles thinly.

"Not so well either," Holiday says.

"Do you believe me?" I ask her. "Do you think we're lying?"

"I think you believe what you're saying," Holiday says. "I have a hard time with some of the stuff you just told us. I think you can see why. But I believe something I don't understand is happening in Dunbarrow tonight. I think Alice does, too, but she won't admit it."

Kirk grunts, takes another swig of beer. "It's totally nuts. Ghosts and magic books and whatever else. But I don't see what they get from lying," he says. "And we all saw what happened down in the town."

"I believe you," Mark tells us quietly.

"All right," Elza says, "we can work with that."

"So what do we do?" Holiday asks us. "You really think we should head to your house?"

"Yes," I say. "I don't see a choice."

"Why not stay here?" Kirk asks. "Wait for it to blow over?"

"We don't know if it will," Elza replies.

Mark nods.

"This thing, whatever it is," I say, "we don't know enough about it. But maybe this is just the beginning."

"And if we get to your house, to this book, you'll be able to stop it?" Holiday asks.

"Yes," I say, more confidently than I feel.

"Staying here keeps us fairly safe, because of my hazel charms," Elza says. "We have food for a few days at least, more if we're brave enough to venture out and raid a corner shop. There's no running water, but I suppose we can drink melted snow. We've got a lot of firewood. Thing is, we don't know how long this . . . event, anomaly, whatever it is, will last. What happens if the snowstorm lasts a week? A month? Longer? Things start to get more difficult."

"Same deal at Luke's place," Kirk replies.

"Right," I say, "but we can make a start at fighting back once we're there."

"Be dangerous getting across," Mark says. "Snow, fog . . . must be way below freezing out there. Like the Arctic. We could die just walking down the road if we aren't prepared."

"That's without whatever else might be out there," Elza adds. "The Knights will be looking for us, plus whatever happened to the people in Dunbarrow . . . it's not going to be easy."

We consider this.

"I still reckon we stay here," Kirk says.

"Don't be a baby," Holiday snaps. He startles. Elza smiles at this.

"We can go across the fields," I say.

"I dunno about that," Mark says. "In the storm there's no way to know where we are. We could go around in circles. That's dangerous."

"All right," I say, "so we go through town. Landmarks, places to shelter if it gets too bad."

"More chance of running into other people or spirits," Elza says.

"I'm with Mark," Holiday says, looking at her feet. "Those fields are so exposed. We could get lost."

"Town, then," I say. "We agree on that."

"Yeah," Kirk says. He finishes his beer and crushes the can against his knee.

"So when do we go?" I ask.

"How'd you mean?" Mark replies.

"I don't know what time it is. None of us do. But it must be four in the morning at least. I'm exhausted. I dunno about you."

"What if this gets worse?" Elza asks me. "What if we run out of time?"

"I honestly don't know if I could make it to my house right now," I say.

"Me either," Holiday agrees.

"I think we need to sleep, regroup, prepare ourselves properly," I say to Elza.

She's still frowning.

"Let's vote," Holiday suggests.

"All right," Elza says. "Who thinks we sleep?"

I raise my hand, along with Holiday. After a moment Kirk does as well. Elza and Mark stay as they were.

"Carried, then," I say. "We stay here a few hours, try to get what rest we can. Then we head out for Wormwood Drive."

"What about Alice?" Kirk asks. "She ain't voted."

"She's not going to want to go outside," Holiday tells him. "Whatever she says about leaving Dunbarrow."

"Well," Elza says, with fake cheer, "sweet dreams, everyone."

We bed down in the front room, bringing blankets and pillows from upstairs, using the sofa cushions as mattresses. It feels like the weirdest sleepover I've ever had. Alice eventually emerges, red-eyed, and immediately lies facedown without speaking to anyone else. There are beds upstairs, of course, but nobody seems to want to be in separate rooms tonight. I feel like we're a litter of puppies, huddled together for warmth. The fire burns itself down, candles sit on the mantelpiece beneath glass coverings. I lie on my back, with Elza next to me, listening to the tidal whisper of her breathing, the empty howl of the wind outside. The ceiling is firelit, deep orange, and every so often a pulse of green or blue will taint the room from outside. I lie awake for a long time, feeling a gentle pulse in my gums where the stone tooth is set. I don't know when I fall asleep.

I'm kneeling on frozen ground. The swans are set before me like a feast. Their necks are broken. They're laid in a ring around the three warding stones. The light circles around and around this clearing, but it can't get out. We're birthing a miracle.

Elza kneels beside me. Her face is rapture.

I'm me but I'm not me. There's something else behind our eyes.

The bird-woman is talking to us. She has two voices, and one is only for special occasions. She takes something from the sky between her fingers and plants it in the ground.

I think it was the Winter Star.

There's something growing from the earth behind her, a stem of ice, veins of light. The swans are moving, dead but moving, flying backward in a circle. Their necks are snapped but they're still flying.

The bird-woman is speaking again. She rests her hands on my chin.

I open my mouth and she reaches inside.

I wake up and nothing has changed. The room is dark; it's still nighttime, the fire burned down to embers and ash. I listen to the wind wailing. No light outside, just fog and snow. I know there was a dream, something about birds . . . but the memories dive out of reach, like slippery fish into a black pond. I remember dead swans, but that's it, and for all I know I'm just remembering the bird we found on the road back to my house, yesterday morning. What happened at the Devil's Footsteps? What is it that happened in those missing hours?

I sit up. My mouth feels dry, the new stone tooth tender but not terribly painful. I can feel my pulse there, a low drumbeat.

"Luke?"

A quiet voice. It's Holiday. She's sitting wrapped in blankets on the far sofa, head tilted toward the ceiling. I thought she was still asleep.

"Still dark," I say, the way you tell people obvious things when you can't think of anything else to say.

"I've been trying to count in my head," she says.

"I couldn't sleep. I wanted some way to know how long it's been."

"How long have you been counting?" I whisper.

"I don't know. Hours."

"Yeah. Time in Deadside is like that."

The wind picks up again. It seems like it's stopped snowing, at least from what I can see.

"Did you really go to the world of the dead?" Holiday asks. I can't see her face properly, just the shape of her head and hair.

"I really did."

"I don't know what to say about that," she replies.

"I've never really known either. Sometimes it feels like a dream."

"So we do live after death," she says.

"Everyone does, yeah."

"So my grandma's still there."

"Somewhere," I say. "And her grandma, and her grandma . . . for as long as there's been people, I think."

"Is it a horrible place?" Holiday asks me. "Where they are?"

"The part I saw was pretty bad," I tell her. "But I think there are other bits."

"Good," she says. "Good."

I don't really know what that's meant to mean. It's

hard to talk about these things. There's another green flash outside. I wish we had some way to time them. I wonder if the gaps between them mean something specific. The room smells stale, musty sleeping bags and last night's sweat. A guy, Mark or Kirk, turns in his sleep and mumbles.

"Where's your mum?" Holiday asks me.

"I don't know. Last I saw she was outside Dunbarrow. Where's yours?"

"Brackford. They went to see the fireworks by the river."

I'd like to say they're OK, tell Holiday her family is fine, but I really don't know. I don't know how far this has spread. Maybe the whole world is like this right now: ice and fog and green ghost light in the sky. Maybe it's just us. Maybe this is all happening in the split second between midnight and the New Year, and nobody outside of Dunbarrow will ever realize anything went wrong.

Elza sits up beside me. Her hand runs over mine, gently touching the gap where my little finger used to be.

"I sort of hoped it would be dawn," she says.

"It's been like this for a long time now," Holiday replies. "I think the blizzard's stopped, though."

"Really?" Elza says. "That's interesting."

"We should go soon," I say. "Before the snow starts again."

Elza stands up, moves awkwardly across the living room, stepping over the other boys. She loudly rattles at the ashes with her poker, then kneels down and arranges fire-lighters and some logs. After a few moments her effort births a new yellow flame, which hungrily spreads over the wood. She rattles the grate again, sparks flying up the chimney.

Kirk raises his head. I can see his face now in the fire-light, Holiday's, too.

"Sorry," Elza says, "did I wake you?"

Kirk just snarls and crawls out of his sleeping bag, stumbles off, presumably to the bathroom.

"It doesn't flush," Elza calls. "Go in the yard! Far away from the house!"

Kirk growls again.

Alice and Mark seem to be awake as well, but they don't say anything.

We eat breakfast, more of the same food from last night: Christmas dinner stuff, a breakfast that doesn't make sense. Green grapes, chocolate cake, a bag of cheese straws. Elza's kitchen is an icebox, cold leaching in through the broken window. Snow has settled on the floor in a thin dusting, with Kirk's footprints leading to the back door. I'm thinking of sweeping it up, but I leave it. More will come in. The snow's piled high in her yard, the shed almost invisible. The fog presses around the house but can't make it inside.

I feel like we're inside in a glass bowl that a giant dropped into cloudy water.

We dress to leave, raiding Elza's parents' closets, looking for woolly sweaters, scarves, anything large and warm. I end up wearing two sweaters, big gloves, waterproof pants over two pairs of jeans, and hiking boots double-lined with socks. Everyone else looks similarly ridiculous, like overstuffed scarecrows.

There are some arguments about light. We can't use flashlights: the bulbs won't work, like anything else electrical. Even though it's not as dark as a proper night would be, nobody likes the idea of going out without anything we can see by, especially with the interiors of buildings being as dark as they are. In the end we take matches and rags and firewood, thinking that maybe we can start a fire or make torches if we have to. We take two long synthetic ropes, kitchen knives, a camping ax, and the four-man tent Elza's dad keeps in the loft.

With nothing left to prepare that we can think of, I push open the door and we step out into Dunbarrow. The wind reaches for us, plunging icy fingers deep into our flesh. The fog swirls and eddies just beyond the hazel charms' reach, waiting for us to join it. Everything is gray and white, a world without warmth or color, a world to vanish in.

(dunbarrow)

It becomes obvious this won't be a short journey. The snow isn't falling anymore, but it has settled in drifts of anywhere between thigh high and taller than our heads. The fog advances on us and then retreats, like a wolf following a flock of sheep, reducing our visibility to mere feet and then lifting to reveal the entire snowbound street. Elza and I are at the front, by unspoken consensus, with Alice and Holiday behind us, and Mark and Kirk bringing up the rear, still wielding their weapons. We're walking in the middle of the road, back down Towen Crescent. The light is low, but it's not the dark you'd expect from midnight; more the dim haze I've come to associate with Deadside, lit from above by some uncertain source. My ears are primed for any hint of hoofbeats or voices out in the snow, but all I can hear is the wind.

After a while, huffing and puffing, sinking in the snow, we reach the end of Elza's street, where it joins with the main road out of Dunbarrow. I can see the car the Knights rammed, still lying on its side, submerged in a snowdrift. My nose feels about ready to fall off, the only part of my face still exposed to the wind. I rearrange my scarf, trying to get better coverage, jealous of Mark's and Kirk's ski masks. Elza stops.

"What's the problem?" I ask Elza.

"Trying to decide which way to go," she says.

"This way," I say, gesturing down toward the center of Dunbarrow.

"Yeah," she replies, "but they said something was happening in the town square. That's where everyone went insane, right? We want to avoid that."

Holiday and Alice almost bump into us. Alice squeaks with outrage.

"So we go along Flenser's Row," Holiday cuts in. "Along by the river path? We can get up onto the bridge, and then we're on the hill up to Wormwood Drive."

"All right," Elza says. "Not bad."

She walks on, with me just behind her. This is kind of Elza's turf—I've been coming up here on the way to her place for quite a while now, but she still knows these roads better than I do. We head downhill, past a row of terraced houses, each with a fat white cap of snow and black unlit windows. Around the corner, things start to change.

Rather than walking past more snowy houses, we

find ourselves in a forest. It happens so suddenly, I don't even register it at first, keeping my eyes fixed on the wall of fog in front of me; it's only when Elza says something about a tree that I look around us and see that we're not in Dunbarrow anymore. Instead of buildings and cars, we're surrounded by twisted gray trees, leafless and crooked, with sickly-looking vines hanging off their branches. The earth is still snow covered, but the drifts are shallower, with gray soil visible around the bases of the trees. The fog is thinner and stiller, a sinister gauze hanging at the edges of my vision.

"What's happening?" Elza asks me.

"Deadside," I say.

"Well, it's definitely not Dunbarrow."

We stop, and Mark and Kirk catch up, breath leaking from the mouth sockets of their masks. Kirk pulls his off when I tell him what's going on, takes a look around.

"Bloody madness," he says, gawping at the crooked trees.

"What does this mean?" Mark asks me. "Where's Dunbarrow? Where are we?"

"I'm not exactly sure," I say. "I should have thought of this. Deadside is spilling through, right? So the town isn't going to look quite the same anymore. There are bits and pieces that'll be different. So what we have to do—"

"What do you mean *different*?" Alice demands.

"I don't know. It really could be anything. Any kind of landscape. It changes."

"We should go back to her house," she says to Holiday.

"Listen," Elza snaps, "we're not in Dunbarrow, Alice. The road behind us isn't there anymore. We can't go back to my house."

"I want to go back," Alice says. Kirk claps her on the shoulder.

"We're right here," he says. "We keep going and we'll be all right. Isn't that right, Luke?"

"Definitely," I say. "We just need to keep going forward."

"Is that really all?" Elza whispers to me.

"I have no idea," I whisper, then raise my voice to say, "But look, what we need to do, as well as keep together, all right . . . What we need to do is think about Dunbarrow. Try and picture it in your mind. When you're traveling in Deadside, you can go anywhere you want if you're looking for it. So just try and think about places in Dunbarrow. Think about the river and the bridge and the clock tower. Think about Vibe or the high school, your house, the park, anywhere we've spent a lot of time."

"And that'll make this go away?" Holiday asks, pointing to the forest around us.

"It should," I say.

Holiday frowns, and then places a gloved hand in mine

and takes hold of Alice with the other. "Let's stick close," she says to Alice. "And think about your house, OK?"

I take Elza's hand with my free one, and we start to walk like this, Mark joining the chain at the other end, taking Alice's hand. We're partly supporting her and partly trying to stop her from running away into the forest. I hate to think what might happen if Alice gets lost out here in the wilderness of Asphodel. I try not to think about the things I saw here last time: speaking snakes and flame-eyed boatmen, the hungry thing that wore Elza's face like a mask. I try to think about Dunbarrow in sunshine: the park, with its duck pond and swings; the town square on Sunday afternoon, with traders' stalls selling homemade jam and jewelry. I tell myself the gray forest around us is an illusion, a veil, something half imagined intruding onto what's real.

The trees persist for a while longer, and we walk slower now that we're essentially supporting Alice. I'm glancing at the ground in front of us when I see a face.

There's a man tangled in the roots at the base of one of the trees. His gray skin blends with the grayness of the roots, making him hard to spot. The roots are looped around his neck, his forearms, his torso, firmly binding him in place. He might be dead, or sleeping, or some strange thing that's not quite one and not quite the other. His eyes are closed.

"Make sure Alice doesn't look down at the tree roots," I

whisper to Holiday. She doesn't ask why but starts talking to Alice loudly, making her look at something up ahead of us. I can see Elza and Mark have noticed the man as well, but they don't say anything about it. The unspoken agreement seems to be that we keep on walking and hope it works out.

There are more of them as we travel, or maybe they were here in this forest the entire time and it's only now I'm noticing them: men and women and children, dressed in gray rags, some almost part of the earth itself, with roots growing into their ears and mouths, as if the forest grew from their heads somehow. Their faces look ancient and weathered, as though they've been sleeping down below the trees as long as the world has existed. I don't like walking among them, but I don't see what choice we have. We can't go back.

"What are they?" Elza whispers.

"No idea. But don't touch them," I say.

The snow is falling again, just a thin dusting, settling on the roots and branches and faces of the awful forest. There's a green flicker in the sky, and it's been a while since we saw one of those. At least we know we're still near whatever's causing that light, wherever we are.

The trees are thicker, more tangled, with more and more bodies visible in the roots. I'm feeling increasingly uneasy about this. I almost trip on an outstretched gray arm. What happens if we wake them? I tug at Holiday's hand to get her to walk a little faster, and she trips Alice, who stumbles, coming face-to-face with one of the bodies.

I can't say a word.

Alice shrieks like a fire alarm, leaping to her feet and setting off at a sprint through the trees.

Shit.

The root-encrusted body nearest to me opens its eyes.

They're blank and white, luminous, twinned full moons.

There's a creaking sound, like tree branches breaking. I can hear hissing voices that aren't ours.

"RUN!" I shout. "GO!"

To their credit, the others don't question me. We bolt along the path we've been following, fog billowing around us, voices that sound partly like trees in the wind and partly like a choir echoing in my ears. The sleepers are awakening, their gray hands reaching at us between the gnarled roots of these trees.

Dunbarrow. That's where I want to be. We're going to turn a corner and find ourselves on the main street. I'm so frightened I can't picture anywhere else. Just the main street on a summer's day, someone selling ice cream, the mobile-phone shop and the Starbucks and the pubs with people sitting outside in the gardens with beers, traffic backed up at the roundabout, kids in shorts and caps slouching on a bench, supermarket parking lot full of weekend shoppers . . .

The fog swirls. I can hear the dead howling, the cracking sounds as they wrench themselves free of the roots . . .

No.

Dunbarrow.

That's where we are. We'll break out of this forest and—

Something reaches through the mist for me, grasping gray arms, white eyes.

I shoulder-butt it as hard as I can, knocking its body aside. The dead thing feels light as paper, a husk of a person. It tumbles to the ground, but there are many more of them, ranks of wispy figures with long fingers and glowing eyes.

Elza shrieks.

Dunbarrow. We're in—

I run slap-bang into a car. I gasp, bent double, trying to catch my breath, legs shaking. A real car, snow covered, with a rear window. Elza grabs me.

"Are we—"

"Come on!"

"Luke—"

"Oh sh—"

Holiday and Kirk and Mark are right behind us, still running, not yet having noticed where we are. The fog thins, revealing familiar shop fronts, traffic lights, a scabby back alley that I know cuts up to the supermarket. I've walked on this road a million times. It's the bottom of the main street.

"We're all right!" I say. "We're all right!" I grab at Holiday and Kirk, trying to stop them from running off into the mist. Kirk looks wildly over his shoulder, convinced we're about to be grabbed by the dead.

"Get off me, man!" he yells.

"What was that?" Holiday asks. "What?"

"I don't know," I say, "but we made it through. It's gone."

Kirk's still looking back down the street, grasping his sword, waiting for the root-dwellers to come rushing out of the fog. Nothing happens.

"It's all right, mate," I say. "We're OK." I pat his shoulder.

"Screwed up, man," Kirk says. He shrugs off my hand.

"You believe me now?" I ask.

He laughs, a little shakily.

"If this is all fake," Kirk says, "you got the biggest budget on earth, man. Yeah, I believe you."

"Where's Alice?" Holiday asks me.

"She was just ahead of us," I say.

We look at the street. She isn't here. No footprints in the snow either, none except ours.

"She's probably just ahead," Elza says gently.

"We'll catch up," Mark adds, squeezing her hand.

Holiday nods, but I can tell she doesn't believe us.

We make our way along the main street in silence. The snow seems shallower here, a thin layer over the cars and pavements. I'm trying not to think what might've happened to Alice. She must be lost in Asphodel, could be anywhere in Deadside. She might already be a gray girl wrapped in gray tree roots, sleeping forever in the dirt. I never really liked her that much, but she definitely didn't deserve that. I'm not sure anyone does.

The windows of the shops have been smashed, broken glass lying half buried in the snowdrifts, just like Holiday and the others told us. There's snow piled up inside the pharmacy, the pubs, the newsagents. I can see myself reflected in the remains of one window, a blurred muffled figure, body wrapped in oversize coats and scarves. I keep checking in every window we pass, making sure I'm still here, that we're all still here, that the street doesn't slip away from us, become something else.

Elza pulls at my sleeve.

"Can you hear that?"

I stop and listen. Fog swirls before my eyes, obscuring the road before us. There's something in the air, voices, people singing. I catch a snatch of it.

"Seven trees of living stone . . ."

No idea what that means, but it's not good. We turn to Holiday and the guys.

"Let's take this slow," I say. They nod.

"The eighth is cast of ice and bone . . ."

It's difficult to tell where the voices are coming from, and I almost don't want to move at all, in case that would take us closer to the singers, but we don't have a choice. We crouch down behind a row of parked cars and walk slowly through the snow. I can hear the crackle of flames, and I see something that could be firelight, shining through the mist.

"Seven trees of living stone . . ." come the voices in the fog.

There are strings of Christmas lights hanging above us, unlit and sinister, like vines ripening with black fruit. We meant to avoid the town square, but that's where we seem to have ended up regardless. Maybe it was the place we were all thinking about hardest. I know it's what I think of when someone says "Dunbarrow" to me.

"The eighth is cast of ice and bone . . ."

We round the corner to the town square, and I can barely believe what I'm seeing.

The fog is thinner here, pierced by the ravenous light of an enormous bonfire. Anything that can burn is being burned: sofas, chairs, piles of magazines and cushions and the new saplings that were planted in the middle of the roundabout. The heat is intense, radiating far enough to warm our faces as we peer around the corner, keeping the snow from settling on the paving stones of the square. Around this fire are people, hundreds and hundreds of them. They're writhing and screaming, and it takes me a moment to realize that it isn't in pain but in joy. Their shadows blend with one another, a many-formed monster, projected over the sides of the buildings in flickering firelight.

"*SEVEN TREES OF LIVING STONE!*"

"Oh my god," Elza whispers. "It really is everyone."

"We said so, didn't we?" Kirk growls beside my ear. "All gone crazy."

"*THE EIGHTH IS CAST OF ICE AND BONE!*"

"We never doubted you," Elza whispers.

"Look," says Holiday, "isn't that Mrs. Gould? You know, from the newsagent?"

I look to where she's pointing. It is indeed Mrs. Gould, the small round-faced old woman who ran the corner shop. Me and Kirk used to buy candy from her every day after school. She's dancing like a puppet, screaming with delight, sweat running over her face. She's not wearing any shoes, stamping the cold wet concrete without a care in the world. She's just one of them. I can see plenty of other people I recognize, and it's like they're turning into something else: the familiar faces are like masks, and I feel like something else is breaking through from underneath, strange new faces grown beyond fear or love. The sky flashes green again, and there's a frenzy of cheering, people tearing at their clothes, throwing shoes and jackets onto the bonfire.

What's happening to them?

"SEVEN TREES OF LIVING STONE!"

They stamp and clap, twirl and wail. The dance has no pattern that I can see, but nobody crashes into anyone else, and nobody hesitates for an instant.

"We'll have to go back," Elza whispers. "Find another way. I don't want them to see us."

"THE EIGHTH IS CAST OF ICE AND BONE!"

I agree. Nothing could make me go across that square. The idea of those faces, those eyes, turning to me is too awful to think about. We turn around and are about to head back down the street, when I see two figures standing in the middle of the road.

"Luke?" one of them says.

"Oh, man, Elza," the other says.

They come closer. It's Ryan and Jack, two of the other town ghosts we know. Their eyes are glowing the same green as the sky, the same green Andy's were.

"You see that?" Ryan says to me, holding up his right hand. He's got a bottle of beer.

This seems like a bad scenario. Holiday and the boys are behind us, using me and Elza as a shield. Kirk's got a sword! Why can't he go in front?

"Yeah, looks good, man," I say to Ryan, gesturing to one side, hoping the others will go around the ghosts and get behind them.

"Nice beer," Elza adds.

"This is incredible," Jack says. "This is the best night of all time."

"I can drink it," Ryan says. "We're holding it. Look at that!"

"You're holding that beer, all right," I agree. "Never seen better beer holding."

"We were so worried all the time," Jack says. "We never wanted to move on, you know? And we don't have to! Deadside's come to us!"

"This all looks good to you?" I ask them, gesturing at the bonfire, the crazed revelers, the snow and broken windows and ghoulish shifting mists.

"It's looking great, man!"

"Yeah, don't you think?"

"We, uh . . ." I begin.

"We love it," Elza says. How are we going to get around them? The town ghosts are blocking us off, and the bonfire is behind us. I don't want to risk them making a noise and attracting more attention. What I want, more than anything, is to get away from these guys without any of the dancing people noticing us.

"*Seven trees of living stone . . .*"

The chant continues behind us.

Ryan takes a swig of beer. "You're leaving already?" he asks.

"Long night, man," I say.

"You can't leave," Jack says cheerfully. "Have you met the Apostles?"

"Yeah, they're, uh, great," I say.

"We love them so much," Elza says, trying to edge around them.

"Me, too," Ryan says, taking another drink.

"Come on, you can't leave yet!" Jack cries, wrapping an arm around Elza's shoulder. "You and your friends! Come join the party!"

The ghosts can touch us now. This is new. It seems like the spirit world and ours really have collapsed into one another. Ryan takes hold of me. His hands are extremely cold, like shapes carved from ice. I can feel their chill even through my thick layers of clothing.

"Come on!" he says cheerfully to me and the others. "No time to waste."

I've always liked these guys. They're the ghosts I've gotten along best with. I don't have any easy way to communicate this to Holiday and the guys; I didn't mention Jack and the others when I told them my story, since they've been a fairly minor part of it. They clearly have no idea what's going on. I don't know what to do here, whether the town ghosts can hurt us or what. Ryan's grip on me is surprisingly strong. He's steering me past the others, toward the bonfire.

"What's happening?" Holiday asks me. "Who are these people?"

"Don't follow us," I say. "Stay here."

"Join the party," Ryan says cheerfully to her, but he keeps pulling me onward and doesn't pay much attention to what they're doing. The others hide behind the car again. Me and Elza are being shepherded into the dance. We're among the dancers now, firelight warming my face, Ryan's cold hand still clamped around my forearm.

"*SEVEN TREES OF—*"

" . . . just amazing," he's saying, "like, everyone coming together, you know? And we can talk to our other mates again, not just you, not that I don't like you—"

"*—LIVING STONE!*"

The dancers howl like wolves. I shudder. I've lost sight of Elza and the others. Ryan pulls me onward, his eyes gleaming with emerald light.

"*THE EIGHTH—*"

" . . . but everyone, man, we're all together, alive and dead, doesn't matter anymore."

"*Please!*" I hear Jack screaming. "*Apostles!*"

"*—IS CAST—*"

"What's happening tonight?" I ask him, hoping we'll

at least start to get some answers. The people around us jostle us, sweaty bodies, faces twisted into horrible masks. Some I recognize, most I don't. I can see now that at least some of the dancers must be the town ghosts: there's a mixture of modern clothing and outfits that definitely aren't from this century.

"—OF ICE AND BONE!"

"I need to speak to the Apostles!" Jack screams again, somewhere in the din.

"It's the Tree," Ryan says. "The Tree brought us together. How do you not know that, man? Have you not been listening to a word they've been telling us?"

"The tree?"

"The Barrenwhite Tree, man."

The Barrenwhite Tree. I don't remember ever hearing about that before. I've seen something in Deadside that the Shepherd said was a tree: a strange being made from shadowy ravens, the awful shrine in the middle of a great field of heads on spikes. If this tree is anything like that one, we're in a lot of trouble.

I can't see any trees here, though, despite everyone screaming about them. Nor can I see anything that might be thought of as a shrine. All I can see are dancers, flames, the mist above us flickering a vivid blue for a moment, and the ghosts' eyes flickering blue with it. I see Elza's distinctive cloud of hair backlit by the bonfire for a moment, just ahead of us. Where are Jack and Ryan taking us? We're heading for the flames in the middle of the square. For a moment I think we're going to keep walking, straight into the fire, and who knows what would happen then, but then I hear an answering cry to Jack's call for the Apostles, and the dancers stop moving and part before us, leaving a corridor all the way to the bonfire in the middle of the square. I see a pair of figures standing before the flames, and I can't take my eyes away.

At first I think they have bird heads, are some new kind of spirit, but as we get closer, I see that the figures are people wearing masks, strange metallic bird head-dresses that shimmer in the light. The shorter figure's head is white and gold, elaborately carved with sigils and magic marks. The taller figure wears a black-and-golden mask, with large eyes and a flatter, wider head. An owl. Both of them wear floor-length robes, like a monk's, woven from heavy dark cloth. These are the riders we saw earlier in the night, crossing the playground on Dumachus's and Titus's backs.

These must be the Apostles.

The shorter figure's bird mask is swanlike but somehow predatory as well, with a sharp golden beak. Firelight glistens over it. I've gone from being too cold to being roasted. Elza's hands are balled into fists, but she doesn't move. Neither of us seems able to. The flames surge and roar, but the masked Apostles never move a muscle. The dancers stand where they paused, mumbling to themselves.

After a long moment a voice comes from behind the swan mask, something cold and utterly inhuman.

"*Yes?*" the thing beneath the mask says.

"We just all wanted to talk to you again," Ryan says cheerfully. "Our mates here hadn't spoken to you. We just wanted—"

"*We have treated before,*" the Apostle says. "*The twice-born and the Speaker's pawn.*"

"Who are you?" I ask the figure.

"*Your throats were cut, or so I was told.*"

"They told you wrong," I say.

"*SEVEN TREES OF LIVING STONE!*" screams the crowd, stamping the cold ground.

"*So it seems. What do you say of this?*" the swan-masked figure asks the second Apostle. I see that this larger being, who hasn't spoken yet, has deformed hands, awful, long fingers with wattled, scaly flesh, ending in hooked claws.

"My master—" the owl-masked figure begins, speaking with a low, hoarse voice.

"*Did not we see their bodies upon the ground? What is the meaning of this?*"

What on earth is this thing talking about? Our throats were cut? It saw our bodies on the ground? Does it mean me and Elza? When is this supposed to have happened?

"I still have pity!" the owl-masked figure screams, making me jump. "Forgive me! Please!"

"THE EIGHTH IS CAST OF ICE AND BONE!"

"I have been good to you," the swan-masked Apostle says, without any warmth. "Still, I see you are unfit for this task." She turns to Ryan and Jack. "Throw these intruders upon the fire."

"She's so great," Ryan says admiringly. "Don't you think she's amazing?"

"Ryan," I say, "don't—"

"Don't worry, mate," he says. "This is all happening for a reason."

The ghost takes a firmer grip on me and starts muscling me toward the Apostles, toward the bonfire. Elza shrieks and claws at Jack beside me. The heat on my face is insane, heat that feels like it's already stripping the top layer of my skin off. The swan-masked Apostle meanwhile takes hold of the owl-masked figure by the throat, lifting him into the air. Despite his larger size and monstrous claws, the owl-headed Apostle makes no move to resist. She crushes the life out of him with one hand and tosses him into the flames like a length of wood.

"SEVEN TREES—"

I take this as my cue to attack Ryan, trying to knock him off balance.

"—OF LIVING STONE—"

Elza's boots scrape along the cement. She bites Jack's hand, to no effect.

"—THE EIGHTH—"

I can see the skeleton of a sofa in the bonfire, springs coiling in crazy fractal whirls in the flames.

"—IS—"

"Luke!" Elza shrieks.

"—CAST—"

"It's all right," Ryan says, trying to regain his footing.

"—OF ICE—"

I slam the back of my skull into his face, my teeth clicking together from the impact. I can see flurries of bright sickly stars.

"—AND BONE!"

Ryan falls flat out on the ground, holding his nose. I think I can deal with Jack, but if the dancers around us take an interest in what's happening, I don't know how we'll get out of this. Elza shrieks again, being pushed closer to the fire. The swan-masked Apostle turns to face me. Do I try and get around the Apostle and hit Jack? I don't know what this thing is capable of.

As I pause, someone surges out of the crowd around us and bowls the masked figure over. Without a word, the Apostle tumbles into the bonfire. Mark steps back, wiping his face.

"Dude—"

"SEVEN TREES—"

I don't hesitate, grabbing Jack around the neck from behind, pulling him and Elza back from the fire. Elza rams her elbow into his side.

"—OF—"

"Listen, Luke, there's no need for this," the ghost says. He still sounds cheerful.

Elza rips herself free. The dancers are all around us, screaming their lunatic chant. I have my forearm locked around Jack's cold neck, forcing him onto his knees. Having a body again has its downside, too, and I guess they've forgotten how to fight.

"Let's go!" Elza screams.

"—LIVING—"

I shove Jack forward and he falls.

"We—"

"—STONE!"

I'm shoving backward, grabbing at Elza's hand, dancers slamming into my back.

The swan-masked Apostle gets back up.

She's standing in the flames, completely unharmed. The fire swirls around the dark robe and golden mask, but never catches, and the Apostle stands in the bonfire as though it were a shower of warm rain.

"THE EIGHTH IS CAST OF ICE AND BONE!"

We turn and push back into the ranks of worshippers,

faces familiar and alien to me leering and howling around us, sweaty bodies pushing against us, like running against an incoming tide. My heart is pounding, and I keep expecting someone to grab hold of us, but none do. The sky flares emerald. I glance back and see the bird-masked figure still standing by the bonfire. The Apostle raises one arm and howls, a sound totally inhuman, and the men and women around us return the scream. I want to cover my ears, but I feel like even if I did, I'd still hear that sound in my bones.

We're out of the crowd now, heading for the street corner where this whole thing started.

As one, the dancers turn and sprint toward us.

"Go!" I scream. "Go! Go!"

The living and dead of Dunbarrow surge across the snowy square toward us. Mark is racing across the road, Holiday and Kirk, too, fleeing back down the road we came up. Snow swirls around us, fog billowing in nightmare curtains.

"—OF LIVING STONE—" the people scream behind us. I look back to see them sprinting after us down the road, hands clutching at nothing.

"Left!" Elza screams.

Mark and Kirk follow her down a side street. Holiday is flagging, and I'm at the rear, glancing behind us to see the shapes in the fog running at full tilt, a wall of people.

I've lost sight of the others ahead.

"Elza!" I shout. "Elza!"

"THE EIGHTH IS CAST OF ICE AND BONE!"

We're running toward the road that Elza and the others went down. I hear hoofbeats thundering; to my horror, Dumachus and Titus emerge from the fog right in front of us, traveling at full gallop. Holiday shrieks. The Knights of the Tree dive right at her. I knock her down into the snow. Dumachus's jaws snap shut in the space where she was just standing. Titus overshoots, galloping past us, seemingly unable to stop, crashing into the front rank of worshippers and bowling them over. Their awful song continues regardless. I drag Holiday up onto her feet. Dumachus snarls and lunges again, breaking the glass of a car's back window with the weight of his armored body. I pull Holiday to the right, into a narrow passageway. I'm desperately hoping it will be too small for the Knights at least, but a bulky form pushes into the opening, armor plates scraping against the brickwork.

"I have them trapped!" Dumachus calls. "Lead the thralls in pursuit of the others!"

Holiday is hyperventilating. I have to remind myself this is the first she's seen of a being like this, and admittedly it's not something you see every day—an armored warhorse with the head of a vile, famished old man. The Knight moves unhurriedly toward us, his broad shoulders just barely fitting through the gap between the two buildings. There's snow underfoot, wadded trash, scraps of plastic bags and old newspapers.

I hear the worshippers shouting, but more distant, as if they're moving away from us.

"You cannot flee me forever, sorcerer," Dumachus says softly.

He's right. This is a dead end. We're in a little alley between the shops, an area for trash cans and fire escapes and not much else.

Wait a second. Fire escape.

"Holiday," I say, hoping the thing doesn't understand English, "there are stairs behind us. Fire escape. Go up them."

As Holiday moves, I grab a plastic bag of trash from on top of one of the cans and throw it at the monster's face. Reflexively, Dumachus bites at the projectile, his long sharp teeth tearing right into the plastic, releasing a shower of rotten food into his mouth and over his face.

"*Aaaairghg!*" he screams, trying to get the plastic bag loose from his teeth.

He lunges at me regardless but not fast enough, and the bag blocks his vision. I'm following Holiday, rushing up the fire escape, the black metal handrails biting into my hands even through the gloves. Dumachus's iron-clad body hits the bottom of the staircase with a terrible crunch, and the entire contraption shakes, throwing me against the brick wall. My teeth click together, and another surge of hot pain starts up in my back gums, where the strange stony tooth is lodged. It doesn't matter. I scramble to my feet, tasting hot blood in my mouth. Holiday is just above me.

"The door's locked!" she shouts.

Dumachus can't climb up after us—the staircase is too small, another disadvantage of having a horse's body, and I'm glad none of the human worshippers came down here after us—but if we aren't able to get into the building the fire escape is attached to, it might not matter. The Knight slams into the metal staircase again and again, and the fire escape's tough, but it was never built to withstand this. The metal is buckling under the weight of his body and armor, and soon it'll collapse altogether. We have to move. I'm beside Holiday now, banging against the fire door on the top floor of this building—a shop, a bank, whatever it is—but the door won't move, and I'm not strong enough to force it. We're stuck up here.

"What do we do?" Holiday asks. "It'll get us!"

"No," I say, throwing myself against the door again, but it might've been painted onto the brick wall for all the good I'm doing.

"I swore to taste your blood, did I not?" Dumachus shrieks from below. "I swore it, and our lady has promised it to me alone."

"Luke!" Holiday says. "What about the roof?"

"What about it?" I rasp. The roof of the building is flat, true, but it's high above us, almost certainly out of reach.

"Give me a boost up," Holiday says, "then I'll lift you."

"Can you lift me? I'm way heavier than you."

"Rope!" Holiday snaps. "I'll tie myself to something!"

"Like what?"

"Anything! We have to try, Luke!"

She's not wrong. We're not getting anywhere with this door. The fire escape shakes again as Dumachus renews his attack, smashing his weight against the supporting columns. There's a lurch as the entire landing we're standing on threatens to come away from the wall. I hunker down and knit my hands together into a boosting platform for Holiday. She stands on my palms with one cold and gritty boot and lunges upward, grabbing hold of the lip of the roof. I strain my muscles and lift her as best I can, feeling the pressure ease as she pulls herself up. With gasps and lots of scrabbling, she manages to fully haul herself up there. The Knight screams unintelligibly down below, and I hear a grinding metallic rasp that I don't like one bit. This whole thing's ready to collapse.

Holiday unwinds the length of blue synthetic rope we took from Elza's garage.

"Is there something you can tie it to?"

"There's a chimney over here!"

"Do it!"

Another impact shakes the staircase. I can't see Holiday, have no idea what she's doing up there. Dumachus bellows.

With an awful grinding noise, the staircase starts to come away from the wall.

"Holiday!" I yell. "Please!"

"I can't get the knot!" she cries.

"I'm going to fall!"

I'm holding as tight as I can to the door's handle, the best grip I have, but there's no way I can keep ahold of it if the whole fire escape collapses.

Dumachus throws himself into the staircase again, howling in a frenzy.

"Holiday!"

She reappears at the lip of the roof, rope tied around her torso. She bends down, reaching toward me. I hope whatever she lashed herself to will hold. There's no way she can lift me on her own.

There's a jolt as the fire escape detaches from the building. It has to be now. I jump as high as I can, reaching for her. For a moment, I think I won't make it, but Holiday grabs my right forearm with both hands. I nearly slip, but am able to hold my position. The fire escape collapses with a grinding crash, leaving me with ten feet of empty air beneath me. My boots scrabble for purchase on the rough brick wall of the building.

"Lift me!"

"I'm trying, Luke!" she yells. My weight is pulling her down, but she locks her feet as wide as she can, the rope taut behind her, and she doesn't let go.

I flail with my other hand, grabbing the lip of the roof. It's cold and slick with ice, but my grip holds. Holiday is leaning back, panting, the rope biting into her body, her feet braced against the edge of the roof, using her entire body weight to counterbalance mine. I pull and pull with my other arm, feet kicking wildly against the side of the building. There's a moment when I think my weight can't be held, that I'm going to fall into the void, tumble down, and feel the Knight's fangs slicing into me, but Holiday won't let go; her fingers feel like they're going to tear right through my sleeve and into the flesh below the fabric, and I pull and pull and finally manage to wedge my foot into a gap where a brick ought to go. The rope is holding. We can do this. I tense my muscles and pull as hard as I can, forcing my body to move.

I heave myself up onto the roof and collapse. Holiday sits beside me, rope lashed around her, breathing hard. She slips the hood of her parka off her head, revealing her long golden hair. Dumachus bellows with rage below us. There's no way for him to get up here. For now, at least, we're safe.

"What is that thing, Luke?" Holiday asks.

"I don't know exactly," I say. "It's a spirit. Something from . . . outside. Something that shouldn't be here."

"But why did they have . . . They have horse bodies," Holiday says. "Why . . . ?"

"I think being in Deadside changes spirits. My dad's ghosts, his Host, had mostly stayed in Liveside, here, after they died. They looked like people, more or less. I think once you cross over, you might start to change into something else. If that's what you want."

I'm thinking of the Fury, my dad's dog-headed demon; thinking about the creatures I met in Deadside, the parade of monsters: a snake with human teeth; the Riverkeeper with its split face, half woman and half man; the shape-changing ghoul with arms longer than its body. Maybe all of them were regular people once.

"Why would someone want that?" Holiday asks. I don't have an answer. We sit there in the snow, getting our breath back. My mind is with Elza, still out there, somewhere I can't see or speak to her. I imagine Titus sinking his shark teeth into her beautiful neck, imagine the blood—

No. There's no time for that. Elza will take care of herself. She knows where we're going.

Elza dead in the snow, the Knights eating her heart—

She'll meet us at my house. We'll see her there. It'll be fine.

Things aren't nearly as bad as they could be.

Elza will be fine.

"Just us, then," Holiday says, as if reading my mind.

I suppose she's thinking about Alice, Mark, and Kirk. I won't say I'm not worried about them, but not in the same way I worry for Elza.

"Yeah," I say.

"So we go to your house," Holiday says. "Stick to the plan."

"Stay away from the town square. Cross the river."

"Definitely," Holiday says. She pulls her hood back up. I look at her curiously. She's taking all of this better than I thought she would. I kind of assumed only me and Elza could deal with things like this, but Holiday's keeping it together. Maybe she was built to keep it together. Maybe the same thing that lets you keep all the popular Dunbarrow girls organized during a night out at Vibe lets you keep your head when your town gets swallowed by the spirit world.

"Sorry I said you were mentally ill," Holiday says.

"What?"

"I'm sorry. I said it back when you stole that DVD from me. I didn't mean it."

"Holiday, I barely remember that happening. It's OK, really."

"Good," she says.

Another flash in the sky. For a moment it's like we're suspended in jade liquid, the fog stained a strange pearly green. A few fresh snowflakes come drifting down out of the gloom. Great. If it starts snowing properly again while we're out here, that alone could kill us. I drag myself to my feet. Holiday fumbles at the knots that keep the rope around her torso.

"They've gone so tight," she says. "My fingers are too cold."

I pass her the knife I took from Elza's kitchen. After a few moments of sawing, the knots are undone. We leave the rope tied to the chimney and make our way across the flat roof, then another, moving away from the bonfire in the town square. The snow up here is thick and undisturbed, and we write breathless stories on it with our feet.

Eventually we find another fire escape and climb down, after making sure Dumachus isn't lurking nearby. I don't like being down at street level with the Knights and revelers prowling around, but there's no way we can get back to my house while staying out of their reach. We'll just have to be brave, and fast, and lucky.

This is a side street, linking the main road with the parking lot outside the riverside leisure center. We make for the parking lot and the river, moving quickly and quietly behind ranks of parked cars, hoping we can sneak along the side of the river and find the bridge that way. The lot is covered in snow, the cars just gentle suggestions under the whiteness. You can see normal stuff still, chip bags stuck in leafless bushes, street lamps, benches, a parking meter. But the leisure center is gone, and instead there's just blackness, silence. We pass between the last few cars like we're in a dream and find ourselves standing on the banks of a river.

The river isn't the Brackrun, the river that flows through Dunbarrow and Throgdown and Brackford on its way to the North Sea. I can't see the pedestrian bridge, the park with its bandstand and swings and ducks. I can't see the other side at all. What I can see is black, silent water, stretching out into the fog-dimmed distance.

"Was there a flood?" Holiday asks. "The snow might've melted upstream . . ."

"No," I say. "This is like the trees we saw, that gray forest. It's part of Deadside."

I walk farther forward. The parking lot fades away the closer you get to the river, asphalt and paving stones becoming sand and pebbles, a barren gray riverbank. There are tiny pale bones from an unidentifiable creature, scattered here and there. No plants grow. The river is silent and immense, larger than any of the rivers I saw the last time I journeyed through Deadside. I have the sensation of infinite space, infinite time, something almost as powerful and mysterious as the Shrouded Lake itself. I imagine this river of shadows lasting forever, a river so long it could loop around the entire universe, something that makes the Amazon look like a trickle of rainwater running over a stone. There might not be an opposite bank. I don't find it scary, either. I think it's beautiful.

"Is it safe?" Holiday's voice comes from behind me.

"It should be. Don't touch the water, though."

I don't know if it would do her any harm, but there's no sense tempting danger. Snowflakes dance past my vision, but they don't seem to land anywhere on the river-bank. Whatever's happening here, it isn't quite part of the river. Unlike the horse spirits and the Apostle, I don't think this river came to Dunbarrow to devour. I think it's here just to be.

"What is this?" Holiday asks, beside me now.

"The river Styx," I say. Nobody told me, but I feel like I always knew. It has to be, right?

"That's a real thing?"

I gesture at the black water.

"I mean, people probably call it different things. But there are eight rivers in Deadside. And this is the big-gest one."

"How do you know that?"

"I can just feel it," I say.

What was it the Shepherd called it? *Backbone of the underworld. River of Oaths.* I assume he stood on the banks of the Styx at some point, looking at this same expanse of darkness.

"What's that?" Holiday asks. She's pointing somewhere out at the edge of our vision. I squint. There's a small white light, moving rapidly across the surface of the Styx, from our right to our left, presumably in the direction of the current. I can't make it out clearly, but maybe it's a lantern on a boat of some kind. I assume the Styx has a Riverkeeper, just like the Cocytus did.

"I don't know," I reply.

It seems like an ember, something moving toward extinction. After a moment it goes out or vanishes from view.

I look down at the shoreline. I think about sitting in gray sand and mist with Dad and Mr. Berkley, back before I understood anything about Deadside. Were we sitting by the Styx? I remember hearing the ocean. The water of this river doesn't make a sound. It's not so cold here, at least.

There's something about the stone next to my shoe that catches my eye. It's small, maybe the size of my thumbnail, dark gray. It has a rough hole bored through it. I bend down and pick it up, look through the hole. For a moment I can see a tiny star.

"Hey," I say to Holiday, who's still looking at the Styx, "check this out. A wyrdstone."

"A what?"

"Stone with a natural hole. They're charms against evil spirits."

"It just looks like a stone to me, Luke."

"Nah, I'm serious." I hold it out to her. "You should have it."

Holiday reaches out and takes the stone. She looks at it critically.

"Magic's in things," I say. "It's really there. Trust me."

Holiday shrugs. "I suppose you were right about everything else so far," she says. Holiday reaches into her jacket and pulls out her golden necklace, a little heart locket hanging from it. She unclips the chain and threads it through the hole in the center of the wyrdstone, leaving it to hang next to the locket.

"How's that?" she asks.

"Yeah," I say, "great. Lucky, right?"

"I don't feel that lucky at the moment."

I think about Elza, remember her wyrdstone, how for ages I thought it was just some weird affectation. I remember her plunging it into the Shepherd's face, scattering him like mist burning off in sunlight. I remember her lying on the ground outside Ash's house. I can't lose her again.

"No," I say. "Me either."

"So what do we do?"

"I think we walk. Let's just walk in the direction the bridge would be and hope we find something."

"We should think about the bridge, then?" Holiday says.

"Yeah. That's right. Just try to imagine us crossing it.

Think about the others, too," I say, as if there were any danger of us not thinking about them. Elza's probably at my house already, I tell myself. She knows what it looks like, what it feels like to be there; she can lead Kirk and Mark there easily.

We walk along the riverbank, ears straining for the sound of voices or hoofbeats. I think the wyrdstone will help us a little against Dumachus and Titus, but I don't know how much. The Knights of the Tree seem powerful, closer to a spirit like the Riverkeeper than a wandering ghost, and I don't know what rules they play by.

The landscape around us seems to only be Deadside now, gray trees and bushes and stones, a constant backdrop of churning gray mist. The cars are gone. I'm still cold, and a sulky crowd of snowflakes comes falling past my eyes as we walk. Another group of the strange lights passes us in the river, but each of them is too far out into the mist to see clearly.

We pass more bones, half buried in the gray sand, some creature that I can't put a name to. I wonder how long they've been there. Time here is strange, and there's a sense that a million years ago and right now are the same thing, that there's no difference between those concepts. The eight rivers will always flow. We walk through a copse of gray willow trees, their branches trailing down into the shadowy water. What did Ryan say to me, back there in the town square? *The Barrenwhite Tree.* If only I knew what that was supposed to mean. We make our way up a low rise, gray, brittle grass under our feet, and in the hollow beyond the rise, we come across three figures sitting around a gray fire.

I don't know whether we should turn around, don't know what we've walked into. The people around the fire look just like that: people, without horse bodies or animal masks or any of the other horrible things we've seen tonight. There's something odd about their postures, but I can't put my finger on what it is.

One of the people, a man, I think, has risen to his feet.

"Who goes there?" he calls to us. His voice is high and musical.

"What do we do?" Holiday whispers.

"Introduce ourselves or run away," I whisper back. "Which do you think?"

"They sound like they're afraid of us," she hisses. "Why don't we ask them for help?"

"Luke Manchett," I call to the people, "and Holiday Simmon. We're lost travelers and looking for help."

"Very well spoken," the man calls back, with a hint of mockery. He's lit from behind, the fire a pale smear of light. "Be you a haunt, Luke Manchett?"

"I don't know what that means!" I shout.

"Be you a ghoul, then? Be you a soul-sucker?"

"We're not dead," I call. "We're alive."

There's a pause, then the man who's calling to us bursts into laughter. "Alive!" he shouts. "The living walk lost along the banks of the Styx now! You hear that, Bald Samson? Rain will be falling upward next! You are not alive, Luke Manchett!"

"We are!" Holiday yells to him. "Let us come closer and you'll see."

The man is talking to the others around the fire. I can't hear what they say. After a while he shouts up the bank to us, "Sit by our fire, then! But be slow about it, and know we are armed!"

We approach the fire carefully, still not sure what to make of these strangers. They must be dead: his laughter when I said we were alive makes me sure of that. Beyond that, I have no idea. I've not been lucky enough to meet many friendly spirits, but I know they do exist. Their fire grows closer, and I can see their shapes more clearly in the mist: two men and a woman, who's sitting at ease in the gray grass. The man who was talking to us moves away from the campfire, walking with a strange gait. He comes closer, and I can finally see him properly through the mist.

He has a thin, aged face, a neck with loose flesh hanging from it, light wisps of hair sprouting from his hands and ears and nose, and teeth that are crooked and graying. But his eyes are bright, alert, and intelligent, appraising me and Holiday with rapid glances. He's dressed in gray rags and walks with an odd limp because of the heavy stone attached to his torso. The rock is big, larger than my head, dark colored, firmly chained to the man. It drags along the ground behind him, twisting his body to one side.

"Welcome, travelers," the strange man says. "Well met upon this dismal road."

He reaches out to me, and before I can think better of it, I take his gnarled gray hand. His palm is cold, his fingers like flutes of ice, but I know he can feel my warmth even through the glove I'm wearing, and his colorless eyes widen.

"You spoke true," he says, and then, "Bald Samson! They spoke truly! They are a living boy and girl! Whatever are you doing, wandering by these dark waters?"

"We're looking for Luke's house," Holiday says.

"I daresay you have gone off course," remarks the other man.

"Join us by the fire," the thin man enthuses to us, shaking Holiday's hand as well. "I am Larktongue, and these are my traveling companions: Bald Samson and the lady who does not speak and thus has not introduced herself to me."

Bald Samson nods to us both, neither hostile nor particularly welcoming. He's enormous, one of the biggest men I've ever seen, built like a bull, with a thick dark beard and dark skin and a wide, smooth scalp that reflects the firelight, and a black scrap of hair above each ear. He's dressed in the same gray clothing as Larktongue, and there's a heavy stone attached to his body as well. Bald Samson seems to carry his burden tightly strapped to his torso, giving him a permanent hunchback. The woman remains mute and doesn't look up from the fire, apparently uninterested in us. She's dressed in gray rags like her traveling companions, but with a veil of thin gray cloth enveloping her face, hiding it from view. She has a smaller rock, perhaps the size of a soccer ball, chained to her left wrist. Holiday grins at these strange people, wringing every drop of warmth from the famous Simmon smile.

We sit by the fire. The flames are bright, but they're the color of a rainy sky, and they cast no heat upon our faces. Larktongue sits with his boulder beside him and pokes at the campfire with a gray branch. He has a long knife in his belt, I notice, and Bald Samson has a heavy wooden walking stick, so they're clearly prepared to fight if they have to. From what I've seen of Deadside, this strikes me as pretty sensible. The veiled woman doesn't seem to be armed.

"Where are you all going?" Holiday asks them. She's taking this remarkably well.

"We are pilgrims," Larktongue tells us. "Sinners seeking peace. We are following this great river to its holy source, the Shrouded Lake. They say the Styx is longer than a man could walk in ten lifetimes, but the dead have all the time they need. One day we will reach that sacred lake of darkness and cast our sins into its depths. Until then, we carry them alongside us."

"Is that what the rock is?" I ask.

"Indeed!" Larktongue replies. "This accursed burden is my sin given form. My pride and sloth and waste and lust. Only once I have borne it all along the banks of this mighty river will I truly understand the weight upon me and be ready to let it go."

"Did you sin a lot?" Holiday asks.

"I am given to understand my sins were modest. Bald Samson here, as you can see, bears a much heavier load, in part due to his long career of iniquity."

Bald Samson shrugs his enormous shoulders.

"I lived how I lived," he rumbles. "I carry what I carry."

"But who made you do this?" Holiday asks Larktongue. "Who chained these to you? Who says that's fair?"

"Made us? Child, we chained these rocks to ourselves willingly. I am glad on it! It is only through this grand pilgrimage that we have any hope of entering Elysium, the lap of the heavens."

"And that's good, right?" I ask him.

"It is paradise," he says. "It will be true bliss."

"Have you seen it?"

"No." Larktongue sighs. "But we have spoken to those who have. It is a kingdom of light."

"If you set out on this journey filled with a hunger for Elysium," Bald Samson pronounces, "you will never see it. We do not think on it overmuch. We think instead on our loads and what we did to incur this weight."

"What brings you to these shores?" Larktongue asks us.

"He is a sorcerer," the veiled woman says softly. A shiver runs through my spine.

"He is what?" Bald Samson asks her.

"You choose now to speak?" Larktongue says.

"He is the Black Goat's favored child," the woman says without anger. She's still looking at the fire.

Bald Samson leaps to his feet, brandishing his staff.

"A servant of the Devil?" he roars. "Does the lady speak truly? Be you a sorcerer, Luke? What business on these banks has one whose heart still pumps blood?"

"Samson—" Larktongue says.

"Sit down!" Holiday shouts. "Luke's a good person."

Bald Samson glares at us. "Magician and his consort. Come to bind some spirit to your Host, or am I wrong? Well, you will not take any of us for your slaves!"

"Look," I say, getting to my feet, "can I just explain one thing?"

"Speak not unto me! You treat with the Black Goat!"

His staff is pointed right at me. Bald Samson's eyes are wide and white in his face.

"He tricked me," I say slowly. "It's not like you think. I don't want a Host. I don't want anything like that. We're just lost is all."

"Does he speak true?" Larktongue asks the veiled woman.

"He does," she says.

I'm looking from her to Bald Samson and back again, trying to figure them out. Is he going to attack me? Holiday has the wyrdstone, but I still don't know how much that can help us.

"I really can explain," I say.

"Luke's not lying," Holiday says.

"It sounds like a tale," Larktongue says. "I am prepared to hear it, if my companions are." He says this with light amusement, as if Bald Samson isn't poised to leap at me and bash my skull in with his staff. After a moment the giant lowers his weapon and shrugs. The chains around his body clink as he seats himself by the fire once more.

I take that as my cue to begin. I tell them the story of my dad and Berkley, how I came into my power without knowing what it was I had accepted. I tell them about my own journey to the Shrouded Lake and what I saw there, and about what's happened to Dunbarrow that we've found ourselves wandering by the banks of the Styx on New Year's Eve.

"To think you have looked upon the Lake," Larktongue

whispers when I'm finished. "You truly spoke to those powers that sleep beneath it?"

"I really did," I say.

"A tall tale," Bald Samson says, but he doesn't outright accuse me of lying. The woman says nothing. There's something about her, I've realized. I feel like I've met her before, but I can't place her, and it's difficult to recognize someone when their whole face is covered like that. Holiday shifts beside me.

"Are we going to sit here to hear everyone's life story?" she asks me in a low voice. "We need to get back."

She's not wrong. We do need to find some way back to Dunbarrow, to Wormwood Drive.

"Do you know of a crossing?" I ask the pilgrims. "We're trying to find a way across the river."

"We do not," Bald Samson says. "None have mapped the course of the Styx, and fewer than none have bridged its expanse."

"Well, it's the Brackrun we need to cross," Holiday says. "We need to find a way back to our town."

Larktongue and Bald Samson give each other a look.

"You may find that difficult," Larktongue says gently. "Those who cross over into the spirit world often find that return is frustrating and elusive."

"Still," Holiday says. "We have to try."

"Naturally," he replies. "Well, I believe we have rested

our burdens long enough. What say you, Samson? My lady? Shall we accompany these young travelers?"

Bald Samson shrugs. "I cannot see as they will walk slower than you, Larktongue."

The small man laughs, a high silvery sound. He leaps to his feet, lurching strangely as the chain tightens around his chest. "Onward, then!" he says. "Onward. With each step our journey shrinks in length, my friends."

The gray-veiled woman gets to her feet. She lifts her small black rock of sin and holds it in her arms like a child, and it's in this gesture that I recognize her: the first time I ever saw her, she was carrying a baby.

The Oracle.

I never thought I'd meet her again. I can't believe it's her. She went through the doorway with the rest of my Host, back when I banished them. Her clothes are different, but I'm certain it's her. I knew I recognized her voice. What's she doing out here? I suppose that explains how she knew I was a sorcerer.

And didn't Ash tell me my father's Oracle was another Ahlgren?

Holiday and Larktongue are looking at me strangely. I realize I've just been staring at the Oracle. I shake my head and grin. Bald Samson is already walking away from the campfire, his boulder riding high on his shoulders. We follow, leaving the strange gray flames to burn themselves out, if they ever will. Larktongue hobbles beside me and Holiday, walking with a strange sideways gait. His sin may be smaller than Bald Samson's, but he's the most obviously crippled by its presence. The Oracle walks behind us, her sins cradled to her chest. Close up I can see that the pilgrims' black boulders are engraved with words, although the script is tiny and dense and I can't make out the exact text.

"Larktongue," I say as we walk, the river flowing black and silent beside us, "have you ever heard of the Barrenwhite Tree?"

"And what would make you speak a name like that?" the ghost asks, sharply.

"Someone mentioned that name in our hometown," I say. "They said there were seven trees made of stone. And an eighth made from ice and bone. Does that mean anything to you?"

Larktongue looks at us strangely. "Now I see what the living wander the lands of Asphodel for. My sincerest apologies."

We keep walking.

"What are you sorry for?" Holiday asks him.

"It is one of the elder spirits," Bald Samson says, without turning. I didn't realize he was listening to our conversation.

"But what is it?" I ask.

"Who can say?" Larktongue replies. He stumbles and his chain bites tighter into his chest. "A great spirit from the Beginning, exiled, outcast by its brethren. That is all I know. It is all I care to know."

"So what does it do?" Holiday asks. "Is it that bad?"

"The elders are not given to us to understand," Bald Samson says. "I know the Barrenwhite Tree is a spirit of the devouring winter and is forbidden from worship, although it is sometimes honored on the night one year becomes the next. Its signs are supposedly a cold and wandering star in the sky, the gathering of swans, certain other dark and wintry omens. As my companion says, I do not wish to know more of such powers, being no sorcerer or other learned man. I am merely a pilgrim."

A spirit of the devouring winter. Great.

"Is that what's come to Dunbarrow? Is that why everything's gone wrong like it has?" Holiday asks me.

"I think so," I say.

"If this power has truly befallen your home," Bald Samson growls, "you would do well not to return there. That is my advice for you."

"That's not an option," I say. "We've got people waiting for us."

I don't know if Elza really is waiting for us. Maybe she's lost like we are, wandering somewhere in Deadside. She doesn't know this place as well as I do, not that I'm some kind of expert. I don't know if she'd be able to get out.

Don't think about that. She's alive, and you'll find her.

Another light passes by in the river, and this time it's close enough to the banks for me to get a good look as it goes by. It's a small floating craft, about the size and shape of a fruit basket, made from dark wood. There's something burning inside the hollow of the boat, a tiny white flame. It rushes past, borne by the current of shadows, and is lost from view behind us in the mists.

"What are those?" Holiday asks the pilgrims. "Why is it burning like that?"

"The Styx carries freshly kindled spirits to Liveside," Larktongue says. "Those lights you see are the unborn."

"But where do they come from?" Holiday asks.

"We do not know. But it is believed they rise from the depths of the holy lake we seek."

Holiday gives me a strange look.

"Are we supposed to know this?" she asks me.

"What do you mean?" I reply.

"I mean, are we supposed to be seeing all of this stuff?" She shivers. "I feel like we've gone backstage."

I shrug. "We see what we see, Holiday. We didn't go looking for it on purpose."

"Still, though. When we get back, it won't seem the same."

"No. I suppose not."

We walk on in silence, at one point stepping over the trunk of a fallen gray tree. The strange fire bowls float past in twos and threes at the most, sometimes far out into the mist, casting only a faint smudge of white light. Bald Samson grunts and shifts the weight of the rock he carries on his back. After a time Larktongue begins to sing as we walk, a chillingly beautiful sound. His voice really is like a bird's, and the song he sings is light and delicate, one of awakening, I think, a song you'd sing in the depths of darkness to remind yourself there will be a dawn.

The bridge emerges out of the mist like the back of a sleeping beast. It's not the traffic bridge that leads to my house; instead this is a stone arch that could've been built by giants, made from slabs of gray rock that are the size of houses. Dead trees grow from the cracks between the enormous blocks. If there was ever a road that led to this bridge, it has long vanished. We stand before it, wondering what kind of creature could need a bridge so huge.

"Who can say?" Larktongue asks himself. "Time in these gray borderlands churns and billows with the fog. Could be that we look upon the ruins of a place yet to be built."

"I think we ought to cross," I tell Holiday.

"Are you sure?"

"We wanted to find a crossing over the river. I think this is it. I certainly don't think we can hold out and hope to find another one."

"Take that path and you'll find yourselves walking alone," Bald Samson says. "Our pilgrimage will continue upstream."

Neither Larktongue nor the Oracle contradicts him. Fair enough.

"I suppose this is good-bye, then," I say.

"A great shame," Larktongue says. "Master Manchett, Miss Simmon, we are glad to have had your company on this leg of our journey."

"Same here," I say.

"Yeah," says Holiday, smiling widely, "it was great to meet you all."

"Keep a strong heart," Bald Samson says to us. "Shoulder your burdens—do not shirk from them."

"Thank you," I tell the giant. "I hope you reach the Shrouded Lake."

"I know we shall," he says. "If it takes a thousand thousand years, so be it."

There doesn't seem much left to say. Larktongue squeezes our hands in his cold palm, then the pilgrims turn to leave, chains rattling as they tighten around their bodies once more. I step out onto the stone bridge.

"Child."

The Oracle has not moved along with the two men. She looks at me through her shroud of gray cloth, sins held tight to her breast.

"Hello," I say.

"Listen to me closely: tree and goat no longer love one another," she says.

"All right," I say.

"The book is the knot of knots, a web that traps minds like flies. But you may unravel it as Alexander did."

"Thank you for your advice."

Holiday hasn't said a word.

"I met your great-nieces," I tell the Oracle. "Ashana and Ilana."

"I did not know them. Magnus sent me away to serve your father before they were born."

"They knew about you," I say.

She doesn't reply.

"Why do you want to help me?" I ask her. "Are you helping me?"

The Oracle reaches up with the hand that isn't bound to her sins and loosens her veil. The gray cloth falls to one side, resting against her cheek and neck, and I see her face.

She could have been called beautiful once, I think. She's pale and young, with blond hair fixed behind her head with a pin. Her features are similar to Ash's and Ilana's, with the same Ahlgren nose and mouth, although her face is smaller than theirs, and her cheeks are fuller. What holds me, though, is the ruin of her eyes. Someone has gouged them out, and all that's left is a pair of wet, dark wounds. Now I see why she hides her face.

"Why are you showing me this?"

"I saw the truth," she says, "or part of it. And I could bear no more."

Holiday swallows loudly beside me.

"I do not see the world. I see beyond. I see beyond you."

"What is beyond me?" I ask her.

"An ending," she says.

"A good ending?" I ask. It seems too much to hope for right now, but I have to ask.

"The end of the one who showed the truth to me. This I hope."

"Thank you," I say, without really knowing how to respond. What does she mean?

The Oracle stares back at me with her ruined eyes. It's difficult to meet her blind, wet gaze. I have no idea what she sees, whether it pleases her, whether anything she said to me was true. Her face betrays nothing. The Styx runs silently beside us. After a long moment she reaches for her veil and rearranges it, covering her face.

"I hope you all find that place you're looking for," Holiday tells her.

The Oracle bows her head very slightly, then turns and follows the other pilgrims. Soon she's lost in the gray fog.

"So she was one of your dad's ghosts?" Holiday asks me, letting out a long breath. "That was so intense. Honestly, things just get weirder and weirder tonight."

"Yeah, she was part of Dad's Host. She was supposed to see the future. I never really believed her. Now I don't know."

"Do you think that's what she told you? Your future?"

"Just now? Maybe."

"We should remember what she said, then."

"None of it made any sense."

"Prophecies never do," Holiday says. "Right? You're supposed to work them out. I feel so bad for her. Who did that to her eyes?"

"Yeah," I say, feeling pretty sure that the Oracle must've blinded herself and deciding Holiday doesn't need to think about that right now. "Well, let's get across the bridge."

We walk. The bridge arcs high above the surface of the Styx. The fog hangs close around us, hiding the bank of the river behind us as we cross. Our footsteps echo dully on the stone. There are towers set at intervals along the bridge, fortified buildings that once had portcullises and bars across their windows, but these defenses have rusted away and collapsed, and gray ivy grows over the ruined walls of the fortifications. I'm half expecting a guardian spirit to emerge from one of the doorways as we pass by, demand some kind of toll, but nothing happens. The silence on the bridge is absolute. I don't think anyone except us has crossed the river this way in a very long time.

The mist thickens as we press onward, until the stones and towers are invisible, and I take Holiday's gloved hand in mine, to make sure we don't lose each other. We stumble forward, unable to see a thing, and I bump smack into a cold metal pole, which at first I can't place, thinking it might be some kind of flagpole or support for a doorway. And then, groping at it with my free hand, I find a piece of plastic bolted to the pole. I look at this object, leaning so close that my nose is almost touching it, and see the words NO FOULING—MAXIMUM PENALTY £1,000. It's a street lamp.

"We did it," I say. The ground beneath my feet is snow-covered cement. I can feel the wind, hear tree branches moving. "Dunbarrow."

"Are you sure?" Holiday asks.

"Yeah, just look."

The fog thins and we can see parked cars, a snow-capped trash can, a muddy bank studded with bare trees. I was right. We're back on the hill that leads up to Wormwood Drive. Nearly home. The enormous stone bridge is gone, and the river behind us is not the Styx but the Brackrun, the surface frozen solid and powdered with snow. I let go of Holiday's hand.

"We really are back," she says.

We head uphill. We're so close to my house now. The sky flares a silent green. I should have asked what the Barrenwhite Tree is supposed to do when it is worshipped, exactly. But the ghosts didn't seem to want to talk about it, even if they did know.

Halfway up the hill, the snow turns red. It's soaked in blood, with scuff marks everywhere like someone has been thrashing around. I can see a cricket bat lying broken in the snow. Mark's. He obviously hit something with it. There's a hard lump in my throat. Did the Knights find their prey? Is this where they caught Elza and the others? I can't see any bodies, but maybe the monsters ate them. We move faster, not speaking. I can see the trees that stand at the gates to my house now. We're nearly there. I'll see Elza again. . . . She'll be waiting there for us—

Voices. I hear voices in the fog and the clanking of armor. I pull Holiday away from the road, and she follows without a word. We push into some snow-fattened bushes and crouch there in the cold, watching the road.

"—my fault, you say, Dumachus?"

The Knights of the Tree emerge from the fog. I see one of them is walking strangely, unable to put any weight on his front right leg.

"My fault that I be lamed and both of us hungry?" Titus says in the gloom.

"If you had been swifter, we could have had all three of them," Dumachus snarls. "Instead we have nothing. I starve, my brother in arms, and the two I chose escaped me on a cunning stair of iron. Now I join you here to find you sorely wounded and the rest of our quarry gone behind their wards. How will we catch them now?"

We don't make a sound. We don't even breathe. They must be talking about Elza and the others. They got away from the Knights? Got into my house, safe behind the hazel charms? How? Titus is clearly injured on his leg, below where the armor stops.

"She has said she will take care of them," Titus says soothingly. "She has many thralls and other ways besides. We shall feed when she is done. She has promised us that much."

"And so much for her promises!" Dumachus snorts. "Her promises are thin and far as the sky! That house is warded with hazel, just as the other was. What can she do against these old charms?"

They're so close to us now. Will they smell us? They seem to be too busy arguing. I could almost reach out to touch Titus. I can see the wrinkles around his eyes, the snowflakes clinging to the lank gray ends of his mustache.

"She has her tricks," Titus says. "Have a little faith, brother in arms. Why swore we to the Tree if not for faith?"

"We swore as exiles," Dumachus says bitterly. "We swore for none else would have us. That is the truth."

They continue downhill, Titus's armor crashing as he lurches and hobbles. Fresh snowflakes spiral down from the fog-dimmed gloom above us.

"Do not speak such, dear friend. Let us return to the Tree," Titus is saying, remarkably cheerful despite his limp, "and see if by her grace I may not be healed."

The Knights continue, out of sight. When they've vanished into the fog, and their awful voices are lost as well, we scramble out of our hiding place. We run as fast as we can down Wormwood Drive, feet pounding on the snowy ground. I can see my front gate, half open, but like Elza's house, the mists of Deadside haven't enveloped my house. The hazel charms have held firm. I expect at any moment to hear the hooves and cries of the Knights behind us, but we make it to the gate and through, past the line where the fog stops. I double over in my front yard, panting, unable to believe we're really here, at the end of our bizarre journey. My house is dark, but I can see firelight glimmering in the front room.

Someone is home.

(wormwood drive)

I unlock the front door and push it open slowly. I'm reasonably sure this must be Elza and the others, since nobody else apart from her and Mum know where the spare key's kept, but on a night like this, there's no way of knowing for sure. Firelight shines from the living room, and there's the buttery light of a candle in the kitchen. Bea hears us and starts barking up a storm in the laundry room. I take a deep breath.

"Hello?" I say loudly.

"Who's there?" comes a voice from the front room.

"Luke and Holiday. What are you doing in my house?"

"Luke!"

A woman emerges from the living room. Red hair down to her waist, wearing brown pants and a purple sweatshirt. It takes me a moment to recognize her.

"Margaux?"

Darren's sister embraces me tightly. She smells of incense and hairspray. Her fingers dig into my back in a way that isn't entirely pleasant.

"Thank goodness you made it here," she says. "They're in the living room."

She takes hold of my arm and pulls me through, Holiday following behind. Saying I'm confused would be an understatement. I'd almost forgotten about Margaux Hart. The front room is warm, the fire roaring, and Mark is lying on the big sofa, his face a grim mask. He's wearing his boxer shorts, a sweater, and there's blood stained all over the cushions and carpets. Elza's crouched beside him, wrapping his leg in what looks like an improvised bandage.

"Mark!" Holiday cries. She rushes over to him and kisses him.

"Hey," he says faintly.

"What happened?" I ask.

"One of the Knights got him," Elza says without looking up. "Kirk saved him. Nearly cut the horrible thing's leg off."

"Where's Kirk now?"

"I don't know—he went upstairs. Now, look, let me—"

"Why's Margaux here?"

"We met on the road here," Margaux says beside me. "Elza was good enough to let us shelter here."

"Us?" I say. This is all going too fast. I thought I'd be relieved, but finding Margaux here has thrown me off. I feel confused.

"I found this girl in the snow," Margaux says calmly, pointing over at the armchair in the far corner of the room. Alice is sitting there, hands folded in her lap, staring into space.

"Where's she been?" I ask. "What happened to her?"

"She won't speak to us," Margaux says.

"Luke!" Kirk shouts from behind me, grabbing me in a tight hug.

"Kirk, what—"

"Mate! I'm so glad to see you again."

"Luke, do you have any antiseptic?" Elza cuts in. "This bite doesn't look good."

"Just hold on," Holiday says to Mark. "You'll be fine."

Mark groans.

Alice stares at the wall.

"Luke! Antiseptic!"

"All right," I say, stumbling out of the room. My head is buzzing like a wasps' nest. I feel like I'm on fire. I stagger into the kitchen, lit by the single candle. It's cold in here. I open the door to the laundry room. Bea bolts past me, yelping, and vanishes into the hallway. She's messed the floor in here. How long has she been locked in here? She's drunk her water dish dry. I step around the dog poo and rummage in the utility cabinet until I find our first-aid kit. I bring it back through to the front room. Margaux is crouched by Holiday, watching Mark intently. Bea is barking at her, hackles raised. The noise is deafening.

"Bea!" I snap. "Not now! These are guests! It's all right!"

She barks at Margaux again. I swipe at her with my foot, and she runs out of the room, yowling. I hand Elza the first-aid kit. I never paid attention when they taught us about it at school.

Mark's face is graying, the skin under his eyes a ghastly purple. Sweat has shaped his hair into a cascade of wet spikes on his forehead.

"How you doing, mate?" I ask.

His eyelids flicker.

"Hurts," he says.

The bite's gone deep into the calf. I can see ragged flesh, dark-red meat. It looks like a shark got hold of him. It must be agony.

"Hang on," I say.

I leave the front room again and head upstairs. It's as dark as anything up here, but I know the layout of the house with my eyes closed. I go into Mum's bedroom. The door is ajar, and Bea is sitting on Mum's bed, a black shape in the dimness. A blue flash outside briefly illuminates the room.

"Hey," I say. "Sorry about that."

I sit down next to her and stroke Bea's soft head. She whines and licks my hand. Her small thin tail thumps on the bedspread.

"You miss Mum, Bea?" I ask her. "Yeah, I do, too. I hope she's OK." I remember Mum crying, walking away from me down Darren's track. What if that's the last time we ever see each other? My stomach churns. I'll apologize to her properly. If I get out of this, that's the first thing I'll do.

Bea grumbles again, rubbing her head on my arm. I think this is the most affection she's shown me since we got her.

"It'll be all right," I say. "I'll be back."

I move over to Mum's bedside table and open the top drawer. I find what I was looking for: plastic prescription bottles, a whole bunch of them. Her headaches haven't come back since the mess with Dad's Host last Halloween, but I knew she wouldn't get rid of the painkillers, just in case. I pick the bottle with the most pills inside and head back to the living room.

"Try some of these," I say, holding the medicine out.

Elza takes the bottle and examines the label in the fire-light. She whistles.

"Persephone had these on prescription?"

"Two a day," I say. "They were bad headaches."

"They must've been. All right," Elza says, and gives

Mark a couple of the tablets. "I don't want to overdose you. Let's try that for now."

"I need some water," he rasps.

"The faucets aren't working here either," Elza says. "I already tried them."

I get up again, go to the fridge, get him a glass of juice. The power might be cut, but the kitchen is an icebox, and I don't think we'll have to worry about the food going bad anytime soon. I hand him the juice, and Mark swallows the pills.

Margaux is sitting at the back of the room, in the armchair next to Alice. They have the air of people who were talking about you just before you came into the room. Margaux is bright-eyed, alert, watching us all with interest. Alice's eyes are like dull coins. Why is Margaux Hart here? How did she get to Dunbarrow from Darren's place? Why isn't she dancing around a bonfire like the others? Does she know what's going on here?

I make my way over to Margaux and Alice. The back of the room is darker, shadows clinging to their faces. I can hear Mark groan with pain, Holiday saying something to Elza that I don't catch. Margaux smiles politely at me.

"How did you get here?" I ask her.

"Oh, to your house? We walked."

"You know what I mean," I say. "We were at Darren's

place. Something happened. I can't remember what. You were there, too, and now we're trapped here."

Margaux shakes her head.

"The last thing I remember is sitting around a bonfire," she says dreamily. "Beautiful firelight. Then I was walking through the snow and fog, and I wasn't sure where I was. And I found this poor girl"—she gestures at Alice, who says nothing—"in the snow. She was lying down. I was worried she might be dying. So I got her up, and we started walking, and we found ourselves on your road. The mist was very thick."

This somehow manages to leave me with more questions than I had before. Margaux doesn't sound particularly worried as she relates this story to me, as if blacking out and waking up during a snowstorm and saving a stranger from freezing to death happen to her on a daily basis.

"Do you know where Darren and Persephone are?" I ask.

"I'm afraid I haven't seen them," Margaux replies. "I could ask the cards if you like."

"The cards—Oh, yeah." I'd forgotten all about her tarot pack. "I think we're OK for now. Are you all right, Alice?"

Alice doesn't look at me. She doesn't react in any way. I'm starting to worry about what might've happened to her out there. She's alive but seems almost comatose, like she's sleeping with her eyes open. Elza just ran into these two in the street outside my house?

"She doesn't seem ready to speak," Margaux says.

"She never spoke that much to me anyway," I say. "Margaux, do you understand where we are?"

"This is your house, isn't it?"

Is she just brain-fried or something?

"I mean, like, Deadside?"

She shakes her head. "I don't understand what that means."

"Do you believe in magic?" I ask.

"I mean, that's quite a broad question," she says. "Are you sure you're all right, Luke? You seem upset."

"My friend's leg nearly got torn off. We're holed up in here, no power, no heating, a snowstorm raging, a night that doesn't seem to end, and the whole world's gone crazy. Or haven't you noticed?"

"We're in the palm of fate," Margaux says calmly. Her tattooed hands are folded in her lap. She has to be drunk or something. I'm not sure if she's taking in anything that I told her. She hasn't gone crazy like the people in the town square, but something's clearly wrong with her.

Whatever. I don't know what either of these two are going to do to help us. I still don't know what we need to do at all. The Book of Eight is upstairs, my sigil and the witch blade, too. I'm hoping the answer, the way out of this, is inside the Book. Otherwise we might all be lost.

I'm sitting upstairs in my room, with Elza beside me on the beanbag. We've got a candle burning in a saucer in the middle of my floor. Bea snuck in next to us and is sleeping by my leg. Elza still has traces of Mark's blood on her arms and hands. We came up here, away from the others, so I could tell her about my journey to the house, and we could try and decide what to do. The Book of Eight, Dad's nine rings, and the bone-white witch blade that belonged to Ashana Ahlgren are on the floor in front of us. Candlelight gleams on the eight-pointed golden star embossed on the Book's cover and the precious stones laid in Dad's binding rings. The octagonal black stone inset into his sigil, the master ring, reflects no light at all.

"And what did the Oracle say to you?" Elza asks me.

"She said tree and goat no longer love each other. Something like that. Then she said the book was a knot of knots, but I could unravel it like Alexander did."

"Strange. Tree and goat . . . does she mean this Barrenwhite Tree?"

"Maybe. Goat . . . I don't know. I've heard people call Berkley the Black Goat."

"OK. So this Tree and Berkley don't like each other."

"According to the Oracle. We think."

"All right," Elza says. She frowns at the Book of Eight. "And the book . . . what else could she be talking about? It must be the Book of Eight, right?"

"What does she mean, Alexander unraveling knots?"

"Alexander the Great," Elza says. "He was a conqueror. There was a famous knot, the Gordian knot."

"A famous knot."

"*Yes*," she says, swatting my ear, "a famous knot. Look, it's a legend—just go with it. It was an impossibly complex knot, and supposedly if you could untie it, you'd become king of all Asia."

"Right."

"And nobody could untangle it, but Alexander the Great cut through the knot with a sword. Lateral thinking, see?"

"Also, I bet whoever was judging the untying was like, *This guy's got a sword and knows how to use it. I won't say anything about how this is definitely cheating.*"

"Well, sure. But back to the Oracle . . . She's saying the Book of Eight is like the Gordian knot?"

"So I'm meant to hit it with a sword?" I say. "Kirk does have one downstairs."

"No," Elza says, "I doubt that's what she meant. It's about thinking outside the box."

"Elza, everything that happens to us is outside the box! We're so far outside the box that the box is, like, no longer visible to the naked eye. We're living people stranded in the world of the dead on a New Year's Eve that doesn't seem like it's ever going to end, and we're trying to work out if it's the Devil or some kind of evil tree that's responsible for it all. We left the box behind a long time ago."

"True," she says. "Why do oracles always have to speak in riddles? Couldn't she just tell us what to do?"

"Maybe it has to come from us. Maybe if she just tells us outright, then what she saw won't happen."

"So what are we going to do now?"

"There's only one thing we can do," I say, putting my hand on the Book of Eight.

"Do you have to? Really?"

"We can't just sit in this house and wait for all this to blow over. You know that. The only way we can find out about the Barrenwhite Tree and learn what's really going on tonight is by reading the Book of Eight. If you've got another idea, now's the time to let me know."

"It just scares me. I don't like that thing. Who knows how long you'll be in there for? Who knows what it'll do to you? Just because you've survived twice, that doesn't mean a third time will be all right! What if it takes you off somewhere and you don't come back? What then?"

Elza stares into my eyes, unblinking.

"I—"

"What if you leave us? What if I'm stuck here with Holiday and Kirk and Alice and Margaux, and your mind never comes back to us?"

"There's no choice! There's nothing else to do!"

"It's already inside you," she says. "I hear you speaking at night sometimes, when you're asleep. You say words I can't understand."

I shudder. I know the dreams those words must come from: dreams of stars and whirling sigils, the secret speech of the universe.

"That's why I should do this," I say. "It already has me. The pages of the Book aren't coming out of my mind. Why shouldn't I look at them one more time, if it might save us all?"

Elza lowers her gaze.

"I know," she says. "I just worry that it must all be building up in there. Ready to, like . . . burst the dams or something. You've already read it twice because of me. I don't want there to be a third time."

"Elza, I read the Book of Eight because of Dad and the Devil and the Shepherd and Ash. It's not your fault. It never was."

"It doesn't feel like it," Elza says. I hug her tightly, kiss her.

"It's not."

She smiles thinly. "I'm dying for a cigarette now," she says.

"No gum left? I mean, I'd offer to go get some from the corner shop, but . . . you know."

"I have some," she says, frowning. "It's not the same, though. I just miss that scratchy-throat feeling, I guess. Oh, why am I even talking about this now? It's not important."

I kiss her forehead. "It's going to be fine," I say. "I'll read the Book, find out what we need to do. We'll make it out of this."

"All right," Elza says.

Bea gets up and wanders over to my bedroom door. She scratches the wood lightly, then noses the crack under the door, whining.

"You OK, Bea?" I ask. She looks back at us, her eyes glimmering in the candlelight.

"Does she need to go outside?" Elza asks.

"Maybe. All right, I'll take her out the back door." I stand up, disentangling myself from Elza. I put on my hat, my scarf, my thickest coat. Bea sits by the door and waits. Elza lies back on the beanbag, holding my sigil ring up to the light. She runs a finger over the black octagonal stone and puts it back on the floor with the others.

"Don't be long," Elza says. I nod. I open the door, and Bea rushes out onto the dark landing, vanishing into the shadows. I hear her soft little feet on the stairs. I close the bedroom door behind me, blocking off the faint candle-light, and stand there for a moment in darkness. I can hear wind outside, low voices downstairs, the crackle of Bea's claws on the kitchen tiles. She knows exactly where we're going. The landing and stairwell are a maze of silhouettes.

I walk downstairs, pausing at the entrance to the living room. Mark is still lying on the sofa, seemingly asleep. If we make it through this, I don't know how I'll explain the blood to Mum. Maybe Bea will take the blame somehow. Margaux is sitting cross-legged by the fire. She's turning tarot cards, but listlessly, without looking down, like she's not interested in what they're telling her. I see one with an image of a man hanging from a post by his ankle, another card with the image of two warriors fighting, and a third that shows white stars against darkness. I can see the tat-toos coiled on the backs of her hands, soft orange firelight playing over the contours of her fingernails and knuckles as she shuffles the deck. Holiday is sitting in an armchair, watching Mark. Kirk is on the floor with his back up against the wall, one hand resting on the hilt of his sword. Alice is still sitting in her chair at the back of the room, star-ing at nothing.

I move past the doorway, following Bea into the kitchen. A silent green flash illuminates the room for a moment, jade light gleaming on the pots and pans and stove. I can see my breath indoors. I wish I had two pairs of gloves. I manage to clip Bea's leash to her collar and open the back door, pushing twice as hard as normal because of the snow piled up in front of it. The Deadside fog boils and churns beyond our wall, the fields invisible. The apple trees in our yard are bare black sketches, their branches and twigs reminding me of the insides of a diseased lung. The snow is up to Bea's neck in some places, and she moves through it by leaping. She eventually squats by a tree, where the snow is shallower, and starts to do her business. I stand there shivering, looking up through the dead branches into the churning sky, a lid of fog set tight over the house. I can see candlelight in my bedroom window, Elza's shadow flickering on the wall.

For some reason I start to think about Margaux's hands. I look at Elza's shadow and then back up at the gray swirling ceiling of fog overhead, and as I do, it flashes blue again, a bleached-denim blue, and we're drowning in a sea of azure fog, and as the flash hits my eyes I remember . . .

The swans are moving again, flying backward in a circle. Their necks are snapped but they're still flying.

The bird-woman is speaking again. Her mask is Power. She rests her hands on my chin.

The bird-woman's hands are marked with curves and lines.

I open my mouth and she reaches inside and I feel the heat of what she planted there.

Around us the seven oak trees turn to stone.

. . . the stone circle. I remember what happened there, or a tiny fragment of it. I nearly drop the leash. I can feel bile rising in my throat and I gasp. I remember the Apostle, a woman wearing a golden swan mask. I remember . . .

Light, hungry light, growing from the ground. Tree is come, feast begun. The owl-man is watching, never speaking. His mask is Wisdom.

. . . the hands of the swan-masked Apostle on my cheeks, remember her planting something in my mouth. But the most important thing I've remembered is this: the Apostle's hands were tattooed, with swirls of ink and lines cutting down the back of every finger.

Margaux's hands.

Margaux Hart is an Apostle of the Barrenwhite Tree. She did this. She's inside the house right now.

I jerk on Bea's leash in a frenzy, rushing back through

the snow to the back door. Bea yelps because I'm pulling too hard, but I can't stop. I drag her inside and slam the door shut. Margaux, it's her. We let her in.

She has her tricks. Have a little faith, brother in arms.

Hands shaking, I unclip Bea's leash and move forward into the kitchen. I take a knife from the knife rack, hide it in my jacket pocket. I walk as calm as I can out into the hallway. Margaux is sitting where I left her, tarot cards forgotten on the floor, tattooed hands resting on her knees, watching the flames. Nobody's moved.

"Are you all right?" Holiday asks me.

"Yeah," I say, "fine. Just letting Bea out. How's Mark?"

"He's resting," Holiday says.

"Great," I say.

Margaux looks at me, eyes filled with firelight. I stare back and smile unconvincingly. Does she know I know? Why is she here? Have I got it wrong? Why would she do this?

I turn away quickly and walk back upstairs, into the shadowy landing. There's still a seam of candlelight around the edges of my bedroom door.

"Elza," I say, quietly, opening the door. "Elza, we need to do something!"

She's sitting on the beanbag where I left her. She doesn't look up.

"Margaux is an Apostle! She was one of the people in masks at the bonfire! It's her fault! All of this!"

Elza doesn't move. What's she looking at? I walk quickly across the room, heart racing, and then a wave of cold comes crashing over me.

Elza is sitting with the Book of Eight on her lap. The pages are open, and she's turning them, her mouth moving, but no sounds coming out. My dad's black ring is on her left hand. The pages are blank, but she's turning them anyway; what's written there is for her now and not for me.

For a moment I'm too numb to do anything. I crouch down in front of her, staring into her eyes. She's not looking at me. She's looking at the Book. *Elza, what have you done? How could you do this? How could I not have seen this coming? I shouldn't have left you alone with the Book. What was I thinking?* I shake her, shouting her name, but nothing. I can't snap her out of this, and I don't know how long she'll be reading these pages. They go on forever. It could be days, weeks, a lifetime. How could she—

No. There's no time for this. Margaux is in the house, and who knows what she wants, what she's capable of. I have to do something. I take the witch blade from the floor and tuck it into my jacket, alongside the kitchen knife. I'm about to race downstairs, then realize how it'll look if I run into the living room. I have to try and be casual, act like nothing's wrong. I need to speak to Holiday without Margaux working out what's going on.

I walk in, smiling, trying my best to look convincing, though there's nothing much to smile about. I step around Margaux, feeling like I'm trying to disassemble a bomb. If she's responsible for breaking open the gateway between Liveside and Deadside, then she's the most powerful magician I've ever encountered. I don't know how a fight between us would go, but I don't have any reason to think it'd turn out well for me. Her long red hair seems like a jellyfish, reaching tendrils out toward me.

I lean down to Holiday.

"Come to the kitchen in two minutes," I whisper. "Important."

I then say, much louder, "Elza's working on something upstairs, so let's give her a bit of time."

"What could she be doing?" Margaux says, almost to herself.

"We're trying to work out what's up with the sky," I say.

Maybe she knows we've got the Book of Eight here. Maybe that's what she's after. I turn and quickly make my way to the kitchen. If I'm in there another moment, I'm going to blow it. I pace the dark tiles, head boiling. I rest my forehead against the cold door of the refrigerator.

"Luke?" Holiday says behind me. I turn.

"Come closer," I whisper.

"What's wrong?" Holiday asks.

I press the kitchen knife into her hand. "You've still got the wyrdstone, right?" I ask. She looks at the knife in blank confusion.

"What are you doing? Is Elza all right? What's happening?"

"Holiday! Do you have it?"

"Yes, I've still got the stone! It's around my neck now. Why?"

"Keep your voice down," I say, then, "Margaux is—I think she's the one behind all of this."

"What? Why?"

"I should have known. She doesn't fit. How could she have ended up in Dunbarrow unless she was involved? Why hasn't she gone crazy like all the others? Trust me, Holiday, she was the one who started whatever's happening here."

Holiday's hand tightens around the hilt of the knife.

"So what can we do?" she whispers.

"We'll have to fight her," I say. "I'm telling you first because you have the wyrdstone. Kirk has his sword, but I don't know how much use that'll be. And Mark and Alice don't seem like they can help us at all."

"What are we going to do? You want me to stab her?" Holiday asks, wide-eyed. "I don't . . . I don't know if I can do that, Luke. I mean, we aren't even sure it's her who's behind this!"

"Look, let me worry about that. I've fought people before." I remember Ash on the shores of the Shrouded Lake, plunging the witch blade into her chest, and wince. "But we have to do something, OK? We need to find out why Margaux came here—"

There's movement behind us. I look over Holiday's shoulder and see a girl's shape in the doorway. She comes closer, into the glow of the candle, and I see short red hair, a sour expression. Alice Waltham is on her feet again.

"Alice," I say, "how are you feeling?"

"We think Margaux is dangerous," Holiday whispers.

Alice doesn't say anything. She stares at both of us, eyes shiny like coins, her hands clasping and tensing by her waist. She seems to be shivering.

"Alice," I begin, "are you—What's wrong—"

"*Oh my god!*" Holidays shrieks.

Alice Waltham's face splits open like a wet paper mask, her skin running and boiling, changing into something else. I'm stepping backward, fumbling in my jacket for the witch blade. It's not Alice. The disguise melts away completely, revealing something like an ape, a lanky predatory beast with colorless matted fur and a ravenous mouth where its face should be. The thing shrieks, an inhuman noise, lashing at me with long sharp talons. I've seen shape-changers like this before, in the deep forests of Asphodel. This thing has been sitting at the back of my living room, waiting for us to let our guard down. It must've come in with Margaux as backup, taking the form of someone we've lost—

Holiday screams as the spirit takes hold of her, slamming her against the wall, long fingers clamped around her neck. The thing is strong; it is holding her with one hand, and the other strikes at my face, driving me back. I've gotten hold of the witch blade, and I lunge at the monster but with no effect. It knocks my arm and the witch blade tumbles out of my grasp, falling to the tiles with a clatter. Holiday is rasping and choking, stabbing the creature's chest with the steel kitchen knife I gave her, but the spirit shows no pain despite its wounds and holds her regardless. I scrabble around in the darkness, trying to find my weapon again.

"Holiday!" I shout. "The wyrdstone! That knife won't be enough! Use the stone!"

I can hear Bea barking and Kirk yelling in the other room, but he doesn't come through to help us. I don't know what to do. Holiday's candle has gone out, and we're fighting in the dark, the scene only illuminated by the strange milky light that comes from the fog itself.

My fingers close over the hilt of the witch blade.

Holiday has managed to grab the wyrdstone, and she

thrusts it into the monster's neck. The spirit screams when the stone touches it, and there's a flare of white light, a tiny supernova. The faceless creature dissolves like smoke caught in a gale, flesh unraveling into gray strands of fog that race away from the point of impact.

"Luke!" Holiday yells. "Luke!"

"I'm here!" I shout.

The screaming intensifies. The spirit must be strong; its body is re-forming in the middle of the kitchen. The wyrd-stone alone wasn't enough to dispel it.

"Is that Alice?" Holiday asks me. "Is that her? Did she—"

"No! It's something else!"

The monster is reknitting its flesh with awful speed. Already I can see its long hairy arms congealing out of the mist. Enough of this. I lunge forward, driving the witch blade into the spirit's body. The creature's hands dig into my back, trying to find purchase, but I twist the knife, and eventually I must hit something vital, some deep terrible heart, because the ghoulish thing stops struggling, and there's a pulse of pure white light that fills the room. The clawed hands fall away from my body. The spirit slumps down onto the kitchen tiles, fading into a haze of gray mist.

"We're OK!" I say to Holiday. "It's dead!"

"What about Mark? Kirk?"

I don't hesitate, rushing out of the room with my knife

clasped in my right hand, not sure what we're going to find in the living room. The room's still firelit, but the armchair Holiday was sitting in is overturned, and Kirk stands in the middle of the room, breathing heavily. His eyes are wild. Mark is somehow still asleep. Bea has her hackles raised, snarling at something on the floor.

"What happened?" I ask.

"I killed her," Kirk says, like he doesn't quite believe it. "She went for me. Then the dog tripped her."

I step around Mark's sofa, take a look at the floor behind it. Margaux is lying there, eyes closed. Her tattooed hands are grasping her stomach, which is slick with red human blood, as is the blade of Kirk's sword. It looks like he keeps it sharp enough, even if he did buy it online.

"She went for you?"

"Yeah," he says, "with that." Kirk points with the tip of his sword at a curved black dagger, in many ways the sibling of the white knife I'm holding, although Margaux's weapon is longer, with a golden handle. "She tripped on your dog. Then I stabbed her and she fell down."

"Good girl," I say to Bea.

"Oh, my god," Holiday says.

Carefully, I bend down and pick up the curved black knife. It's definitely another witch blade, made from a sharpened bone that's been turned black by methods thankfully unknown to me. I pass it to Holiday.

"Use that instead of the kitchen knife," I say. "It's probably magic."

"You think she's dead?" Kirk asks.

"Why, do you think she isn't?"

"Dunno what I think anymore," he says, shaking his head.

Margaux makes a gurgling noise and I jump back. Kirk raises his sword. Holiday moves around behind us, holding the black dagger and the wyrdstone.

Margaux opens her eyes and gasps. The sound is inhuman, a wet gurgling wail. She sits up. Bea sets up a storm of barking again.

"What the . . ." Kirk begins.

I keep my knife held close to my body, ready to attack if I need to. Margaux laughs hoarsely. She gets to her feet. Her eyes have rolled up into her head, exposing only the whites.

"This flesh will be restored," she says. *"I am more than you know."*

"What are you?" I ask Margaux's dead body. This is a different voice, nothing like the voice of Darren's sister as I know her. This is the voice I heard from beneath the swan mask.

"I am the Barrenwhite Tree," Margaux's head says. *"I speak through my Apostle."*

Margaux's blank eyes flicker between us.

"What do you want?" I ask.

"I want to be loved."

"What does that mean?"

"All love me. All dance. You do not."

"No," I say, "we don't love you. None of us do."

"This night will live eternal, just as I do," the thing says. *"You are lost."*

"We're going to beat you," I say. "We've got the Book of Eight."

"You may try," the thing tells me scornfully. Before I can say another word, Margaux screams and dives at me, teeth ready to tear into my throat. Holiday holds up the wyrdstone and it flares again with white light, and the possessed woman shrieks in pain and anger. Margaux comes close enough for me to feel her long hair flap against my face, and then whirls around and heads for the window, bursts through the glass, and vanishes into the snow and fog.

"What the hell?" Kirk's asking me. "What the hell?"

"We just spoke to the Barrenwhite Tree," I say.

"That means, like, less than nothing to me, man. What are you talking about?"

"The Tree is the spirit that's causing this, I think," I tell him, moving over to the window. I look out, but I can't see any sign of the red-haired woman.

"Why did they come here?" Holiday asks.

"To get the Book maybe," I say. "Perhaps just to kill us. Make sure we didn't stop whatever's going on here tonight."

"Oh my god," Holiday says. "Oh my god . . ."

Kirk puts an arm around her, but she shrugs it off. The room is getting colder, the freezing air leaking in through the smashed glass.

I move out into the hallway, holding the witch blade, and push the front door open. There's churned-up snow and blood outside the living room window and footprints leading to the front gate. I follow them, wary, keeping my eye on the darkness underneath the trees by our gate, and then there's a silent green flash in the sky and I stop dead.

The house is surrounded. There are people outside in the road, pressing against the barriers, staring at me with empty eyes. People from Dunbarrow, spirits, worshippers of the Tree. They seem grayer than before, losing definition in their faces and bodies, as though they're made of the mist around them. I can't tell the difference between the living and the dead anymore.

Jack, Andy, and Ryan are standing at my gate, watching me with glowing eyes.

"Just let us in, yeah, Luke?" Andy calls. I see that he has a thin root growing from the side of his face, like someone planted a seed in his head.

"Come on, mate."

"It's not so bad out here," Ryan calls. The roots, slim as hairs, are sprouting from his nose and his fingers.

The crowd begins to chant as they see me.

"Seven trees of living stone . . ."

I don't say a word to any of them. I check the perimeter, shivering in the cold, witch blade held in my good hand.

"The eighth is cast of ice and bone . . ."

No breaks, and they clearly can't cross. We're safe in here, at least. But I don't know how we'll ever get out.

When I come back inside, stamping snow from my boots in the hallway, I find Holiday and Kirk sitting by the fire. Mark is staring up at me blearily from the sofa.

"Got cold in here," he says, slurring.

"Yeah, mate," I say.

"Did I miss something?" he mumbles.

"Nah," I say. "Nothing exciting. Get some rest, yeah?"

Kirk and Holiday don't freak out as much as I expected when I tell them we're surrounded. I suppose we already felt under siege in here anyway. Kirk helps me tape some cardboard over the hole in the window, which helps a bit with the draft, but not much. Our only room with a fireplace has been compromised. We stoke the fire as much as we can. Mark has fallen back asleep, breathing heavily, his eyes moving under bruise-dark eyelids. His face is still shiny with sweat. It doesn't look good.

"But how could those things get in here?" Holiday's asking me again. "I thought your house was protected? Can those people out there get in? Shouldn't we try and go somewhere else?"

"Elza must've invited them," I say. "They can come in if Elza lets them, because she made the hazel charms. She already knew Margaux. I guess she just didn't think about it. But no, the crowd outside now can't get in here. If they could, they would've already."

"Where is Elza?" Holiday says.

"She's, uh, reading the Book. I don't know how long that might take."

"Didn't you say it does weird things to you?"

"Yeah."

I lead them upstairs, to my bedroom. The candle's still burning. Elza is still frozen, staring into the Book of Eight's endless pages. Her mouth moves soundlessly. She turns another wafer-thin page.

"This is . . ." Kirk starts to say.

"It looks worse than it is," I tell him, without believing it myself.

"I thought you were going to do this?" Holiday asks me.

"I was. She didn't want me to. I left her alone with the thing for a moment and—"

I'm surprised to catch myself crying. This is the thing that took me over the edge? After everything?

Holiday folds me in a hug, and then Kirk does, too.

"I'm sorry," I say, "sorry—"

"It's not your fault," Holiday tells me.

"This is all my fault."

"Mate, don't talk bollocks," Kirk snaps. "How's it your fault? She chose this, man. Lotta other people doing bad stuff tonight. Don't put everything on your back, you know?"

"Elza's going to be fine," Holiday says.

"It should be me," I say.

"Honestly, man," Kirk says, "I'm glad it's not, 'cause if I had to spend a couple days cooped up in here with her, waiting for you to wake up, I'd go mental, man. No offense, I know she's your girl and all. We just don't click."

I do laugh at that. "Well, I feel much better now."

"Seriously, mate. She'll snap out of there. You did, right?"

"Yeah. I did."

"So will she," Holiday says. They release me. I take a deep breath.

"Thanks," I say. "Sorry. I don't know—"

"Look," Holiday says, "are we safe here? That's the main thing right now. Are we safe?"

"I don't know."

"What if they come back?" she asks. "Margaux, this thing, it knows we're here. If it lets the rest of them in, that are waiting out there . . ."

"Not without being invited," I assure her again. "They can't come back in."

"But you're sure?"

"They shouldn't be able to break the wards. And where else can we go? Unless you want to take Mark and Elza out, somehow get them through the people in the snow, back to Elza's house . . ."

"No," Holiday says, "there's no way. We can't."

"Yeah," I say. "So, we're stuck here. We've just got to keep alert and wait for Elza to snap out of this."

"All right," Kirk says. "So we wait."

It could be hours or days. Snow and fog swirl outside, and cold leaks in through the broken window. We sit with Mark by the fire, wrapped in our coats, with Bea snuggled against our feet. We eat stuff from the fridge: leftover Christmas food, cold lentil soup that Darren cooked before we went to his place, however long ago that was now. I play cards with Kirk. Holiday reads some of Mum's spirituality paperbacks. Sometimes Mark turns over in his sleep and whimpers. At times I pace the dark halls of my house, witch blade in hand, making sure there's nothing else that crept in here from outside. There are flashes of light outside, in the sky, irregular pulses of blue and green. The candle in my room where Elza sits burns down, going out completely. I replace it with a fresh candle and sit with her for a long time.

I think at some point I must fall asleep on the beanbag chair beside my bed, with my head resting against Elza's leg, because the next thing I know, she wakes me with a start, her legs kicking and spasming. She's back from wherever the Book of Eight took her. I leap to my feet.

(the manchett host)

Elza coughs and heaves, and I think she's going to throw up, but nothing comes out. Her hands clutch at the bedspread. The Book of Eight has fallen to the floor and lies there, its green covers spread, pages facedown.

"Are you all right?" I ask her quietly.

She swallows.

"I feel like I grew a new brain," Elza says. "I feel like I got shot in the head and survived. How did you do this twice?"

"Why did you do this at all?" I ask.

"You know why," she says.

"I can't believe—How could you do that?"

"I wasn't about to let you go in there a third time. No way."

"I can't believe you did that! How could you leave me?" I feel angrier than I have in a long time, and it surprises me.

"You're not the only one who gets to take risks!" she snaps. "Now you know what it feels like! It's not nice, is it?"

I look back at her. She's pale and trembling, sweat dampening her forehead.

"No," I say. "It's not."

"Please, let's not fight about this now," she says softly.

"How did you . . . I didn't even think it would work for you."

"I had the sigil. I remembered the sequence, the start of it anyway. I was the one who read it out to you the first time. Why wouldn't it work for me?"

She blinks, looking into the candle.

"Can you still see them?" I ask, remembering the first time I came out of the trance, the way the sigils and symbols crawled over everything.

"Yeah," she says. "Your face was made out of . . . something. I don't know. I felt like I could see through you. Like I could see right through everything."

"Did you find what we need to know?" I ask.

"I did."

"Can you walk?" I ask. "We should go down where it's warmer."

"We should," Elza says faintly. She tries to stand and nearly falls. I catch hold of her, press her body against mine. She breathes in and out. "Give me a moment . . ."

"If you need to lie down—"

"No," she says. "No. I want to walk. Let me walk."

"All right, all right."

We make our way across the room, leaving the candle burning in its dish, and across the landing, downstairs, stumble into the living room. Holiday and Kirk stand up as we come in.

"Is she—"

"I'm OK," Elza says. "Just a bit weak."

She slumps down into the armchair Holiday was sitting in. Her eyes are unfocused. She chews on one finger, not seeming to know she's doing it.

"Elza," I say, "are you really—"

"I'm fine! Stop fussing over me!"

"You just don't seem that well," I say.

"Nothing we can do about that," she replies.

We stand in awkward silence. None of us seems sure what to do. Elza doesn't look at anyone, instead devotes a solid minute to looking at her forefinger. Dad's sigil is still on her hand. I reach down to take it from her, and she jerks her hand away.

"We're in bad trouble," Elza says after another moment.

Nobody replies.

"Very bad trouble. This thing . . ."

"The Tree," I say. "The Barrenwhite Tree?"

"Yes," Elza says. "It's . . . it's from the Beginning. Before the worlds were broken."

"What do you mean?" I ask.

"Before there was life and death. The spirit world was all there was. Everything was one. The split happened so long ago, almost nothing exists that remembers how things were before. But the Tree does."

"OK," I say. "So what does it want?"

"It reaches out and makes things how they were before. Living and dead are one. The worlds collapse into each other. But it isn't allowed. It can only do these things certain nights, in certain seconds, when the Winter Star is here and the old year becomes new."

"The Winter Star?" Holiday says.

"The comet," Elza replies. "Every eight centuries. It comes back. It comes back and then the stars are right and the Tree's Apostles can open the gateway."

"Margaux—" I say.

"We helped her," Elza says.

"What?" I say.

"We opened the gateway. The Devil's Footsteps. We broke it open, and the Tree came through. We helped her."

"Why would we do that?"

"I don't know."

Is this what we don't remember? The gateway opening—we helped Margaux. Why? I try to remember what I was thinking, but I can't. All I remember is stars, frost, Margaux's tattooed hands. White swans flying backward.

"You did this?" Kirk asks me.

"I don't know why we'd want to," I say, holding my hands up. "Trust me, man."

"You did this to us?" he barks.

"The Apostles made us," Elza says, wheezing. "They drugged us or something. We couldn't protect ourselves."

"How did we get away?" I ask her.

"I don't remember."

"So the gateway is open," I say. "Haven't we opened it before?"

"Not properly. The stones . . . they're locks. It could only open a crack. The real circle . . . I don't know. But we broke the locks. The standing stones are gone."

"And that's how the Tree came through?"

"It grows there," she says. "While the Tree is still there, the gateway is fully open, like a dam burst. Deadside has spilled out into Liveside, covered the whole of Dunbarrow. That's what it does. In the moment the New Year is waiting to be born, that's its chance."

"What does it want?"

"Dunbarrow. The people here. They'll be stuck here, in this moment, worshipping the Tree, until the next time the stars are right. And then it'll choose somewhere else, take that town into Deadside instead. This is how it feeds."

I think about the gray people surrounding the house, the roots growing from their faces and bodies.

"That's what's happening to everyone?"

"Yes. They'll be stuck here, being eaten away to nothing, for eight hundred years. And we'll be stuck here, too. The night will never end."

"But what can we do?" I ask.

"We have to close the gateway. We have to place the standing stones again."

"What do you mean, place the standing stones? What happened to the Devil's Footsteps?"

"In our mouths," she says.

I don't understand for a moment, and then I run my tongue over the flinty new tooth in the back of my mouth, and I do.

"The stones are . . . but that's impossible."

Elza laughs.

"Everything that's happened to us, and you can't understand how a standing stone could become a tooth?"

"That's crazy," I say, but I know she's right. I can feel the shape of it with my tongue: the flattest stone, the one like an angled table. That's the one I have stuck in my gums.

"I have another," Elza says. She opens her mouth wide, so we can all see the dark stone stuck in her gums, right at the back on the left. Hers is the second-largest one.

"So who has the third Footstep?" I ask.

"I don't know. One of the Apostles, maybe."

"Margaux."

"What happened to her?" Elza asks.

"We messed her up," Kirk says. "Then she got away."

" . . . All right," Elza says weakly.

"Margaux went back to the Tree," I say. "I'm sure of that. If the third stone is in her mouth . . . we'll have to go find her and get it out."

"It won't be easy, Luke," Elza says. "The Barrenwhite Tree . . . it's powerful. So powerful."

"We've got the Book of Eight," I say. "We've got a sigil. We've got two witch blades—"

"It won't be—I don't know if that's enough," she says. "This thing, Luke, what we'll be able to see of it, is just a tiny fraction of the spirit. It's like something reaching down into a rock pool, and we're the fish. I don't know how we'd go up against something like that."

"It's either that or we're trapped in this house in a snowstorm for eight centuries. I mean, I know which option I prefer."

"I know," she says. "I just don't . . . I don't know if we're coming back from this one."

"We have to try," I say.

She nods. "We need to close the gateway," she says. "That's where we have to go. Back to the Footsteps. We need to go soon," Elza says. "The Barrenwhite Tree will find a way to break through the hazel charms. They were never meant to stand against something so strong."

"We need a better plan than this," Holiday says. "I mean, how are we even going to get out of the house, for starters? Did you forget all the awful people out there? How do we get past them? Is Luke going to do magic at them?"

"I can't," I say. "I don't have a Host. I'm a necromancer — we take power from our Host. Without one —"

"So your magic ring won't work?" Holiday says.

"Basically."

"I mean, don't you think you should have a Host? If we're going up against Margaux? And this Tree thing?"

"Well, they're not just lying around," I say. "I don't know nearly all the spells to find the right spirits. I just used my dad's."

"Why not use mine?" Holiday asks.

"What?"

"My spirit? I mean, we all have one, right?"

"Because you're alive," Elza says, running her fingers through her hair.

"So it has to be a ghost?" Holiday says.

"Yeah," I say. "I did explain all of this. A Host is eight dead servants and one living master."

"Well," Elza says, "everything's upside down right now."

"Yeah?" I say.

"Midnight never ends. We're stuck between the old

year dying and the new year being born. Dunbarrow's been taken into the world of the dead, but we're all still alive. Kirk cut into that spirit with a normal sword."

Kirk nods with pleasure.

"Mashed its leg up," he says.

"Right," Elza says, agreeing with Kirk for maybe the first time in history. "'Mashed' is a good word. The two worlds have been mashed together. In a way, there is no life or death now, or not as we normally see it. It's like it was before the worlds were split."

"So?"

"So maybe Holiday's right. She does have a spirit. Maybe right now, that's all it would take to put some power into your sigil."

"You really think?" I ask them.

"It might be worth a try," Elza says to Holiday. "You're putting your life in his hands, though. Like, a necromancer can destroy his Host completely if he wants to."

"I'm already trusting you with everything," Holiday says. "If this would help us stop whatever's happening tonight—"

"It's not going to work," I say. "Nothing will happen if I try and do this. It's not how my sigil works."

"OK," Holiday says. "So if it doesn't work, then nothing happens. We lose nothing. But if you were going to try this, what would you do?"

I look around us. Elza and Holiday and Kirk wait for me to speak. I have to try something. Elza and Holiday are right: if this doesn't work, then we're only as bad off as we are now. But if it does work . . .

"Well, you'd be my Shepherd, I suppose," I say. "The first member of a Host. That's like the leader."

"OK," Holiday says, grinning slightly for the first time in a while. "I like organizing stuff. I'll be a Shepherd."

Maybe this isn't the stupidest idea in the world. Holiday does like arranging things, taking charge. Maybe she's not the weirdest choice for being the Shepherd.

"So you have to accept that name," I say. "This is the easy version, when you're willing to become part of the Host."

"All right," she says.

Elza pulls the sigil ring from her finger and hands it to me. I turn it over in my palms, examining it in the firelight. Silver band, eight-sided black stone, reflecting no light. I put it onto my ring finger for the first time since last Easter and feel the cold embrace of the sigil. Elza's hands are far smaller than mine, but it fits me just as well as it fit her.

I motion for Holiday to stand in front of me. I stand up too, and Elza and Kirk stay sitting, watching us. I feel like we're about to start playing a game, charades or something.

"*Honorable leader,*" I say, raising the sigil, keeping my

eyes locked on Holiday's. *"Beloved left hand. Speaker for the dead. I name you Shepherd."*

"Your voice has gone all weird," Holiday says.

"No," I say, lowering the sigil, "then you say, 'I accept this name in turn. I bind my soul to the Manchett Host, now and for eternity.' All right?"

"Got it," Holiday says.

"Honorable leader. Beloved left hand. Speaker for the dead. I name you Shepherd."

"I accept this name in turn," Holiday says. *"I bind my soul to the Manchett Host, now and for eternity."*

Nothing happens. I stand for a moment longer, sigil raised. On a whim I move my hand forward and down, resting the ring on Holiday's head.

"Hey—" she starts to say, and there's a rush of heat, like someone lit a fire inside my hand. I snatch it away from her, try to tear the sigil ring from my finger, feeling like it must be searing into my flesh, but there's nothing wrong with my skin or the ring, just this crazy heat boring into my hand, spreading down my arm, like I replaced my blood with gasoline and someone held a match to my veins—

"Luke!" Elza shouts. I raise a hand, trying to make an *I'm fine* gesture, but I can't. Sweat pours from my forehead.

Holiday's eyes are flickering. She breathes raggedly.

"Are you OK?" Elza asks me.

The sigil pulses with power, not with cold, like normal,

but with golden heat. It doesn't hurt anymore; it feels good. Bea whines, looking at us anxiously.

"You've gone pale," Kirk says dubiously.

"Yeah," Holiday says. "God. I could see stars."

I stretch my hand out, and with a flick of my wrist send a blast of golden fire arcing into the air. Kirk flinches away from the flames. I laugh. Elza and Holiday look at me, astonished. Warm shimmering flames play around my sigil ring.

"That," I say to Holiday, "was a brilliant idea."

Elza and Kirk become members of my Host as well, to give me as much power as possible. Kirk says the words and becomes my new Vassal, Elza my Heretic. With each binding, the sigil ring glows with brighter heat on my finger, and I feel more confident. I can't believe this worked, but it seems that it has. Sometimes you need somebody without any specialist knowledge to innovate. Three spirits isn't the strongest Host you can make, not even by half, but I only had one ghost to my name when I went into Deadside to face the Ahlgrens, and I came out of that in one piece. We have a chance.

Elza hasn't gotten up from the chair since the binding. She sits with her eyes closed, fingers tapping on the arm-rests.

"This feels so weird," she says quietly.

"Are you really all right to travel?" I ask. She's insisted she'll come with me.

"I'll be fine. I'll have to be."

I bend down and kiss her. Her lips are soft.

"What about Mark?" Holiday asks us.

"How do you mean?"

"He can't come with us," she says.

"Oh yeah," I say. I hadn't even thought about that. Mark's still asleep, and there's clearly no way he's going anywhere on that leg. He'll have to stay here.

"I don't like leaving him," Elza says, "but I don't see what choice we have. This is about as safe as anywhere in Dunbarrow at the moment."

"You just said they could find a way to get in here," Holiday says. "There are hundreds of ghosts and who knows what else outside Luke's house."

Elza smiles thinly. "I'm hoping we'll give those things out there more important issues to worry about. We're going back to the Devil's Footsteps, and we're sending them home."

"So we just leave him here?" Holiday asks.

"Me and Luke need to sort this out," Elza says. "You can do what you like."

"I'll stay with him," Kirk says.

"What?" I ask.

"I mean, I'll stay. I don't . . ." Kirk trails off.

"You all right, mate?"

"I'm not cut out for this," he says. "No way. I don't . . . I don't think I can. I can't go out again. Too many monsters, man. It's screwed up. I'll stay with Mark."

"All right, mate," I say. "That's OK."

He stares at me, gripping the sword, daring us to laugh at him.

"You've done more than anyone could ask," Elza says quietly. "Someone does need to look after Mark. That's brave, too. You'll be on your own here with him. I'd be afraid of that. Nobody thinks worse of you."

"That's right," Holiday says, putting an arm on his shoulder.

"You'll have Bea with you," I say. "There's food in the fridge. Give Mark some of those painkillers every twelve hours. . . . Well, that won't work. No clocks. I suppose whenever he's in pain."

"What about you?" Elza asks Holiday.

"I'm coming with you," she says grimly.

"You're sure?"

"I don't see how I can do anything else," Holiday replies. "And you're going to need help."

"That's fine with me," I say.

Elza nods. She rises from her chair with a lurch and starts to head for the kitchen.

"We'll need food," she says. "I don't know how long this'll take. Weapons too. You say we've got another witch blade now?"

"The one Margaux was using."

We gather our supplies. Warm clothes, backpacks with food and cans of soda. Sigil, Book of Eight, two witch blades, Holiday's wyrdstone on a string. Rope, a hammer, first-aid supplies. The standing stone—I can't quite believe that's what it—but I still carry it in my mouth. Elza hasn't explained to me yet how we're going to get them out of our gums, but I suppose we'll cross that bridge when we come to it.

We're gathered in the hallway, Kirk holding a candle in one of the candlesticks Mum uses at Christmas dinner. Nobody seems sure of what to say.

"Well," I say at last, "we'll see you in the morning, I guess?"

"Yeah," Kirk says. He doesn't sound convinced.

"You know where stuff is, right?"

"Haven't been here since we were thirteen."

"It hasn't changed much." Has it really been that long? I suppose Mum got worse after that, so I kept people away from the house. I never once had Mark over, I remember that.

Holiday hugs Kirk tightly. "It's going to be fine," she says to him. "I'll find Alice."

"Be safe," he says.

Elza and Kirk shake hands. There's a silence.

"Sorry about calling you a lesbian that one time," he says.

"It was more than one time," Elza replies.

"I dunno what's wrong with me," Kirk says, looking at the floor. "I'm sorry, man."

"That's OK," Elza says. "It doesn't really matter now, does it? I'm sorry I busted your nose that time. For what it's worth."

Elza turns and unlatches the door. Cold air blows into the hallway. Kirk's candle goes out. Elza steps out, followed by Holiday. I stay where I am.

"She'll come around," I say. "Elza's really cool, honestly."

Kirk laughs bitterly. "Mate, I'm never gonna see you guys again."

"We'll be back," I say. "Trust me."

"Yeah," he says, not sounding convinced. "Look, I wanted you to have this."

He hands me his sword.

"Authentically forged in Japan," he says. "Got a certificate with it and all. You see them horse things—"

"You sure?" I ask. I raise my sigil ring. "You've already given me power, Kirk. You gave me your spirit. You can keep the sword."

"Nah," he says. "You might need a weapon, man, no matter what magic you got in that ring there. Maybe you'll find a sword's exactly what you need. You're gonna be in more trouble than me. I'm just the lad sitting on his arse inside 'cause he's scared."

"Don't be like that, man," I say. "You've done really well."

"Your girl's braver than I am," he says.

"Elza's braver than most people," I say. "And she's been living with all this way longer than you have. Don't feel so bad."

"Yeah, well. I'm sorry for making fun of you both and stuff. Dunno why I do half the stuff I do half the time. If I get out of this—"

"It's all right, man."

We hug. Kirk's stubbly head rubs against my neck. He smells of cigarettes.

"Go do it," he says. "Kick this tree-thing's head in. And you see them horse monsters, you know what to do. Carve them up good. Tell them I sent you."

"I will," I say. "I'll see you and Mark soon."

He smiles properly and claps me on the shoulder.

"You've always been positive like that," he says. "It's good. I always liked it. Now get that door shut, man. I'm freezing my balls off here."

I laugh and step out into the snow, sword still held

in my right hand. The front door clicks shut behind me. I imagine Kirk standing there, hand on the door. I wonder what his face looks like now. Does he really believe we'll come back? What will he and Mark do if we don't?

I shove the sword through my belt. It's pretty awkward, but it'll have to do. I tie my scarf up around my face for warmth, and then I set off, with the strength of three living souls burning inside my sigil ring, ready to face the dead.

Holiday and Elza are waiting for me by the front gate. Just beyond them, the fog of Deadside beckons us. Ranks of the Tree's servants surround the house, twisted gray bodies in the grayness. Elza looks at the crowd with a worried frown. They stare back, chanting in a whisper.

"*Seven trees of living stone . . .*"

"So how do we get through this?" Elza asks me. "They've got us pretty well trapped."

"Elza!" Ryan calls from the dimness beyond the garden gate. "Luke! Great to see you! Let us in."

He lurches closer to the boundary of the hazel charm's protection, close enough for us to see him properly. Holiday gasps. Ryan's body is a mass of roots, some now thick as my fingers, trailing down to the ground. The Tree really is eating them, bit by bit.

"I don't think so," Elza says.

"The eighth is cast of ice and bone . . ."

"There's nothing to be afraid of," someone says in the crowd.

"Yes," I say, raising my sigil, "there is."

I draw power from my new Host, draw from the living spirits of Elza and Holiday and Kirk, and a warm golden light blossoms from my sigil ring, like someone attached the sun to my hand. The light cuts through the fog, dissolving it away. The crowd screams, revealed in the light, covering their glowing eyes with their root-gnarled hands. They're forced away from us, cowering into the fog. Holiday raises her wyrdstone, and white light shines from it, matching the radiance of my sigil.

"Follow me," I tell Holiday and Elza, and they do, holding their witch blades ready for an attack. My heart pounds as I step outside the garden gate, into the fog, but the crowd of worshippers does nothing to hurt me. They can't even look at me, as long as the light from my sigil shines.

We walk back to back, pushing our way through the throng. They're a terrible sight: skin gray and cracked, losing their hair, gray roots pushing through their flesh. It's no longer possible to recognize my neighbors, to pick out who each figure used to be before the Tree came here. One brave worshipper makes an attempt to grab at us, one hand covering its eyes, but its skin starts to smoke as it comes closer to my sigil, and the creature backs off, howling.

There's a commotion behind us, and the sound of a dog barking. A black shape slips between a pair of gray legs and jumps into the ring of light around us. Bea.

"What are you doing out here?" I yell. "Go inside!"

"She got out!" Elza says, keeping her eyes fixed on the creatures around us. "You spent so long with Kirk . . ."

"*Seven trees of living stone . . .*" the crowd mumbles.

"Bea! Go home! It's not safe!"

"You can't send her back through this!" Holiday shouts at me, pushing the shining wyrdstone into a worshipper's root-furred face. "They'll grab her!"

She's not wrong. I had hoped we'd have broken free of the crowd by now, but they're still packed as tightly as possible around us, shielding their eyes with their hands.

"I don't . . . I already lost Ham! It's too dangerous! She can't come with us!" I say.

"We don't have a choice now," Elza snaps. "She's here! Now how are we getting out of this?"

"*The eighth is cast of ice and bone . . .*"

The light from my sigil is still shining, but it's starting to feel uncomfortably hot on my hand. I can see Holiday's wyrdstone is starting to fade. How long can I keep this alight? When it goes out, they'll surround us and tear us to pieces. Bea runs around me in a circle, barking furiously at the worshippers. I can't tell where we are anymore, how far or near we are to my house. All I can see is fog, hands covering gray faces, dark bodies.

"We need to break free!" I shout. "We can't do this forever!"

"Can we jump?" Holiday asks me.

"What?"

"Can we go somewhere else? Like we did crossing the bridge?"

"I don't know how to make that happen!" I reply.

"We ought to try," Elza says. "We'll never get free of the crowd like this."

"Grab Bea," I tell her. "Think of somewhere else in Dunbarrow! The school, maybe? I don't know!"

The creatures around us howl.

"Seven trees of living stone!"

My hand feels like I'm holding it in a furnace. I don't think I can stand this much longer.

"The eighth is—"

I squeeze my eyes shut, think as hard as I can of the high school, imagine us walking across the playing fields, gray mist swirling around us.

"—cast—"

There's a rush of coldness, and when I open my eyes, we're not on Wormwood Drive anymore. We're in a snowy field, with leafless trees visible in the fog. The creatures around us are gone. Holiday takes a deep breath. I let the burning light fade from my sigil, a welcome relief.

"Well, that's not where I was thinking of," I say. "But it's a start."

"Where is this?" Elza asks. "I was thinking of Dunbarrow."

"Uh," Holiday says, pointing to a street sign sticking out of the gray grass, "I think this might be it."

"You're kidding." Elza whistles, looking at the bleak grassland around us. "Is this the main road?"

We walk farther and come across the shells of buildings I recognize: the bank by the roundabout, the pet shop. Dunbarrow is coming apart, unraveling like an old worn-out rag. There are trees where houses used to be, enormous gray trees with scaly bark and icicles hanging like vicious fruit from their branches. When there are buildings, they look a hundred years old or more, ruins clouded with ice. Time runs strangely here, I know that. Perhaps some of these buildings really have stood for a hundred years now, slowly collapsing under the weight of the snow. I don't know. We pass Dunbarrow's clock tower, the clock stuck at exactly midnight. Nobody seems to be around; I assume Margaux sent them all up to guard my house. I'm on alert for any sign of the Knights, but I can't hear any snatches of their voices or the telltale clank of their armor. We move quickly through what remains of the streets, Bea following us like an extra shadow.

We pass the pub, doors still open, with snow blanketing the tiled floor inside. They must've been doing good business when midnight struck. We cut across the bus station, double-deckers standing abandoned and dark in their bays. There are thorny gray trees growing through the blacktop in the parking lot opposite, splitting through the earth.

"It's like it's all turning back into forest," Elza says as we pass by.

"England's memory of itself," I say.

"What?" she asks.

"I dunno. Something the Shepherd told me about Deadside, I think."

We pass along a snowy road surrounded by trees. This is the route we used to walk to school in the mornings, when I went to Dunbarrow High. I think this is the tree where we threw Nick Alsip's sports bag as a joke, and it got stuck in the highest branches; and bizarrely, of all the things in Dunbarrow that have remained, that bag is still caught up there, a ragged shape in the dimness. Our feet crunch in the snow. Bea takes the lead, crossing back and forth across the road in a zigzag pattern, as if she's scenting for something.

"Why did you stop talking to me?" Elza asks Holiday after a period of silence.

"What do you mean?" Holiday replies.

"I mean—" Elza sighs. "God! Don't act like you don't know what I mean. We were best friends. Remember going to Devon? Do you remember your dad finding that crab in the rock pool and picking it up to show us, and it pinched his thumb so hard it bled? We were screaming. I know you remember that."

"Yeah," Holiday says. "He still has a scar there."

"Do you remember the Pony Castle?"

"Of course," Holiday says. "The tower is still in our garage."

"I think Queen Goldenmane is in our attic," Elza says.

There's another of those green flashes in the sky, brighter I think now that we're closer to the passing place. Bea is trotting along next to me, apparently no longer worried about me grabbing her collar and making her go back home.

"Just checking, anyway," Elza continues. "I mean, we've barely spoken for, like, five years. I wasn't sure if you remembered any of that or if it was just me."

"Of course I remember," Holiday says quietly. "But we were little girls, Elza."

"Of course," Elza says. "People change."

"I mean, like . . ." Holiday grasps for words. "School's

tough. You think it was fun for me? Half those girls are horrible. Everyone smiles at you, and then when you're not in the room, they all start talking about you. It's a nightmare. I couldn't have done it and kept things how they were with us when we were little. You kind of freaked them out. I mean, I didn't mind how you'd look at stuff that wasn't there—"

"Hey, there was stuff there," Elza says. "You know that now."

"All right, I know now that you weren't just talking to nothing but I didn't back then. I mean . . . you're kind of intense, Elza. I'm sorry. It wasn't always easy to be friends with you."

"I'm intense," Elza says.

"You are a little intense," I say gently.

"Plus you were kind of bossy," Holiday says quickly.

"I'm bossy?" Elza asks, looking at us hard.

"You're, like . . . you have strong opinions," I say.

"I mean, I don't know," Holiday says. "I wanted people to like me. You didn't seem like you cared. That's fine for you; it's not great for people who . . . I mean, I dunno. You're so brave, Elza. I thought you'd be all right."

Elza nods.

"I mean, I'm sorry. I wish I hadn't just ditched you. We were eleven. We weren't grown-ups. We're not even grown-ups now. It was hard to talk about stuff like that."

"No," Elza says, "that's fair. We are different people. I guess if I had more friends, it wouldn't have bothered me so much." She reaches out with a gloved hand, knocks a lump of snow from a car's side mirror as we pass by. "I don't know if we'll make it to the Barrenwhite Tree. I certainly don't know if we'll make it back. It doesn't seem likely. This seemed like my last chance to ask you about any of it."

"It's OK," Holiday says. "For what it's worth, I think Alice and the others were really horrible to you. I never wanted to—It's hard, you know. To tell people not to be like that. I wasn't brave enough."

"Yeah, well," Elza says, "Alice is . . ."

"She might find her way back," I say.

"She's not a bad person," Holiday says. "She's got problems at home and stuff. Like, she's really unhappy."

I think Alice has problems period if she's lost out there in Deadside, but I decide not to say that. It's not as if Holiday doesn't know. We're at the gates to Dunbarrow High, I realize. They're locked, with a gleaming padlock and chain. This is more or less the first place I spoke to Elza, that day when she was smoking by these gates. Bea slips underneath, her snout cutting through the snow like a plow. She watches us through the bars, ears cocked, as if asking, *Well?*

"Come on," I say, and we climb the school gates again, more awkwardly in my case, as Kirk's sword rattles and bangs against the cold bars. Holiday nearly falls off the top, but steadies herself and drops down next to me. The trees seem thicker, like a forest. Fog moves between their trunks in slow waves.

Up past the high school, through the staff parking lot, into the far yard where I used to play soccer before class with Mark and Kirk. Three quick flashes in the sky illuminate the fog, the buildings, green blue green, and I see the school is coated with gray ivy, the windows broken, the front yard knee high in colorless grass. Fresh snow spirals in the air, and frost gleams on brickwork. The place is derelict, a hollow shell of a school. Everything is falling apart. The longer this lasts, the longer Dunbarrow is sunk into the swirling chaos of Deadside. Like a sand castle collapsing at high tide, the harder it'll be to put everything back like it was. We've broken the bones of the world.

We need the third stone from Margaux's mouth. We find her, take it from her, and shut the gateway. This can still be mended. That's what I tell myself.

The playing fields are a frozen waste, unkempt and tangled, being reclaimed by forest. It's barely recognizable as the same place me and Elza ran across earlier tonight. Bea sniffs the air and growls. Her ears go back against her head.

"Something's coming," I tell Elza and Holiday. I expected this sooner or later. Elza unsheathes her witch blade. I draw out Kirk's sword, feeling heat in my hand where the sigil rests, the Book of Eight held in my coat's breast pocket, a pressure against my heart. Holiday has the wyrdstone held in her right hand. We're as ready as we could be.

Heavy footsteps. The clank of armor plating. Two bulky shapes emerge from the fog, walking with slow purpose. The Knights of the Tree.

"And what is this that we find?" Titus calls to Dumachus. He halts, knocking at the frozen earth with one hoof. It looks like the Tree did heal his wounds, because his lame leg seems perfectly functional. "Did I not say to you that we shall eat tonight?"

"They be armed," Dumachus says doubtfully. "The blade that bit us before and more besides. The sorcerer bears his sigil now."

"They do hold to the old ways, this be true," Titus agrees. "But do we not hold terrible form, Dumachus? Is our shape not powerful? Are we not true Knights, armor forged in the fires of Tartarus?"

"You don't even have thumbs," I tell them.

"What are you saying?" Holiday hisses to me. "I don't understand."

"It's spirit language," I say. "I'm insulting them."

"Oh my god! Guys and your macho bullshit! Just tell them to go away!"

"We have business with your master," I tell the spirits, staring them down. "Let us through."

"You have no business with our lady," Titus hisses. "Do not presume to give us instructions, sorcerer. We have devoured far greater souls than yours. You have found your magic ring, I see? I have the measure of the strength there. It is not enough."

While Titus is speaking, Dumachus is moving slowly around to our right, eyes locked on my sword. He's trying to get behind us. I know Bea's noticed, at least. I hope Elza has as well.

"If you don't let us through, I'll destroy you both," I say. "This is your last chance."

"We cannot allow you to reach the gateway," Titus says.

I release the golden light from my sigil, and the Knights howl, but they don't shrink back from it like the crowd of worshippers around my house did. Instead they shut their eyes and trample toward us, snapping their jaws. Without eyesight their aim is bad, and we stumble backward, Bea barking crazily, trying to keep out of their reach.

"Luke!" Elza screams. "What can we do?"

"It's not enough! I need more power!" I shout. My sigil

is burning as bright as I can make it, but it doesn't stop the Knights. Dumachus is very close to me now, rearing up on his hind legs, striking at the air wildly.

"You think to blind us with your tricks?" he snarls.

I feel Holiday grab my arm. Fresh heat surges through my sigil.

"I know you can do it!" she shouts.

Dumachus, hearing her voice, lunges at us.

I strike back with the full strength of my will, directing my anger and hatred at the creature, drawing deeply from Holiday's spirit. Golden fire erupts from the sigil ring, a surge of heat that engulfs Dumachus, and the knight bellows in terror, not expecting this power. Flames sear into his face, into his muscular shoulders and legs, the thick plates of armor no protection against my attack. The Knight falls back, stumbling in the snow, screaming with pain. I unleash another golden lash of heat so bright, I can't stand to look at it, and when the light has faded, Dumachus is nothing but a horse-shaped cloud of mist and ash, drifting to the ground. I burst into laughter, raising the glowing ring above my head. Titus rears and wails.

"Oh! You have destroyed him! Noble Dumachus! Oh! Oh!"

"Yeah, tell me again how you have the measure of our strength!" I scream at him.

"My friend! My love! No!" The monster is crying now, pounding the earth with his hooves.

Elza is shouting something that I can't hear. The ringing in my ears is too loud. I don't care. I channel Holiday's spirit through my sigil again, and a blast of golden flame courses over Titus's body. These Knights are nothing; they're weak—

The spirit screams and thrashes as the fire consumes him. I gather my will for the killing blow.

"Luke!" Elza shrieks. "Stop!"

She grabs my arm, tipping me off balance. I lose my concentration. The cloud of fire around my sigil evaporates.

"Holiday," she's saying. "Holiday!"

I look behind us to see Holiday collapsed in the snow, eyes open, not moving. I didn't notice. I hadn't even noticed when she let go of my hand.

"What—"

"You took too much from her—Luke! *No!*"

Elza screams and a shock of pain runs through my body as I fly into the air. I land with a crunch on the earth, searing pain running through my torso, my right leg. I think it's broken. I dropped the sword when the Knight hit me. I try to use my sigil again, but the power I felt a moment ago isn't there anymore. I hurt too much. I can't concentrate. The power's far out of reach, faded away.

What did I do to Holiday?

Titus looms over me. The Knight's awful colorless eyes run with tears.

"My oldest friend," he says in a whisper. "Dumachus was worth ten of you."

"Told you to let us pass . . ." I say.

Titus bends down and sinks his jaws into my left leg, the one that isn't broken. I scream. This is the worst pain that I've ever felt, worse than anything that's ever happened to me. Being stabbed hurt less than this. The Knight lifts my entire body into the air, and I'm upside down, suspended by my leg from his jaws, my hair brushing the cold crust of snow over the playing fields. Titus shakes me, a terrier with a rat, and then flings me into the air, and I'm tumbling over and over as the world flashes green and gray and green again, a jade wall of fog above me and the ground—

I hit the earth and shriek. Everything hurts. My body is a searing map of pain. I have pain highways running down my back, pain cities buzzing in my hand and face and legs and my stomach; there's blood running down my face—

Titus comes stalking out of the fog again. I can barely move, I'm trying to get up, and I can't move, and all I can think about is getting away, it's all going to end here . . .

The Knight's gray face is dark with my blood.

"I will feast upon you slowly," he pronounces. "I shall start at the feet and work up."

Titus bares his teeth. I can see the dents and scratches on his armor, the lank hairs of his mustache. He has no smell, I realize, feeling absurd to be thinking about that right now. None of the spirits do.

"Better you had died when our master decreed. Better you had submitted then."

He looms over me, blood drooling from his jaws.

"Better—AAAH!"

I hear Bea snarling and Titus jerks away from me, legs flailing.

"Damn beast! Begone!"

I raise my head. Bea has torn into the Knight's back leg, her teeth finding purchase in unarmored flesh, biting deep into the thigh. He tries to stamp on her but she dances aside, snarling and snapping at the monster. Pain pulses through my broken body. Bea's brave, but it's only a matter of time before he catches her. She's just a mouthful to Titus. A single snap of his jaws. She'll die like Ham did, and not even to save me. I'm already done for.

Titus tries to bite Bea, but she's just out of reach. He rears up for another strike, legs flailing in the air, roaring unintelligibly, and that's when Elza appears.

She darts out of the fog, moving fast and light as a panther, the witch blade a white fang in her hands, and she strikes Titus's flank with all her strength, sliding the blade into a chink in his armor. He roars and turns to face her, and without hesitation Elza plunges the witch blade into his exposed face, right between the eyes.

There's a blinding flash of white light, and Titus falls to the ground, wailing. He thrashes and churns, his outlines already fading, his gray body becoming one with the gray Deadside fog as I watch. The Knight's armor falls into a disorderly heap, snow already starting to cover it.

Elza rushes over to me. Her hair is an explosion, her breath ragged.

"Luke," she says. "Luke . . ."

"Hey," I say. Even speaking a single word hurts my chest.

"Can you—"

"Can't move," I whisper. "Got me good."

Bea licks my face, a welcome warm tongue. I try to smile.

"Luke," she says, "I'm sorry. It's my fault—"

"No."

"I distracted you! I'm sorry!"

"Holiday. Shouldn't have . . . Is she alive?"

"Luke, you're dying!"

"Is Holiday alive?"

"I don't know! Everything's gone—what am I meant to do? You're all broken up. I . . . What can we do?"

Breathing feels like a knife in my ribs. I grimace.

"You have to shut the gateway, Elza. You and Bea."

"I can't leave you here!"

"I'm not gone yet," I say. "If you do it in enough time, you might be able to get an ambulance up here for us. Get things back to normal—"

"You can't see yourself," Elza says. Tears glitter in her eyes. "No, don't try and look. Just lie still, OK? You look like . . . oh, Luke. It's like you were in a car crash. It's bad. You're not going to last that long."

"I'll be a ghost," I say. "Give me . . . few minutes. I'll come with you again."

"No," she says.

"What else is there?"

"Nothing," Elza says. "I just . . . I don't know. I don't want to put Dunbarrow back together if you won't be there with me."

"I could be there. I'll stay with you."

"And you'll still be seventeen when I'm seventy."

"Look," I say, my breath searing my chest like steam as I speak. I try to breathe as shallow as possible and not to grimace so Elza won't see how much I'm hurting. "What else can we do?"

"Nothing."

"Where's Holiday?"

"She's over there," Elza says, gesturing off into the fog.

"Move her indoors. Don't leave her in the snow."

"I'm not leaving you here."

Bea whines.

Snow is drifting down toward my eyes. I want to close them. The sky flares emerald.

"Bring her over here at least," I say. "Can't leave her alone."

"What if you—"

"I'll hold on while you're gone," I tell her.

"All right," Elza says. "I don't see what good it'll do, but all right."

She gets up and runs off into the fog. Bea stays beside me. I breathe in and then out. The agony orchestra is playing a symphony inside me. The full repertoire: the molten-hot pain of broken bones, the cold pain of my skin against the snow, the dull pain of defeat. I didn't think I'd die right here, on the school playing fields. I told Elza I'd stay with her, but will I even remember her? Not all ghosts remember their lives. I hope I will, but what if I don't?

Someone is coming through the fog. I can hear light footsteps, the crunch as snow compacts under shoes. Bea pricks up her ears and growls. What now? Did something get to Elza and Holiday? Is it Margaux? Something worse?

The mist flares sapphire blue along with the sky. I see a tall shape approaching us, a man walking with a confident, carefree stride.

Is that . . . ?

Him.

I should have known.

The figure becomes clearer, emerging from the fog, a tall, honey-tanned man with a neat white beard and white hair that's slicked back from his forehead. He's wearing a wolf-gray suit, an open-collared shirt that's midnight blue. Shiny black shoes and a snakeskin belt with a golden buckle. Eyes the color of summer skies, and a warm, welcoming smile.

"I hope I haven't caught you at a bad time," Mr. Berkley says cheerfully.

(a horsehide tent)

A flame emerges newborn from his line-less palm, like the yolk from a cracked egg, dropping onto the ground beside me and Bea, where it becomes a small bonfire, spreading warmth over my tired, broken body. Bea growls louder and yelps as Berkley moves close to me.

"And who is this?" Berkley asks.

"Beatrice. Bea. Mum got her this summer," I say.

"Charmed to meet you, Beatrice," he says with a honeyed tone. He reaches a long finger out to her snout, and she sniffs his hand and her fear seems to fade away. She grumbles contentedly and settles down beside my head, like a living pillow. Berkley's charm won her over already. We're indoors now, I realize, inside a tent that seems to be made from animal skins and long wooden poles, the kind of tent you can imagine the first people living in. I'm lying on a bed of dried grass, with bare earth underneath that. The snow is gone.

"Where is this?" I whisper.

"We haven't moved. I merely thought you could do with some shelter from this awful weather. This was the first shape that came to mind. Horses' hide for walls. I thought you might appreciate that detail."

"I know you've come because of my debt—"

"Let's not worry about all that right now," Berkley says, waving his hand. "How are you feeling, Luke? How is life treating you?"

I try to laugh and can't.

"Bad," I say.

"I have seen you in better days, it pains me to admit."

The shadow Berkley casts on the wall of the tent is not the shape of a man. His teeth gleam in the firelight.

"Everything's—" I cough. "Everything hurts. It's all gone wrong."

"I know," he says soothingly. "Bodies. Sometimes I wonder what they were thinking when they housed you all inside these crude sheaths of flesh—anyway, no matter. What's done is done, whatever some might wish for."

"Dunbarrow," I say. "It's all gone crazy. We were trying to fix it."

"Yes," Mr. Berkley says. He sits down opposite me, crossing his legs. "I know."

"Did you . . . ?"

"I can assure you, Luke, nothing that has happened to your home is any fault of mine. I take no pleasure in making the living into thralls by force, nor do I have much interest in breaking open gateways between our realms. I walk where I will; this has always been true."

"The Barrenwhite Tree."

"Yes," Berkley says, grinning. "You really are very clever, Luke. Have I said that before? Terribly impressive. Setting off to beat back one of the great spirits from the Beginning armed with a sigil and a small dog!"

He chuckles.

"Look . . ."

"I do not mock you, Luke Manchett. It is impressive. If you knew how many would tremble at the mere mention of that name, how many would bow rather than fight. . . . At every turn you prove my initial impression of you correct."

"What was that?" I ask. Pain bites into my sides as I breathe.

"That you are remarkable," he says.

"This really hurts," I say. "My body hurts."

"Yes, well," Berkley says. "It'll have to hurt for a little while longer, I'm afraid. Let the pain sharpen your wits, like a bracing draft of flame. You have choices to make."

There's no pity in those blue eyes at all.

"Luke?" comes a voice from outside. "Luke, what the hell is this?"

"Can Elza . . . ?" I ask Berkley. I can barely finish the sentence. I don't know what to do.

"Come in," Berkley says in a welcoming tone. "I'm just speaking with Luke."

Elza pulls back the entrance flap of the tent and peers inside. Her eyes widen as she sees Mr. Berkley. She stands there, speechless.

"Please do enter, my dear," he says. "You're letting cold air in."

"Is this—" she asks.

"Yeah," I say. "It's him. Come inside."

She doesn't move. Snowflakes spiral around her face. She's firelit, the world behind her a dark haze. She looks like a beautiful bleak painting. She bites her lip.

"Where else can we go?" I ask her.

Elza breathes out heavily.

"You know what?" she asks me. "I think I always knew it would happen like this."

Elza moves away from the front flap, letting it fall closed, and I hear scraping sounds. She comes in backward, fresh snow settled on her shoulders and hair, pulling Holiday after her. Holiday is still limp and unconscious, half dead from whatever I did to her, her back and thighs caked with snow. Elza lays her down on the ground beside the fire and turns to us, still standing by the doorway, as if she's prepared to flee at any moment.

"You must be Berkley," she says. Her voice is flat and miserable.

"Yes!" he says. "Admirable deduction. My name is Mr. Berkley, and I am Luke's late father's solicitor. You must be—"

"I know all about you. I know exactly what you are," Elza replies.

"Manners," Mr. Berkley says with a smile. He gets to his feet.

"Elza," I say. "Please be polite to him."

She swallows. Looks at Berkley with a fear I've never seen in her before.

"I'm sorry," she says.

"Oh, don't be!" Berkley replies. He rests one hand under her jaw, turning her face to the firelight. He appraises her like she's a priceless sculpture, his eyes hungrily absorbing every detail of her body. "You are, after all, correct, and I happen to believe there is no rudeness in speaking truth. Yes, I am other things besides a solicitor for a deceased conjurer. I am a scholar, a poet, a philosopher king. I hold dominion over the ancient lands known as Tartarus. I am the Speaker of Secrets, the Black Goat who whispers in the woods on moonless nights. As you say, you have heard of me. All men have, by one name or another.

"And you are Elza Moss. Blood of Lilith, who slew my child and was slain by it in turn. It was for love of you that Luke journeyed to the Shrouded Lake and made his offering there, or am I wrong? Elza Moss, the twice-born."

"Yeah," Elza says. "That's me."

"Come," Berkley says. He lets go of her chin, gesturing toward the campfire. "Sit and speak with us."

His tone makes it clear Elza has no choice. She sits down on the grass inside the tent, Holiday's feet right next to hers, and Berkley sits again as well. Bea sighs contentedly. It's really warm in here now. The snow on Elza's hair is melting, plastering her bangs against her forehead. She looks half drowned, exhausted. This has been a night of bonfires, strangers huddled around a fading light. I think of Elza's house, of sleeping on the floor and eating Christmas cake for breakfast, think of Larktongue and Bald Samson and their gray, heatless campfire. And now we find ourselves here.

Like Elza said, I think deep down I always knew it would happen like this. I don't know how we imagined we could ever beat Berkley. He's had me where he wants me from the first day. He beams at both of us, radiantly happy.

"Holiday," I say to Elza.

"Your friend is alive," Berkley says. "Just about."

"What happened to her?" Elza asks him.

He shrugs. "There are many good reasons not to bind

living souls to your Host," he says. "Foremost amongst them are that the process destroys them irrevocably. The dead are a near-inexhaustible source of magical power. The still-living spirit, however, is eminently exhaustible."

"Will she die?" Elza asks.

"It could still happen. If Luke were to relinquish his hold over her, that would be an excellent start in reversing the process."

"Why do you care?" I ask Berkley, confused.

"Who said that I do? I was asked a question and answered it."

I focus my will into the sigil ring. I try to block out the pain, the fear, and find the spell that's keeping Holiday and Kirk and Elza bound to me. I find it there in the darkness, a slender thread of golden light, and I untie it in my mind, breaking my Host. If it's going to kill them, then I don't want that power. I'll do this without it.

Holiday breathes in audibly for the first time.

She might still make it, at least. I don't know what's going to happen to us.

"There," I say.

"Still, an interesting application of your power. Creative," Berkley says. "Was she coerced?"

"No," I say. "Her idea."

"The greatest servants are those who take the position willingly," he says. "Something your father never quite understood, I feel. He had power, sure enough. But you have power and a quality that wins you followers through love, too. You inspire loyalty."

I think of Ham, vanishing into the waters of the Shrouded Lake. My heart hurts, to match the rest of my body.

"What do you want?" Elza asks Berkley. "I know Luke promised you something."

"He did, after I let his bloated wretch of a father go free. He promised me something worth as much as his father's spirit."

"And now you're here," Elza says. "To collect."

Berkley grins at us.

"I don't know what you want," I say.

"Of course you do. You have known ever since you agreed to it."

Mr. Berkley's shadow covers half the wall of the tent, a seething awful shape. I focus on his human face. His white teeth and white beard. I feel like any moment the mask might break, and I'll see what's beneath it.

"You want me," I say.

"I want you to work for me," he says.

Nobody speaks. The wind howls outside the tent's horsehide walls.

"You've already done great things, Luke. I do not think you understand the power that is within you. Of course, as things stand, you are only the spark that might start a great fire . . . or might be extinguished, had I a mind. But I see true potential within you, my boy, the way a gifted sculptor sees his masterpiece within a chunk of unworked stone. If you will submit to my teachings, I believe you would be a great asset to me."

"What would I do?" I ask.

"Come to Tartarus with me. Abandon this broken flesh. Study the high mysteries at my side. I will show you secret patterns within the weave of the world. You will learn the first language, the speech of the stars, and we shall walk in the graves of forgotten gods. You will be a prince, Luke." Berkley's eyes flare like sky-colored embers. "We can build whole worlds each morning and raze them to dust when we are bored. Your voice will make the mountains shudder like frightened beasts. You shall have an honor guard of demon lictors, a chariot swifter than thought, a palace filled by beautiful wives, a garden of incomparable beauty, a feasting table that is ever full. Fountains of wine, fine robes in colors men cannot name. You will be worshipped by innumerable children, just as I am. You will be undying, invincible, fierce as the sun. Think, my boy! You would live your life and slip unremembered into death, becoming a base, hungry ghoul, a lost phantom? You would walk the banks of the Styx with a boulder chained to your body, hoping for salvation? I think not, Luke. Take my hand. The darkness awaits a new prince."

"This is a trick," I say. "You want to torment me."

"My boy! My reputation is poor, I know, but I thought you had grown to know me better than that! I admire you, Luke! I admit that I have placed you into difficult circumstances, but I have tried only to hold up a mirror to show you your own strength, your own willpower. I gave you your father's Host to see whether you would rise to the challenge, and how magnificently you did! How deep you drank from my well of secrets! How loyal you were to Horatio! You put yourself irrevocably into my power to rescue him, even knowing how awfully he had treated your family, your very brother! You traveled to the Shrouded Lake to save a girl you had not even known a year! I admire loyalty, my boy. Do you think I am without enemies? The Speaker of Secrets, master of Tartarus? Do you think there are no spirits who covet my position? I need acolytes that I can depend upon."

"What about Elza?"

"What would you like to do with her?" he asks me. "The witch girl can come with you if you like. She has a pleasing aspect, I certainly understand why you would be spurred to feats of heroism by her. And she has Lilith's blood. . . . She would make a suitable consort for you within my court, I suppose. She might need new clothes, a new form? The shape of a golden lioness is fashionable at present, I am led to understand. Or perhaps a gown of black flame . . . My wives can help her choose something, certainly. What do you think about that, my dear?"

Elza's face is unreadable. She's pulling at a wet strand of hair, winding it around her finger.

"I'd rather not," she says quietly.

"Well, if you're certain." Berkley smiles carelessly, then turns his attention back to me. "You could bring the blond one if you prefer, my boy—it's all the same to me. As I have said, you will not lack for companionship in Tartarus. You will not lack for anything."

"OK," I say.

Elza starts like she's been shot.

"What?" she asks me.

"OK," I say. "I'm about to die. I'll go."

Berkley's smile is wider than I've ever seen it. He reaches out toward me.

"There's one thing, though," I say. "Before I go. I don't feel right otherwise."

"Ha!" Berkley exclaims. "Anything, Luke! Ask me anything! The world is yours, my boy."

"We're going to turn this all back like it was. We're going to save Dunbarrow."

Berkley's smile fades away. He folds his hands in his lap.

"Well," he says, "it's not quite so easy as that."

"Why not? You said I could have anything."

"You will, you will. But it is not a simple thing you ask for. Dunbarrow has been submerged into the spirit world by the will of the Barrenwhite Tree. Another elder spirit. My influence is somewhat, shall we say, compromised in this matter."

"How do you mean?" I ask.

"Picture a chessboard," Berkley says. "You are familiar with the game? Good. Picture a white bishop upon a white square, and a black bishop on a black square. Each able only to take pieces that stand upon similarly colored squares, and thus unable to move directly against the other, separated by fundamental and immutable laws. Each reduced to watching and hating, unable to strike, forever separated. Do you follow so far? This is the Barrenwhite Tree and me, the Speaker of Secrets. This is how it has always been. The Tree has claimed your town, for reasons known only to itself, and I cannot easily compel it to release Dunbarrow."

"So we kill it," I say.

Berkley roars with laughter. "Ha! This is why I like you so, Luke! Your drive! The will for power! A mighty elder spirit stands in the way of what you want, so you propose we destroy it! You are very precious to me."

"You think we can't do it?"

"I know I cannot," he says. "I cannot harm that ancient being, and vice versa, by the terms of a concord made long ago. I have wished I could a thousand times."

Tree and goat no longer love one another. That's what the Oracle told me. This is what she wanted me to do, but I don't know if I'm getting it quite right. She must have seen this point in time, this conversation. I press on, hoping I'm doing the right thing.

"But I can," I say. "I could do it. I'm not bound by those rules, right?"

"You are not. However, I feel that fighting against one of the great spirits might be somewhat beyond your abilities at this point," Berkley says gently. "I said that I see potential for true greatness within you, not that you are a great power at present."

"Please," I say. "I've been thinking about what you said, last time we met. About how evil's a point of view. I think you're right. I think we could do great things together, sir. I think I want what you're offering me. But this is my home, it's where I grew up, and I can't leave it in the hands of a spirit like that Tree. It might look weak. Surely there's something we can do?" I look into Berkley's eyes, lying with my face, my entire spirit. I pray and hope he sees what I want him to see. "Imagine if we managed it. Nobody would dare stand up to us after that."

I think Elza sees what I'm trying to do. I hope she sees it. Even if it's the end for me, the end of Luke Manchett as anyone would understand that concept, I want Dunbarrow to go free. I don't want the Tree to consume everyone, drive them into root-choked madness. Even if I have to get the Devil's help to do it.

"Perhaps," Berkley says. "It is possible that . . . if a formal challenge were issued . . . there are protocols for this sort of thing, unusual as it is. We may issue a challenge, by the power of eight, and demand that the Tree relinquish this territory. That is possible."

"Act through me," I say. "I want . . . I want you to be like my father. That's what I never had. What you could be for me."

Did I go too far?

Berkley is silent, looking into the flames.

"That is a beautiful sentiment, my boy," he says softly. "I would be honored to think of you as a son. I think there is much we could accomplish together."

"I agree," I say.

"So you'll really help us?" Elza asks Berkley, in a voice barely above a whisper.

"More than that," he says. "I will ascend you. Transform you. Grant you every pleasure you've ever imagined, and many more you haven't. Have you rethought your position on coming with us?"

"Sure," she says.

Berkley frowns. "You still do not sound very enthusiastic, Elza."

"No, it sounds great. Who wants to hang around in this shithole? Sign me up for the flame dress," she says.

"Language," he says indulgently.

"I'm in a lot of pain," I say. "Can we—"

"You don't need that body," he says. "Leave it behind. It's no use to you."

There's no way of getting around this one. If I die then I die, I suppose. This body didn't have much life left in it.

"Help me," I say. "I haven't been able to get out of my body like I used to."

"Ah, naturally. A side effect of the two worlds colliding." Berkley reaches down with a long-fingered hand and pulls me out of myself. The pain fades instantly, replaced by pleasant warmth. I sit up and realize I'm sitting on top of myself, a broken bloody copy. My brown eyes stare uselessly at the tent's ceiling. I touch Elza's hand and find that I'm still really here, the way the Knights or Berkley are. I'm still present. She shudders a little.

"You OK?" I ask.

"You're cold," she says. "And your eyes have gone black. Like the Shepherd's."

"Oh."

I feel great, even if I look scary. I feel powerful. Berkley did more than pull me out of my body; he made me stronger, gave me a little jolt of something. There's lightning in my limbs.

"So what's the plan?" I ask Berkley. "Father."

"You will need a weapon," he says. "One befitting my apprentice. Would you mind . . . ?" He gestures at Kirk's sword, which is lying on the ground next to Holiday. I pass it to him. He examines the blade. "This is a shadow of the weapons I have in my court, but the basic form is adequate. If you would give me the enchanted blade you have in your jacket, please."

Silently Elza passes him the black witch blade, the one we took from Margaux. She keeps the white one for herself. Berkley turns it in the firelight.

"This will suffice," he says, and then inhales a great gulp of flame from the bonfire before him. It's drawn up into his mouth like juice through a straw. He holds the flames inside his mouth and then lets them dribble out onto the blade of Kirk's sword. He presses the witch blade into the flames, too, and speaks a word I don't understand.

The outline of the sword blurs and melts under the flames, the knife sinking into the longer blade of the sword. It no longer looks like metal, instead taking the form of shadows lined with fire. Berkley works the blade with his bare fingers, twisting and adjusting the shadow stuff, until he has a sword longer than Kirk's and thicker, with a cross-shaped guard and a sinister edge of molten-red flame that reminds me of the surface of the Phlegethon, the fiery river that runs to Tartarus. Finally, he draws a strange mark at the base of the blade with his index finger and then hands the weapon to me.

I take the sword. My sigil ring blazes with cold, with more power than I've ever felt before. My head is spinning. I nearly black out.

"Not my best work," Berkley remarks. "But it will suffice for now. How do you like the blade?"

"It's perfect," I say, and I'm not actually lying. This thing feels good to hold.

Holiday and Bea are still asleep by the fire. I stand, the sword like an extension of my hand. Bloodred flame drips from the tip and sears the earth.

"My son," Berkley says, "my newest son. What a picture you make. You will certainly command respect in the feasting halls of Tartarus. Is he not a figure of terrible majesty, Elza?"

"Yeah," she says. "Strong look."

I don't mean this, I'm thinking to her, as if she can hear it.

"Well," Berkley says, getting to his feet, "our foe

awaits. My long-hated foe. Onward, my son. To the Barrenwhite Tree."

The snow is fierce outside the horsehide tent, but I can't feel the cold anymore. Elza is huddled up in her coat, hood raised, the only skin exposed her eyes and the top of her nose. We left Bea to keep watch on Holiday, who seems to be breathing more normally now, color returning to her face. They'll live, I hope, no matter what happens to us. I notice the snowflakes that land on Berkley melt instantly, and his feet leave pools of water as he walks. His eyes are blue stars. He seems to be losing his human shape, piece by piece. His shadow stretches out behind him, a rippling dark stain on the snow.

"This way, my children," he says. "We do not have far to go."

We follow Berkley silently, away from the tent, into the mists and snow. The forest is consuming the playing fields, and we move between great gray trees, strung with vines and armored in thorns, but it all seems to move aside as Berkley passes, without any sign of anything ever actually shifting. He walks, and the forest always has a path ready for him.

The trees grow thicker still, and I can see people tangled

in their branches and roots, the same forest we found ourselves in after we left Elza's house. Gray shapes, sleeping
or else moving with drugged, lazy spasms, people quietly
singing to themselves with roots burrowing through their
chests and faces. As we walk they become more numer-
ous, until the trees seem to be mostly made of these bodies,
strange twisted pillars of lost souls.

"What are these?" I ask Berkley as we pass a particularly large mass of roots and people.

"Thralls," he says. "Worshippers. The remains of the
mortals the Tree has pulled into its realm."

"This is what'll happen to everyone in Dunbarrow?"

"Great power requires a great appetite," Berkley says,
stepping on a singing face without a downward glance. "It
would behoove you to accept that. I have consumed many
lesser spirits to become as mighty as I am. Countless mil-
lions. You will need to do the same."

The light has changed, becoming greener and brighter,
like we're walking underwater. Frost glitters on the bodies
of the damned and the roots of the gray trees. The fog
shimmers. We must be closing in on the gateway. I clasp
Elza's hand tightly. She hasn't spoken a word since we left
the tent.

"In fact," Berkley says, "this should provide an excellent opportunity. Let us raid our enemy's larder, shall we?"

He reaches into one of the masses of souls and pulls one out, mewling, a withered old man with blank silver eyes and colorless wrinkled skin. He looks like an ancient newborn. Mr. Berkley holds him by the neck, appraising him with one blue eye.

"You want me to eat him?" I ask.

"No, my son, I want you to wear him for a scarf. Of course we are going to eat him. He is aged and weak, and the Tree has drained most of the succor from him long ago. I chose this example in the same way a mother cat will bring her young a wounded bird; in order to teach without risk. He has no will remaining and is easy prey."

I look into the man's eyes. There's nothing there. He's barely a person at all; he's the husk of a dead one. There's no way Berkley will buy this if I don't do as he says. I'm lucky he's even letting me try to save Dunbarrow at all. But this . . . he was still a person once. What am I if I do this?

I'm like him.

What will Elza think?

I can't even look at her.

I have to do this.

"My son," Berkley says, "why do you hesitate? Do not grieve for him; he is weak. Were he wise and strong, he would not find himself in this unenviable position. We are above him. We may do as we please. His spirit is yours."

He holds the man's face out to mine. The gray lips move without a sound. He doesn't seem to know where he is.

I close my eyes and lunge forward, biting the spirit. My teeth tear through him easily, and I gulp his spirit down. It's like drinking glacier water, a cold refreshing draft, mixing with the heat inside me and fizzing into every part of me. My sigil flares colder than ever. I bite again, taking more, drinking deeper, until there's nothing left.

I can't believe I did that.

I think I'd do it again.

Berkley's eyes are pinpoints of azure flame in the dimness. "There," he says, "your first taste of true power. Why bind a spirit to your sigil when you can consume it entire? And this was only a weakened thrall, already drained of its succulence. Imagine eating a strong spirit, feasting upon them in a great banquet. Imagine eating a prince of demons defeated by your own hand. Oh, the meals we have had in Tartarus, my son. The feasts yet to come. You cannot yet know."

He claps me on the back.

"I can't wait, Father."

"You look larger already!" he says. "Doesn't he look strong, Elza? You must be proud."

I still can't look at Elza. I hear her clear her throat behind me.

"Yes," she says, almost a whisper.

"Perhaps we all have room for a little more," Berkley says, reaching into the tortured mass of people again. "How would you like some, Elza? Your beauty will only grow."

"We're wasting time," Elza says.

He looks at her, and she stares back.

"I beg your pardon?" Berkley says softly.

"This is a waste of time," she says. "I'm not eating someone's hand-me-downs. Did we come to challenge the Barrenwhite Tree or go through its larder like thieves?"

Berkley's eyes flare brighter. He removes his hand from the mound of gray people.

"You would instruct me in matters of courage and cowardice? You are Luke's consort, nothing more, witch child. Remember your place."

"I don't want to be anyone's consort if they act like this," she says. "We came to issue a challenge, I thought. Or are we here to hide in the woods?"

Berkley's jaws drip with blue fire. I clench the handle of my sword. He's melting, turning into something else, and for a moment I catch the glimpse of something like a horned bear made from shadow.

"Please, Father," I say. "Forgive us. She has a sharp tongue."

He starts at the sound of my voice and snaps back into focus, a tanned, white-haired lawyer again.

"No, no," he says. "The girl is right. As I said, it is no insult to speak truth. There is nothing to be gained here. But I might suggest she express herself more delicately in the future. There is indeed richer food than the Tree's thralls in these woods, if one only knows where to look." He grins ferociously at Elza and she drops her gaze.

"We are sorry," I say.

"All forgiven," he says cheerfully. "Come. We are close to the gateway."

We follow him through endless ranks of trees, through drifts of snow that melt beneath his feet, past wailing masses of gray thralls, their twisted bodies piled high into the sky. The green and blue light grows stronger, shimmering walls of light in the fog, like we're walking through the aurora, and there's a high ringing tone in my ears.

In the path before us, we come across the bodies of two deer, their throats cut open, blood staining the snowy earth. There's fresh snow settled on their fur.

Elza puts a hand to her head.

"I remember something," she hisses to me. "I've seen these before."

I look at the corpses. Nothing comes to me. Berkley has already stepped past them, his eyes fixed on the glimmering brightness we can see between the trees.

"Just a little farther!" Berkley calls to us.

"Come on," I say. "We can work this out later."

Elza shakes her head, like she's trying to get water out of her ears, dislodge the memory, but evidently nothing occurs to her. I take her hand in mine, four-fingered, and squeeze.

"We'll get through this," I say. "I know we will."

She doesn't answer, but she doesn't take her hand away either. We move through the nightmare forest, following Berkley. The gauzy light grows brighter and stranger, veins of blue-green lightning running through the air around us, coiling about branches like vines.

After a few more moments, we come to a clearing in the forest, a cathedral of wintery light, and I know that we're in the presence of our enemy.

(the barrenwhite tree)

The passing place has changed beyond all recognition. The Devil's Footsteps are gone, and the ground is coated with snow. The oak trees that always encircled the standing stones have turned to stone themselves, and I realize that these trees must always have been the real passing place, the gateway that the people who put the standing stones here were trying to keep closed. Seven trees of living stone line the clearing, and in the middle stands an eighth.

The Barrenwhite Tree grows from the ground where the Devil's Footsteps once stood, a splintered white mass that towers over the clearing. I was expecting it to be ugly and frightening, but actually it's beautiful. It does look like a tree, but there's something of a heart about it too, a swollen growth with veins of ice reaching up into the shimmering sky. The Tree does emit the light we've been seeing in the sky all night; some of the branches glow with green and blue streaks of power that drift up to tint the fog above us. The ringing tone is louder still, like someone struck my skull with a bell. I weigh my sword in my hand. We have a chance, I tell myself. This wasn't all for nothing.

Two figures wait for us before the Barrenwhite Tree. One is Margaux, seeming to be unharmed, dressed in a dark robe, her white swan mask held under one arm. The other is hung upside down from one of the Tree's branches, its feet bound together with rope, wearing a dark robe and a black owl mask. It's the second Apostle, the one Margaux threw onto the bonfire. It doesn't seem to be burned, but the Apostle's body is lifeless and limp. What this means, I have no idea.

Berkley comes to a halt just past the nearest stone oak tree. He surveys the scene with undisguised loathing. I stop beside him, with Elza behind me.

"Is that truly you?" Margaux says, in the voice of the Tree. Her eyes have rolled up into the top of their sockets, exposing only the whites. *"What shape is this now? This is how you come before me, after so many years?"*

"I wear the shapes I please and walk where I like," Berkley replies. "It has always been the way."

"What business have you here, Speaker of Secrets?"

"Relinquish your hold over this town," Berkley says. "Release the thralls you have captured here, and return to your rightful place."

"A strange demand. You love menfolk so much that you wear their skin now? You order me to release what I have rightfully taken? Never. Begone from here, Speaker. Take your morsels with you."

"Relinquish your hold on this realm," Berkley says again.

"This is my right. You know this. It is the Feast of Winter. When my star rises above this world, I take a piece of it back into our realms. I teach the mortals new ways to live and love, beyond fear or death. I am beloved of them again, as it was before the worlds were divided. It has always been the way."

"I challenge you," Berkley says to the Tree. "I defy your will."

There's a silence. The green-blue shards of light that project from the branches of the Tree glimmer and flash, sketching sharp shapes in the mist that churns about us. Then Margaux's body laughs, her mirth sounding almost like cries of pain.

"What care you about my thralls, Speaker? What care you for the living or the dead, or anyone besides yourself? Or is it that you have worn the shape of a man so long, you have inherited their cares?"

"This is the birthplace of my apprentice," Berkley says. "He demands that you remove yourself, and I give him authority to do so."

I wasn't actually born in Dunbarrow; I wasn't even born in the northeast, but it doesn't seem like the right time to bring this up. I feel the Tree's attention fall onto me, the full weight of its cold gaze.

"I know it is the home of Luke Manchett," the Tree says. *"Do you think I chose this place at a whim? It pleases me to consume his house and kin, to use him so easily as the agent of my own arrival. He broke the gateway open himself, at my Apostles' urging. He bears one of the locks within his own mouth."*

Berkley turns to me, eyes flickering with blue firelight.

"Is this true?" he asks me softly. "You aided this spirit? You wish for two masters?"

"I don't remember!" I say. "But I wouldn't do something like that! Why would I want to? Why would I let it free?"

This is bad. Why didn't I think about this before?

Berkley grabs hold of my face and wrenches my mouth open, reaching inside with his other hand. I hold completely still as his fingers sear into my gums, pulling out the stone lodged there. He holds it up to the green-tinted light.

"They put a spell on us," Elza says. "We don't remember what happened. We ran away as soon as we could."

Berkley turns to look at her, then back at me.

"This is the truth?" he asks.

"Yes," I say.

He thinks for a moment, turning the stone over in his line-less palm.

"You are untutored," he says lightly. "It would be no great matter for the Apostles of this exile to compel you into opening this gateway. I will teach you how to defend yourself against such assaults." He tucks the shrunken standing stone into his jacket pocket. "As for you," he says, addressing the Barrenwhite Tree again, "you presume to use my own apprentice for your designs? Knowing full well my mark is upon him?"

"Your apprentice? The Manchett boy? This is how low you find yourself now, Speaker? An idiot child who has drunk from your well of secrets. I used him easily and discarded him."

"I got away from you," I tell it. "You haven't killed me yet. I'm still here."

"For now."

"Enough idle talk!" Mr. Berkley says, raising his voice so it booms through the clearing. "Barrenwhite Tree! Lost Child of the Winter Star! I challenge you! I defy you! Your will is not your own, but mine! Your acolytes are weak and fearful, where mine are great and terrible! By river and by heart, by stone and by hand, I expel you! By tree and by eye, by sky and by tooth, I defy you! By the power of eight, I challenge you!"

"You are a fool, Speaker of Secrets," says the Tree. *"You*

challenge me by the power of eight over a scrap of a town in the living realms? This, of all things?"

"I do challenge you, exile."

"Then you know I must accept," Margaux says in that terrible voice. Her face grimaces. *"Name your champion, fool."*

"I name as champion my apprentice, Luke Manchett," Mr. Berkley says. "Our champions will battle to the death, as it always was. Only one will leave the circle with their spirit intact."

"And what shall the victor receive, O Speaker of Idiocies?"

"Idiot, am I? Fool, you call me? I would like to know, if you fancy yourself so sharp, how you found yourself stuck inside that grave of ice in the first place? If you are so powerful, how is it you must resort to speaking through the stolen tongue of a chattel? Why you may only come sneaking through cracks into the living world to feed, whereas I rule a great empire of spirits and do as I please?"

"Because I have never bowed," the Tree says, *"and you did, Scraper of Foreheads."*

Mr. Berkley's eyes flare so brightly, they go beyond color, white-hot furnaces. There's heat streaming from his body, turning the snow around his feet to steam. Elza covers her face with her scarf, cringing away from him.

"We could never have won," Berkley hisses. "You saw it, too, but blinded yourself."

"You feared her."

"I WAS NOT AFRAID!" Berkley screams. "I FEAR NOTHING! I AM SPEAKER OF SECRETS! I AM LORD OF TARTARUS! YOU ARE A BROKEN RELIC TRAPPED WITHIN A TREE OF ICE! YOU ARE NOTHING! YOU NEVER WERE!"

My hands are clasped over my ears. Berkley's voice could split the sky in half. There's nothing human about it anymore, nothing cheerful or charming.

"You are a craven, miscarried shadow, Speaker of Secrets. Mother always said as much."

"Do not even say her name," he snaps, recovering some of his composure. I've never seen anything get under his skin like this before. "Do not *dare*. I challenge you, by the power of eight, and this fight shall be not only for our champions' lives, but for ours!"

"Tread carefully," the Barrenwhite Tree says. *"Challenges such as this cannot be revoked. Are you sure you do not wish to simply gamble for a small town? You will not be able to break your promises to me so easily this time."*

"Whoever's champion loses this fight, they will submit to the blade! They will submit to destruction! THEY WILL LOSE ALL!"

"I accept," the Barrenwhite Tree replies. There's a moment of stillness, and a circle of blue-green flames erupts on the ground before us, about the diameter of a boxing ring. If I had a heart, it would be pounding. Mr.

Berkley lays his hands on the sides of my face and takes hold of me, forcing me to stare into his glowing eyes.

"I may have overplayed our hand," he says, soft and urgent. "If I had not already named you champion, I would name another, one proven, but this is no longer possible. Do not fail me, or as my final act I shall ensure the witch girl perishes alongside me."

I look back at my unlikely ally: his face masklike, the mouth no longer even moving convincingly in time with his words, his form unstable, with darkness seeming to leak from around the edges of this false body. He—it—is losing control. Whatever's really lurking at the heart of Mr. Berkley, the Barrenwhite Tree knows exactly how to turn the screws. Seams of blue fire flare across his body. His fingernails sizzle, burning my spirit flesh, tiny fragments of hot stone.

"What will it choose?" I ask him. "What will I have to fight?"

"The Tree is old and powerful," he says, "but hardly well followed in the recent ages of the worlds. The Apostles you see before you may be its only remaining servants."

Margaux, then. I'll be fighting Margaux. I wait for her to step into the ring, but she doesn't move. Instead the other Apostle—the one I had almost forgotten about, hanging upside down from the icy branch of the Tree—speaks.

"Allow me, Lord . . . I beg. Let me stand for you," it rasps.

"*My Apostle,*" Margaux replies in the Tree's terrible voice, glancing upward at the dark-robed figure that hangs above our heads. "*My Wisdom. You presume now to speak to me? You lied. You swore the boy was dead.*"

"I did," the owl-masked figure says in a hoarse, croaking voice, distorted by the mask. "I could not—I implore my master. I found there was still a shard of kinship and pity within me. The pain you inflicted upon me has given me ample time to reflect. I was mistaken. It will not happen again. Allow me to redeem myself."

"*You permitted them to escape. You intentionally deceived me. Am I to forget this?*"

"Am I not your beloved servant, O Tree? Do I not love and worship you as none other does? I beg of you this last chance. Do not cast me aside so easily, after I have made but one mistake. Allow me to destroy the boy and prove myself to you. Let me shed the last of my humanity."

There's a silence. Margaux, the Tree, seems to be caught in thought. Then the owl-masked Apostle falls from where it hangs, the rope that keeps it tethered to the Barrenwhite Tree breaking. The robed body hits the snowy ground with a thud, and then rises to its feet, like a broken puppet. Limbs snap back into place, and the owl-masked Apostle flexes long, clawed fingers.

"You are indeed my beloved servant and sought me out when all others had long abandoned me," the Barrenwhite Tree says. "Your falsehood was grievous, but the situation may be salvaged still. . . . Very well. I offer this as your one chance to redeem yourself. Kill your son, and you will ever be in my favor. I name you champion, Horatio."

What?

It's just a name, surely.

Other people have that name, too.

The second Apostle removes his black owl mask. A shiver of panic runs through me.

It really is him.

It's Dad.

I'm lying in cold grass, Elza beside me. My mouth throbs and there's blood on my chin. The sky is a boiling cauldron of light. The bird-people stand over us.

"It is done," the bird-woman says. "The gate is broken."

"What do you wish?" the owl-man asks her.

Green light crawls across our bodies. I can't move.

"We have no more need of them. Body or spirit."

"As you command," the owl-man replies.

He reaches down with terrible clawed hands and picks me and Elza up by our necks. Our arms and legs dangle. He's so strong.

"This one is my kin," the owl-man says to the bird-woman.

"I know," she replies. "We did not choose them by chance."

"Such actions are not for the light of the great ones," he says. "May I have a moment of privacy?"

"Of course, my Apostle," the bird-woman replies. "I will allow you a last moment with your son. But his blood must flow. I demand this."

"I remain your servant," the owl-man says.

Horatio Manchett steps across the line of blue-green fire and into the ring. Last time I spoke to him, he looked just like he did when he was alive: white suit, purple shirt, hands heavy with rings. Now his shape has begun to change. His long, thinning hair, which was as dark as mine, has bleached snow white. His eyes are ten times larger than any human's, grotesquely stretching his face, wide and golden orange, with slitted black pupils. The eyes of an owl, I realize. His hands have become monstrous talons, the skin of his palms wattled and pitted, the claws thick and vicious-looking. His mouth has been transformed into a hooked beak, the hard bill pushing through the flesh of his face. He looks deformed, awful, caught between man and beast.

"What happened to you?" I ask.

"Your humanity is the first thing to disappear," Dad

says in that strange hoarse voice, "when you make the promises I have made."

"Horatio," Berkley says. "This is a surprise."

"I wish I could say the same," Dad replies. He flexes his talons.

"You found a new master, then," Berkley says. "Why ever did I let you go, Horatio?"

"Because I asked you to," I say to Berkley. "And I told you I never wanted to see you again," I say to Dad.

"I didn't choose this, Luke. Any of it."

"Your son calls me Father now," Berkley tells Dad, smiling again. "He has proven himself greater in spirit than you ever did, and I have decided to raise him higher than you could have dreamed."

I grip the sword. Is this Dad's fault? After everything I did, after letting him go, did he bring the Barrenwhite Tree to Dunbarrow? Helped it swallow the town where me and Mum live? How could he do that? I wouldn't even know Mr. Berkley if it wasn't for him. I should've sent him to the darkness and been done with all of this. He's a monster.

As the anger grows, I see my sword ignite, bloodred flames spitting from the edge of the black blade.

"You know, I find this fitting," Mr. Berkley says to me, loudly, so Dad can hear. "Fitting that your first act in my service will be to overcome this false father. Ancestor of your discarded flesh. Show no quarter, Luke. This is your new birth."

"Enter the circle, Speaker's pawn," Margaux says in the Tree's voice. *"I tire of talk."*

I'm about to step over the line of green fire, when I remember I haven't even spoken to Elza. I turn to look at her, standing beside Berkley, as lost and miserable as I've ever seen her. Her hood is down, snow settling in her black hair, and she looks at me like I'm a ship vanishing into a storm.

"I'm still me," I say to her.

"I know," she says.

"I'm coming back," I say.

I want to grab hold of her, kiss her, but something in the way she's looking at me stops me. Does she really believe I'm pretending to work for Berkley?

Am I even pretending now?

I can't look at her. This will work out. I know it will. I turn away and step over the line of flame, into the circle.

"The circle closes," the Tree says.

"The circle closes," Berkley replies.

"Let what may be, be."

"Let what may be, be," Berkley says.

The azure-green flames flare higher, a heatless barrier around the arena. Dad's bare feet crunch in the snow as he moves to my left. The sound from outside seems muffled, far away. I can hear Berkley talking again but can't make out his speech. The world outside the arena barely exists for me anymore. I can feel strength from Berkley's sword flowing through me. I feel like I could count the scales on the backs of Dad's awful hands. I can see the flesh of his face shift as he speaks, his beak moving in a gross, puppet-like motion in time with his words.

"They cannot hear us here," he says.

"So?" I say, holding the flaming sword out before me in both hands.

"What passes between champions is theirs alone."

"Why are you doing this?" I ask. "I hate you. Why did you come back?"

Dad swipes at me with one clawed hand, startlingly fast, and I leap back, snow spraying around my legs. I swing with the sword, suddenly feeling panicked, hitting nothing. I've only seen people sword fight in the movies. I know you're meant to hit people with the blade and that's about it. I've got power, mostly borrowed from Berkley, but I don't know what to do with it.

"I do not wish you harm," he says.

"Oh yeah?"

"I swear on it. But only one may leave here alive."

I lunge forward with the flaming blade, bloodred sparks spraying into Dad's deformed face as the sword passes just in front of him. He doesn't even flinch.

"I let you go free! I made a deal with Berkley for you!

And you run off to this Tree and betray us! You bring it here!"

"I know," he says. His wide golden eyes don't convey any emotion, but he sounds sad. "But it is never so simple."

"I let you go! All I asked was you leave us alone!"

"Attack me again," he says. "This must look like a true battle."

Is this a trick? I can't tell. I thrust forward with the sword, and he bats it aside with one clawed hand. There's iron force in those arms. The dad I knew was no athlete, could barely run upstairs without getting winded, but we're not fighting with our muscles, and whatever's happened to him in Deadside has strengthened him. If he really wanted, I think he could destroy me. I swipe again, not even pretending, really trying to hit him, and he ducks easily under the blade, slicing upward with his claws and scoring a terrible cold slash across my face. I yell out and fall back, clutching at the wound. He stalks toward me.

"I was left alone in the hungry wilds of Deadside," he says, talking quickly in his raspy, quiet voice. "I was alone. Do you know what Asphodel is like for a newly dead necromancer? Do you know how many enemies I had made? Those who bind the dead are not beloved by the dead themselves, Luke. Many spirits wished to claim they were the one who devoured Horatio Manchett."

"I don't care!" I shout, swiping at him with my sword.

"I needed a patron. I needed protection. And in the forgotten reaches of the spirit realms, far beyond the borders of Asphodel or Tartarus, the cold corners of the exiled and lost, I discovered a power I had long heard whispers of: the Barrenwhite Tree. An elder spirit, one that remembers the Beginning—"

I swing at him again. My sword runs with crimson, thirsty for battle, and it feels like the blade that Berkley forged is pulling me forward of its own accord. Dad counters, a flurry of wild swipes that somehow always manage to miss me. He's so fast, I can barely follow the blows. I stagger backward. He could end this at any time, I'm sure of it.

"I needed strength. I needed a master. I could not survive otherwise."

"So you did something bad to help yourself. What's new?"

"I took an oath and became the Tree's first Apostle in countless ages. I swore to serve and aid it, in return for protection. For a time the situation benefited me. I was safe, with a new master, and I learned much about the two worlds from the stories the Tree told me, truths I had never even suspected in all my research during my time among the living. It told me stories of the Beginning, the great war between the elder spirits, the division of the two worlds. . . . But the Tree came to doubt my loyalty. Many had betrayed it before. It demanded . . . the Barrenwhite Tree demanded to swallow Dunbarrow for its Feast. Nothing and nowhere else would suffice."

"So you just let it?" I scream. I stab the black sword at his deformed head, not faking the blow at all. He dances aside, dark Apostle's robe flowing as he moves.

"I begged and pleaded, but the Tree would not be moved. Only Dunbarrow would do. Only the home of my wife and child. To prove my true devotion once and for all."

"And you went along with it?"

"There was nothing else to do! If I refused to help, I would be destroyed and the Tree would take Dunbarrow regardless! Please!"

"You don't care about me! You never did! You left me! You killed my brother! You would've killed Ash and Ilana! You don't care about anyone but you!"

The blade slices into his clawed hand, severing a finger. No blood runs from the stump, just a trickle of ashen gray mist.

"I saved you!" he rasps, not seeming to notice the injury. "I saved you and Elza! I took you into the forest after the gate was opened and lied to the Tree, saying that I had killed you both! My hands were reddened only with deer blood. I let you live, hoping you would find a way to escape!"

"You—what?"

As he says this, I remember . . .

The owl-man takes us past the trees of stone, away from the writhing light. He carries me and Elza into the darkness of the woods. When we're far from the bird-woman, far from her sight, he places us on the ground. The owl-man holds his clawed hands out to the trees and calls. I don't understand him.

A pair of deer come out of the blackness. They're not afraid of us. They're small and brown and tender. The owl-man reaches out and slices their necks. They die without a sound.

"I do this for you," he says. I don't understand.

He touches each deer once behind the ear, with his long claws, and the bodies change, becoming a boy with brown hair, a girl with a black storm cloud around her head. Their throats are cut, their eyes blind.

Me and Elza are on our feet.

"Run," the owl-man tells us.

. . . him cutting our bonds, telling us we could go free. I remember the deer, how they walked up to him and he killed them instead of us. I remember running into darkness without looking back, not knowing who was under the mask or why they saved us, running from the light behind us, and after a time I regained my true self, the Tree's spell broken, and I found myself alone in the frozen woods with a hot pain in my jaw.

He saved us, me and Elza.

"I will not kill my son!" Dad says. "I will not!"

"You killed my brother," I say.

"And it was the worst mistake I ever made," he says. "Were I to attempt pilgrimage along the Styx, I would be given a mountain to pull at the end of my chain."

I scream and whirl at him with the sword. Red flame scores a crescent in the air.

"You think you can apologize and I'll forgive you?"

"No," he says, dancing backward, "no. Never. But I love you."

"Bullshit!"

Dad leaps at me, bellowing like an animal. His clawed hands rake at my face. I scream and fall to the ground, snow spraying around us. I hear Berkley's voice roaring something, but it's muffled and far away. Dad's right hand clamps over mine, pinning the sword down against the earth. His left hand is clasped around my neck.

"It is the truth," he says, his golden owl's eyes unblinking. He's heavy and cold as stone against me. "Whether you accept it or not. I am your father, and I love you. I always have."

"You're a monster! You're disgusting!"

"I could end this now," Dad says. I force myself to look right at him, at his glowing orange eyes and his horrible beak. "I could rend your spirit apart with my claws. The Speaker of Secrets itself would be undone, by its own vows. Would the two worlds be better off without that dark being?"

"They would," I say.

"So much good I could do with one terrible blow," he says. "But I will not. I will not lose my other son. I have lost too much already."

"What do you want?" I ask. "What do you want from me?"

"I wanted to explain myself. I thought maybe—no. No matter. The time for forgiveness has passed." The back of his throat glows with the same golden-orange light as his eyes, I see as he speaks. "Destroy Berkley," he says to me. "Destroy the Speaker of Secrets. Only then will you be safe."

"You think I don't want that?"

"It claims you call it Father now. Do not be fooled. The Speaker will tire of you eventually and leave you behind."

"He thinks he knows what I want," I say. "He doesn't. I'm only doing any of this to save Dunbarrow. To save the people you were willing to let the Tree consume."

"Show my master mercy and it will be in your debt," Dad hisses. "Promise me. Show it mercy."

"What are you talking about?"

"Struggle against me, Luke. This must seem real!"

I try to prize his claws away from my throat. I struggle to raise my flaming sword. There's just no way—he's far too strong. I can see Berkley and Margaux and Elza watching, from beyond the green flames, but they seem far away, distorted, like I'm viewing them through molten glass.

"I do not wish to go on," Dad whispers, face close to mine. "This must be the end. It has all been a mistake. Beginning to end. I wish I had never found that tomb, never set eyes upon the Book of Eight. But it is too late."

The frozen boughs of the Barrenwhite Tree intersect the sky above us. I watch the cold flecks of light that glitter between the branches, the larger streaks of green and blue that flicker up into the mist.

"Strike now," he says, releasing my sword hand.

"What?"

"DESTROY ME, LUKE!" Dad roars. "Before I lose my nerve! END THIS!"

I feel like my arm moves on its own. The black sword swings in an endless moment, bloodred flames eating into Dad's wattled neck. His eyes widen. I see the black slits of his pupils contract. He gurgles, white fog leaking from his mouth.

"Good-bye," I say to my father.

"Good-bye, Luke," he says, a tiny croak of a voice. "Grow up good."

Dad's monstrous body dissolves into gray mist. His weight falls away from me, and for a moment I can't see anything. I'm buried in a cloud of fog. I get to my feet. The end of Horatio Manchett swirls around me. I raise my sword in victory, and a crimson stream of fire erupts from the blade, washing over me like rain, burning away my father's remains.

The sound of the outside comes back all at once. Berkley is roaring in triumph. Even Elza seems to be shouting. Mr. Berkley rushes forward and embraces me, picking me up off my feet. His body is as warm as tropical seawater. He almost purrs.

"Spectacular, my boy! Outstanding! A triumph!"

"Thank you," I say, "Father."

"Dare I say it looked bleak? Dare I say I doubted you? Especially since you previously showed Horatio such undeserved mercy. I worried that you might spare him the blade."

"He got what he should have gotten long ago."

Elza is waiting behind him. I reach out to her, and she grabs my hand.

"Are you all right?" she asks. "Your face—"

"I'm fine," I say. "I'm OK."

"I'm sorry," she says. "Your dad—"

"Don't worry about that now."

"What do you think of that, you twisted revenant?" Berkley shouts at the Barrenwhite Tree. "What say you now?"

Margaux the Tree makes no reply.

"Get away from here," I whisper to Elza while Berkley is distracted. "If he works out what's going on, he'll kill you first, and I don't know if I can stop him."

"What are you doing?" she hisses.

"I'm going to get rid of him. The Tree, too."

"How?"

"I don't have time to explain! Just go!"

"Oh, fantastic."

"You are undone!" Berkley screams. "Finally you are undone! Submit! You swore by the power of eight you would submit to my acolyte's blade."

"*I did and shall,*" Margaux says.

Berkley claps me on the back, drawing me close to him. "A great prize, my son! A great prize. I knew my faith in you was not misplaced! I have an eye, you know. It is a gift—I was born with it. I see potential, the oak within the acorn. And I have seen it in you since the day you sat across that desk from me."

"I hope to surpass your faith in me," I say, gazing into his flaming eyes with what I hope appears to be admiration, trying to hold every bit of his attention, hoping Elza is escaping as we speak.

"You shall, you shall. Quickly now. Plunge your sword into the heart of our foe. Destroy this wretched thing. Do what should've been done long ago."

I turn and walk across the clearing. Margaux is silent, and she steps aside as I move toward her. The Tree makes no attempt to stop me. It comes closer with every step, a tangled mess of icy branches and veins of light. I see a multitude of colors swirling beneath the surface of the ice, like the rainbow sheen you see in an oil slick. The snow on the ground merges with the base of the trunk. The coldness here is overwhelming, cold so deep and hungry, I wonder how the blade of my sword can keep alight.

I stand before the Barrenwhite Tree. Light ripples and flows around me. In the depths of the Tree's frozen trunk, I think I can see a figure, a dim distorted shape. There's someone frozen inside the Tree, upside down, with their arms outstretched and pointed toward the ground. I can't make out anything more about the figure, whether they're old or young, male or female, or something else entirely. I think this must be the being that speaks through Margaux, trapped inside the tree of ice. Berkley called it an exile.

I rest the tip of the black sword against the ice, and a tiny fragment melts off with a hiss of steam. If I strike hard enough, the ice will shatter, this tree trunk will break open, and I can destroy the power contained within the Tree. It promised to submit to the blow. I can kill it if I want to. Destroy an elder spirit from the Beginning.

But if I do that, my apprenticeship with Berkley begins for real. I'll never escape him. I'll become something like him, monstrous, undying, devouring the souls of other beings to grow larger and stronger. I'll become the worst version of myself.

Dad said I should show his master mercy. Admittedly, he hasn't been the greatest help to me in life, but maybe he was right about this.

I place my left hand against the trunk of the Barrenwhite Tree, my four-fingered palm covering the spot where the figure's head seems to be. I know I need to speak to the spirit inside the Tree, but I don't know how that's going to happen. If I speak out loud, Berkley will hear me. So instead I focus my mind on the shape inside the trunk, sending my willpower through my hand and into the ice, hoping this gets its attention.

End this, pawn. Do what is already done. Or do you wish to torment me?

The voice insinuates itself into my mind. It's like I'm remembering someone speaking to me, but without them having spoken out loud. This voice could almost be my own thoughts.

I keep my hand resting on the Tree's frozen trunk.

What if I spare you? I think, hoping it hears me the same way I hear it.

Your master has instructed you otherwise.

He isn't my master yet. I've sworn nothing to him.

I promised to submit to the blow. I swore by the power of eight.

You did. But I never promised to deliver it.

Very well. Spare me and I am in your debt. What can I give you?

If I spare you, then I want you to let Dunbarrow go. Everyone. All the people. Put the town back how it was before you took it under your control, and make it so they don't remember a thing.

The Speaker of Secrets will destroy you regardless, pawn. For betraying him, he will raze your homeland to the ground. All will be lost.

No. I'm going to destroy him.

And how do you intend to do that?

With your help. Give me your strength. You leave this place, return it to Liveside. In return I let you live, and Berkley is destroyed instead.

You cannot overcome him here. Even if I lend you my power.

How do I do it?

We eldest of spirits cannot be killed, not in the way you understand. But he might be unmade.

How?

There is only one place it can be achieved: within the boundless forge of our creation. The depths of the Shrouded Lake.

Great. That's a long way away, right? How do I get from here to there? I'm going to be pretty short on time. I can hardly run all the way there and jump in with Berkley chasing me.

Listen: in the Beginning there was born a jealous spirit who seized the secrets of the sleepers and made them his own. He transcribed the language of the stars so that even mortals could understand it and use that power, which should be the right of the first spirits alone. He did this not for charity but for might, so that he would be exalted and worshipped as those sleepers once were. And indeed he rose far above his station and became mighty—

We don't have time for this! Any moment he'll realize something's not right. Tell me what to do!

What I am trying to tell you, boy, is this: The Shrouded Lake is bound in green leather within your breast pocket.

The Book of Eight?

Yes. It is fitting the Speaker be undone by his own creation. Release the Lake. Face him within its infinite depths. Unmake him.

I'm about to ask how I'm supposed to release the Shrouded Lake from the Book of Eight, when I remember something the Oracle told me. She said the Book is a knot that can be undone, in the way Alexander did. She really was talking about a sword after all.

"My son! Why do you hesitate? Strike our enemy down!" Berkley yells at me.

We have to do this now, I think to the spirit within the Tree. Quickly. Swear to me you'll release Dunbarrow. Send it back to Liveside. Swear by something unbreakable, or I'll destroy you.

I swear by the power of eight itself, I will release the town of Dunbarrow and all the thralls I have claimed from your home. I will return them to their rightful place, without knowledge of my actions. I swear this by the Styx, great River of Oaths.

I swear by the Styx to spare you and let you return to your place in Deadside. Now give me your strength.

It is done.

Coldness runs up my hand from the icy trunk of the Tree, coldness like the deepest reaches of the sea. My head feels like it might burst. My sword flares beyond crimson to white, pure white like the heart of a star, so bright I have to shield my eyes. Frost and pale fire play over the sword in unison, patterns forming and devouring one another as fast as my eyes can track, neither force quite having the upper hand.

I turn away from the Barrenwhite Tree to face Mr. Berkley. The Devil. The Speaker of Secrets.

"What is the meaning of this?" he asks me, still smiling.

I take another step toward him, frozen fire flickering along the edge of my blade.

"I defy you," I say. My voice is surprisingly steady.

"Luke, my son, please. This is entirely the wrong time for—"

"I'm not your son. You're not my father. You'll never teach me anything. I want nothing to do with you. You thought I would really call you Father? You thought I would follow you?"

"I saw great things in your future," he says sharply, adjusting his cuffs. "I think that if you would only follow my instructions and destroy our common enemy, there might yet be greatness ahead of you. I am still willing to forgive this lapse."

"You told my dad to take my brother out of Mum before he was even born. You taught him to do that. You thought I'd forget about that?"

"Luke, your father came to me with a problem, and I gave him a possible solution, one of many. He chose to act upon my advice. Just as you chose to—"

"Shut it. I don't care. You're a monster. I want you out of my life. Leave now, or I'll destroy you."

Berkley laughs thunderously.

"Did that Tree put these ideas into your head? You will destroy *me*? The Speaker of Secrets? Please, my boy, do not be a fool. This is madness. I am eternal. I was made in the Beginning, born when the One divided and became many. You might as well declare war upon the darkness between the stars.

"Destroy the Tree, Luke," he snaps. There's no smile anymore. "You are a fool. Destroy the Barrenwhite Tree now, and I might allow the witch girl to survive to mourn you."

I take the Book of Eight from my breast pocket, weigh it in my left hand. I turn it over, looking at the embossed golden star, the silver clasps, the pale-green leather.

"This is your weapon? That store of secrets? My boy, I created that artifact. I am its author. You seek to use my own revelations against me? What do you imagine you would find within those pages that would let you withstand my anger?"

I try to steady my nerves. What if this doesn't work? What if the Oracle was wrong, the Tree lying to me? Why should I trust them?

"Or is it that you think this is the first time a great spirit has tried to destroy me? You think the meager power that withered Tree has lent you gives you a fighting chance?"

He still sounds carefree and jovial, but I can tell he's preparing to attack. It will come any moment now.

There's no choice. I have to go through with my plan. I don't have anything else left.

"If you made the Book," I say, "then you know what it really is. Where it could lead us."

Mr. Berkley doesn't say another word. He explodes, the shape of the smiling man erupting into an avalanche of shadow. The gray suit, white hair, tanned handsome face; all are gone. In their place is a ravenous storm of darkness that sweeps across the clearing toward me.

"*Now, boy!*" I hear Margaux cry. "*Now!*"

I toss the Book of Eight into the air, like I'm serving for tennis.

The nightmare cloud that was Berkley is almost upon me. I see a thousand terrible faces in the blackness, a million mouths yawning wide to devour me.

Either this works, or a moment from now there won't be a me at all.

The Book is at the top of its arc, clasps gleaming in the light.

I swing the black sword, fire and ice at war inside the blade.

The Speaker of Secrets closes around me like a fist.

My sword slices through the Book of Eight, cutting it in half.

Without a sound, the world vanishes.

(speaker of secrets)

I'm falling through a void, stars spinning around me, molten white points of light against velvet blackness. This must be the depths of the Shrouded Lake, the endless expanse of sky that lies beneath the mist. Infinite space, infinite time. There's no up or down, no way to say I'm even falling at all. The stars write and rewrite stories, they form into sigils and signs that I can almost understand but never quite hold in my mind before they become another shape.

Something is cutting through the blackness, a billowing torrent of firelight and shadow. A voice like a thunderclap.

"YOU DARE? YOU DARE PROFANE THIS PLACE?"

I still have the sword, the power of the Barrenwhite Tree burning white-cold along the blade's edge. I hold it with both hands and try to face the thing that Mr. Berkley became—his true shape. It's easier said than done, as I spin wildly in the void, with no gravity to pull me, no air or water to push against. He's bearing down on me like a tidal wave, black against black, obscuring the stars with his formless body.

Willpower. Will and wisdom. That's how I move. I force myself not to panic, to will myself to steady. The world stops spinning so fast. I'm holding myself still in this void. I'm still here. I can fight him. This is what I planned for.

"I WILL DEVOUR YOU, PIECE BY PIECE, LUKE. I WILL UNMAKE YOU SO COMPLETELY, NONE WILL REMEMBER YOUR EXISTENCE."

A mouth of dazzling flame, coming at me like a shark through a vast black ocean. I steady the sword.

"YOU THINK TO DEFEAT ME? I WHO TRAN-SCRIBED THE SPEECH OF THE STARS INTO PROFANED TONGUES? I WHO HELPED BREAK THE WORLDS IN TWO? I WHO SIRED DEMONS IN AN UNENDING STREAM? I WHO LAID THE FOUNDATIONS OF URUK AND DIS?"

"I don't even know what any of that means!" I scream.

"YOU ARE NOTHING," the voice replies, and the thing is upon me. As Berkley envelops me, I plunge the sword, blazing white with power, deep into its dark body. The being screams with rage, and the blade glows brighter still, so bright I can't look directly at it. We're spinning off into the depths of the Lake, traveling faster than I thought possible. The stars around us are streaks of light. Berkley sends tendrils of flame and shadow burrowing into my spirit flesh, but the cold power the Barrenwhite Tree placed inside me resists his heat. I have time. Not much, but a little. In these depths, I can unmake him.

Berkley changes in an instant, becoming a white serpent with eight heads, each head crowned with eight golden horns, their faces the cruel withered faces of ancient kings. His white body is wrapped around me, his thick tail coiled around my legs and torso. My sword is still lodged deep within him, white fire leaking from the wound. The eight royal faces scream with rage and bite deep into my hands, my neck, my legs, gouging chunks from my spirit with golden fangs. I keep my grip on the hilt of the sword. Stars whirl past. I punch one of the heads in the face with my free fist, the four-fingered left hand. It roars in fury.

"You're afraid of me," I shout, "aren't you?"

"I FEAR NONE LIVING!" the white snake screams.

"You didn't expect this! Did you?"

"I AM ALL-SEEING! ALL-KNOWING! ETERNAL!"

"You're a shadow! You're just a shadow on the wall!" I yell at the serpent. The blade of my sword is still burning in the monster's chest, streams of smoke flowing behind us as we fall. Another head lunges at me, and I grab hold of the face and squeeze, trying to rip it from the neck completely. The searing gold fangs of six other heads are still buried in my body.

As I tear at one of his heads, Berkley starts to change again, his spirit flesh shifting like liquid, becoming a lion with crimson fur and a mane of peacock feathers. His eyes are bowls of fire, his teeth are silver blades, but my sword is still buried deep into his body. The lion roars and tears at me with its fangs and claws, but I don't let go, don't let the fire-cold sword shift from its position in his heart.

He can't destroy me. The power the Tree lent me is too great. If it weren't for that, he'd already have swallowed me whole, like I was a raindrop falling into the ocean.

My sword blazes brighter still, as bright as the stars that hurtle past us. The flame-colored lion bellows with pain and lashes at me with the barbed tail of a scorpion, but I don't let go, even though the fiery venom flows through my body like cursed blood. I ignore the pain, focus on my sword, keeping the blade steady. His claws tear ribbons from my back; he plunges his silver fangs into my shoulder, but he can't consume me and the pain doesn't matter. I won't let go of him. We're falling faster and faster, the Shrouded Lake's depths expanding around us, a vastness beyond vastness.

Berkley changes again, becoming a huge black goat with a fleshless white head, human hands gripping my throat, a tongue coated in barbs that lashes at my face as he roars, but I won't let go. He can't destroy me, so long as I don't let go.

We're falling toward one of the stars, I see, as we twist in space; a beacon in the blackness, smaller now than a mote of dust but growing fast.

Berkley becomes a woman made from molten glass, who hugs me close and whose skin burns worse than anything I've ever known, but my sword is still stuck into her heart, and I don't let go of the hilt.

"I WOULD HAVE RAISED YOU HIGHER THAN MY OWN CHILDREN!" the thing bellows through a white-hot throat. "YOU WOULD HAVE BEEN WORSHIPPED!"

"When did I ask for that? Do you think that's what I wanted?"

"YOU WOULD THROW IT AWAY FOR WHAT? A SHARP-NOSED SCHOOLGIRL? THAT CREDULOUS WRECK WHO BIRTHED YOU? WHAT DID YOU THINK THEY COULD GIVE YOU THAT I CAN'T?"

"They *love* me!"

He changes into something like a jellyfish—a nightmare net of stingers and tendrils and eyeless faces—that glistens in the light of the sword and bores a thousand holes in my skin, injecting venom into every tiny cut, and it hurts worse than ever, but my sword still burns inside him and I don't let go.

"I LOVED YOU!" the writhing monster screams. "YOU WERE TO BE MY MASTERPIECE!"

"You were wrong," I say.

"UNHAND ME! I WILL DESTROY YOU!"

Berkley changes faster and faster, becoming a proud knight in golden armor who stabs me with his own cruel swords, and then an ancient blind monk who bites into my neck with hollow teeth, and on into stranger shapes still, a bird made of blue fire that cries out the most beautiful notes I've ever heard, so beautiful that it almost seems wrong to hurt it, but I keep my sword stuck into the bird regardless, and Berkley becomes a white tiger with the round face of a newborn child, wailing so loudly, I feel like my head will split apart, but I hold him all the tighter, and the sword is eating straight through him, his spirit flesh burning away like mist when the sun rises, and I know that he's truly afraid.

He flickers and shifts, unable to settle on a form, merging into different shapes like tides breaking across a beach, becoming spider and wolf and human all at once, impossible bodies that I can barely hold in my mind before they're gone. Now Berkley is a child made from smoke, now he's a howling dog without skin, and now an ox with the wings of a dove. He becomes me, my eyes pools of dark oil, and just as soon, he's a monstrous squid, crimson tentacles scrabbling at the hilt of my sword, trying to pull it out of his body. I don't let go.

The star fills the world now, a searing wall of white light. We're plummeting toward it. I see surges of pale fire erupting from the star's surface, white splatters of paint against a black canvas.

"YOU WISH FOR BOTH OF US TO BE UNMADE? IS THAT WHAT YOU DESIRE? LET ME GO!"

"You don't want to go into this star, do you?"

"IT WILL BE OUR END! WHAT MUST I DO TO CONVINCE YOU TO RELEASE ME? LUKE!"

He becomes Elza, beautiful, green eyes and freckles, hair done the way it was the first day we spoke to each other. She tears at my hands, trying to prize them away from the sword hilt.

"DON'T YOU WANT TO SEE HER AGAIN?" the false Elza screams. "UNHAND ME! WE BOTH CAN RETURN TO OUR HOMES AND FORGET THIS AFFAIR!"

"No," I whisper. The star is singing to me as we fall, a beautiful high chiming noise, and I feel a growing coldness in my sigil ring. I know what I have to do. I need to unforge Berkley, destroy him with the same fire that created him. This is the moment.

I reach out with my left hand, toward the star, and will that power into me.

"YOU CANNOT! I DEFY YOU! I AM SPEAKER OF SECRETS! LUKE! I AM—"

A thread of fire rises from the surface of the star, so slender at first that I can barely see it, but as soon as it touches my sigil, it becomes a pulsing artery of white flame.

For one awful moment, the power is flowing through me, into my sigil, consuming it, trying to consume me, but I close my eyes and will it out into the black sword. It's like forcing an ocean through a keyhole. I pour the star's power into Berkley, sending it through the blade of my sword right into the core of him.

"I—AAAAAAIIIEEEEE!"

I can't see a thing, can't feel anything, I feel like I'm being broken down and rebuilt atom by atom

> moment
>> by moment
>> is this
>>> forever
> no
>> i'm still here
> i'm still
>> who
> speaker of secrets
>> no

I'm floating. I'm floating in space. I'm—Am I alive? I don't know.

Where did the star go?

There are points of light around me, constellations. I'm still inside the Shrouded Lake.

My sigil is gone. Whatever happened, it was too much for the ring to withstand.

Did I destroy Berkley as well?

I can't see him.

Have I won?

"Luke," a tiny voice says.

I'm still holding the sword, and I think the voice comes from there. I move the blade closer to my face and see that my weapon is stuck through something, a shape like a glob of oil that moves on its own. Living darkness. The glob grows arms the width of matchsticks, forms something like a head, a smudged remnant of a face.

"Luke," it says again, trying and failing to pull itself off the blade.

"Berkley?"

"I want to say something," the scrap of darkness whispers.

"It's over," I say. "This is the end. I won."

"One last thing."

"What?"

"I ate your brother, Luke."

I don't say anything.

"After you gave your Host to us. You sent them through my doorway. I had no use for the Innocent, so I ate it. A moment's work."

"Liar," I say, but I know it's true.

"*A scrap, a tiny bite,*" the blob whispers. "*I want you to think about that.*"

I reach out with my left hand, my four-fingered hand, and I pull the scrap of shadow from the point of my sword and crush it. I crush the life out of Mr. Berkley in my palm, and anything more he has to say is cut off. I crush him until I can feel that he's gone, until all that's left of the Speaker of Secrets is a pale pebble the size of my thumbnail, a pebble that looks a little like a goat. I put it inside my jacket, where the Book of Eight used to sit.

And then I drift.

The depths of the Shrouded Lake move around me. Constellations ebb and flow in the darkness. My sword has dulled, the flames and ice fading from its edge, the molten shadow stuff cooling into smooth dark metal. The power the Tree lent me seems to be used up. I drift, listening to the hum of the stars.

Berkley gone. Dad gone. The Book of Eight and my sigil are gone.

I'm still here.

What do I do now?

How do I get out of this place?

I should've asked the Tree that, but I had no time.

I remember the Shepherd and Ham falling into the

Lake's depths, and my instinctive knowledge that there was no way out. I suppose this was always a one-way trip. Is that the real reason the Tree told me to do this? It knew I wouldn't be coming back.

Sorry, Elza.

I hope the Tree keeps its word at least, lets Elza and everyone else in Dunbarrow go. That was the point of this.

What will happen to me? What happened to Ham and the Shepherd and the Widow when they fell into this place?

I want to go home.

I ate your brother.

You're gone. You're a figment. You were the one that was nothing, in the end.

I watch the sigils and magic marks forming in the darkness, a story without a beginning or end. Constellations spiral silently around me and then break apart.

Maybe I'll become part of this place. Dissolve into the black space around me, like a grain of sugar into coffee. I think if I wanted to, I could. Let it all go and disappear. It wouldn't be the worst end.

No.

Elza and Mum still need me. I need them. I have to find a way back.

I can't tell which way is up or down, or how I could get back to the surface of the Lake, but I have to try. The problem is there's nothing to fix on. The stars are moving all the time; you can't use them to navigate by. Even if I try to head toward another point of light, it might just be leading me in circles.

In desperation, I choose a direction that at least feels like upward and move with a purpose.

I'm starting to accelerate, I think. The stars are streaks around me, threads of light rather than points.

I will myself faster, onward, imagining myself breaking the Lake's misty surface and finding myself on that silver-lit shore, the same spot I fought against Ash and the Widow.

There's something forming ahead of me, a darkness against the void that's blocking out the stars.

I move toward the shape, losing it when it merges with the sable darkness, then finding it again as it obscures the constellations.

This thing, whatever it is, is enormous. I feel like I'm approaching a black planet.

Wait . . .

Is that a person?

The thing comes closer, and I want to stop but I can't. I'm still accelerating.

That is a person, I think. It's a human shape at least.

Every time I think this place can't get weirder.

As it grows closer, approaching now at enormous speed, I can see the being more clearly in the chalky starlight. It looks like a child, or maybe an immeasurably old person, coiled in on itself, in a fetal position. It makes me think of a newborn, held inside a womb of immense darkness.

Is it asleep?

I can't slow down. I'm going to hit it.

The being's face fills the world: a hairless scalp the size of a planet, an ancient sleeping face, intermittently lit by the constellations shifting around us. I see the ridge of a nose, a tightly closed mouth. Skin that's as dry and gray as moon dust.

I fall closer and closer, trying everything I can to slow down, but I can't. The thing is drawing me in, I realize, although for what purpose I can't imagine. The Shepherd spoke once about sleepers below the surface of the Shrouded Lake, I remember now. Is this what he was talking about?

The thing opens one eye, an eye that must be hundreds of miles across, and I fall into the darkness at the center.

I'm standing on a plain of pale stones, some just pebbles, others larger and streaked with dark flaws. Each one is smooth and edgeless, as though eroded over millennia by the tide. They rattle as I move my foot. Far above me I can see the stars of the Shrouded Lake moving in their silent patterns. There are curved black walls around me, and the starry sky is just a circle above. I'm at the bottom of a pit, a stone well hundreds of miles in diameter.

This doesn't make sense.

Is this place inside the enormous being's eye?

I look down at myself. I'm dressed in jeans, hiking boots, my raincoat. I still have two hands, nine fingers, a frayed woven belt. My coat and skin are the same gray, without hue or tone. I'm not casting a shadow. I slide the black sword through my belt and start to walk.

This plain has the feeling of a tomb, a place you're not meant to be walking. There's no sound but the dry scraping of the pebbles underneath my feet as I travel. There's no way I'll be able to climb the walls of the well—they're smooth and flawless, unscalable. I can't fly anymore. I'm stuck on the ground. Whatever power drew me down here, it doesn't want me to leave. There's something in the very middle of the plain of stones, a far-off domed shape. For lack of anywhere else to go, I decide to head toward it.

I have the same feeling as I walk that I had when I first looked at the Styx: of a place beyond time, a vastness beyond vastness.

The domed structure comes closer. It's a building, made from gray stone, and I feel like it has a religious significance, a place of worship. I fell into the eye of a sleeping giant, and now I've found a temple inside it.

Of course I have.

I walk closer still. The temple is a low octagonal building with a domed roof. The stone it's built from is the gray of cold ashes. There are no decorations or carvings on the temple walls: it's very simple, almost like something that was abandoned before it was completed. There's a round black doorway in the side facing me, although I can't be certain it was there a moment before.

Something luminous emerges from the blackness, like a miniature constellation, a being constructed from tiny points of white light that shift and swirl as the creature bounds toward me. The thing is sinuous and strange, running across the expanse of gray stones with lunging strides. I don't know whether I should be scared or not. I draw my sword regardless, but I don't feel like it would do me any good in this place.

Hello, boy, the star creature says. I hear its voice in my mind, like I heard the Tree's.

A tail made from stars lashes wildly behind it.

Good boy. Hello hello.

" . . . Ham?"

Of all the things I expected to meet down here, this wasn't it.

Yes yes. Am Ham.

The star creature rears up and places its front paws on my shoulders. Its glimmering flesh shifts and swirls before my eyes, a fog of white light. There's no face exactly, but now that I know what I'm looking at, the outline of my dog is easy to make out. I break into a grin.

"What are you doing here, Ham?"

Sleep.

"You're sleeping?"

Many sleep. Big sleep.

"I don't understand."

Follow boy. Follow follow.

Ham drops back onto all fours and trots away, back toward the gray temple. This is so bizarre. What happened to him when he fell into this Lake? Is this what'll happen to me as well?

Good boy. Follow follow.

I follow him across the stones. He doesn't seem to have become much better at stringing words together. Not knowing what else to do, I walk into the temple, through the dark doorway.

The temple interior seems much larger than it was from outside; a high vaulted space with floors the color of dust and gently curving walls that stretch high overhead. Ham's shape lights the way in front of me, gentle milky star glow. The floor is smooth stone, a single unbroken surface without cracks or seams or signs of tiles being put down. This place seems like it could've grown out of the rock. I can't see the ceiling overhead. Ham leads me deeper into the

cavelike building, and I see another source of light glimmering in the darkness, something bright and white.

We come closer. Ham's starry paws make no sound
against the stone. The light is cast from a stone bowl set on
the floor, an enormous gray basin whose rim is higher than
my waist. I could climb inside it easily and still have room
for more people to sit in there with me. There's something
like white fire held inside it, a shifting radiance that ebbs
and flows within the bowl.

"What is this?" I ask the star-fleshed creature.

Allwell.

"I don't understand you."

Allwell. Old place.

"This is old magic?"

First spell.

I rest my hands on the rim of the bowl of flame. I
don't understand what I'm supposed to do here. Why did
Ham — the thing that wants me to think it's Ham, at least —
bring me here? Now I look closer, the substance held in the
basin reminds me of the stars floating in the depths of the
Lake; it's the same pale fire.

I glance down between my hands, at the bowl's thick
rim, and I notice that there's a mark engraved in the gray
stone, a small sigil. I recognize this mark. I've seen it before,
carved into the edge of the shrine in Deadside that juts out
over the edge of the Shrouded Lake. It's a special kind of

mark, a word that can mean anything the person speaking to you wants it to mean.

At the moment the mark means WELCOME. I can understand it like I'm reading English.

"Hello?" I say, projecting my voice into the darkness around us. I'm still not exactly sure what I'm speaking to. Is it the sleeping creature whose eye I fell into? Is it the fire in the bowl? Is it something else entirely?

The mark's meaning hasn't changed.

"Why am I here?" I ask the blackness. There's no echo to my voice, which feels strange. A huge empty building like this should reverberate with sound. I suppose there aren't sound waves in this place; I don't even know if there's air to breathe. Different rules apply. The white fire churns in its container. Ham sits beside me.

The mark cut into the stone now means this: YOU HAVE DESTROYED THE SPEAKER OF SECRETS.

"I did."

DO YOU CLAIM THAT POWER?

"I . . . no. What?"

A SPEAKER OF SECRETS MUST EXIST.

"You're asking if I want to take his place?"

YES. A NEW SPEAKER MUST BE BORN. DO YOU OFFER YOURSELF?

"No. I want to go home."

THERE MUST BE A SPEAKER OF SECRETS.

"Why? Berkley was a monster."

THAT IS NOT FOR YOU TO JUDGE.

"Why do you want a new Speaker?"

THERE MUST ALWAYS BE A SPEAKER OF SECRETS. IT IS NOT ABOUT WANTS.

"So make a new one, then."

WE REQUIRE A SOURCE. DO YOU OFFER YOURSELF?

"No! I want to go back to Dunbarrow."

VERY WELL. BUT A SPEAKER MUST BE BORN.

"How can I help you? I don't understand what you want."

YOU DESTROYED THE SPEAKER OF SECRETS. The sigil can't communicate tone, but I detect a twinge of exasperation on the part of whatever's speaking to me. THEREFORE IT IS YOUR DUTY TO OFFER THE KERNEL OF THE NEW.

"A kernel?"

I am absolutely lost. I feel like I walked onstage halfway through a play and everyone's expecting me to know my lines. I have no idea what this thing is talking about. What does it mean by *kernel*? Isn't that like a seed? At a loss, I reach into my pocket and bring out the pale stone that Berkley became when I crushed the life out of him. The small white stone that looks a little bit like a goat. I hold it out to the basin of fire.

"Is this . . . ?"

THIS WILL SUFFICE. IF IT IS YOUR WILL.

"What will this do?" I ask, still holding the white stone.

BIRTH A NEW SPEAKER.

"Do you mean Berkley will come back if I give you this?"

THE SAME PATTERN WILL NOT BE REPEATED. THE SPEAKER WILL BEGIN ANEW.

"I won't be in its debt? It won't come after me?"

YOU WILL BE ITS ARCHITECT. HOW COULD YOU OWE IT A DEBT?

I hesitate. I still don't understand this. I think I'm being asked to assist in creating a new great spirit. However horrible I found him, Berkley must've performed some role that was vital to the spirit world; or at least, that's what the being talking to me through this stone sigil thinks. I want to go home, and I feel like I don't have enough of a grasp on what's happening to argue a case against doing what it wants me to do.

I lower the white stone into the pool. The flames rise in silent surge and swallow the stone. My hand is left empty, unburnt. Pale fire swirls undisturbed in the basin. Ham nuzzles his starry snout against my thigh.

Good boy, he says.

"What's Ham doing here?" I ask the dark temple.

HE CAME TO US. HE HAS A PLEASING FORM. THE YOUNG ONES ARE FOND OF HIM.

"The young ones?"

YES.

"What is this place?"

A PLACE OF RENEWAL.

"Are you the sleepers?"

NO. WE SPEAK FOR THEM. WE TEND TO THEIR AFFAIRS WHILE THEY DREAM.

"What are you?"

No answer.

"What happens when the sleepers wake up?"

ALL THINGS WILL CHANGE.

"Will it happen soon?"

THERE IS NO REASON TO THINK SO.

I don't know what to say to that. Even though it's easy to understand the words the being wants me to understand, the meaning behind them is anything but simple.

"Can I go home now?" I ask the dark, empty temple.

YOU MAY.

Follow follow, Ham says, prancing in the blackness. *Follow boy.*

I turn away from the sigil, the stone basin filled with silent fire. Whatever this place is, I feel like I've gone deeper into the mysteries of the spirit world than Dad or the Shepherd ever managed. I feel like I've seen something almost nobody, living or dead, has ever caught a glimpse of. Back on the banks of the Styx, Holiday said that she felt like we'd gone behind the scenes, seen things we weren't meant to see. I think that's a good way of putting it.

Whatever power is speaking through the mark on the edge of the bowl makes no good-byes. Ham, a luminous constellation, lights the path deeper into the darkness. I follow him, the bowl of flame receding behind us. He leads me to a staircase that spirals downward below the floor of the temple. The light of the basin is lost. There's only blackness, and the faint glow of Ham's stars.

"Do you like it here?" I ask my dog, whatever it is he's become.

Yes yes.

"Do you miss me?" I ask. "I miss you."

Meet again.

"You mean right now? Or we will meet again?"

Again again.

"I don't understand."

Good boy, Ham says in my mind. *Meet again.*

We walk farther down. I can no longer see stairs below my feet, or walls. If the temple was inside the sleeper's eye, then this stairway must be leading us down through the cord of the eye, into its mind.

Ham's shape is wavering, stars winking into existence around him, no longer looking much like a dog. He's a vein of light.

I'm falling into the stars, pale galaxies whirling around me, and I'm losing sense of where my body is, of how big or small I am, and I see shifting gray landscapes beneath me, small as the maps of a board game, like rough panes of smoked glass, and I see ancient mountains of gray stone and gray forests with black rivers running through them, plains and prairies and deserts without color, and I see a girl walking through fog with her coat wrapped tight around her, a girl with short red hair and a fur-lined parka, and I reach out with a hand beyond size or form and I twist the world so she finds herself at a stone circle, a seam between the gray place and ours, but before I can see what happens to her she's gone, and now I see black deserts scarred with a river of bloody red flames, tall keeps with walls and gardens in sickly nightmare colors that none living could name, and I hear terrible bells ringing and see mourning processions of creatures I can't describe, and I fall farther still through bottomless deeps of silver mist, and I see three pilgrims chained with black stones walking by the side of a great river, two men and a woman who covers her face, and I reach out again and shorten the river, drawing it tight like a string and bringing them closer to the lake they seek, before I'm gone again, falling into an ocean of warm sunshine, a river of golden light, islands with flags flying in colorful rows, I see fruit trees with people sitting under them, beautiful fields of animals grazing, rainbow-hued creatures I never saw in my life, and like that it's out of reach and I'm flying through layers of fog and ash, frozen light, seething walls of fire, all the wards between this place and others, and I find myself landing on cold wet ground, with mist around me and tall gray trees, with a girl with black hair and wide green eyes standing before me, and she opens her mouth to speak.

"Luke? Is that you?"

"Who else?" I ask.

"I thought—" Elza gapes at me. "For a moment you were different."

"How do you mean?"

"You were made out of stars. Like a hole cut into the night sky."

I reach out to her, and she throws herself into my arms. I crush her tight against me. She kisses me and then pulls away.

"You're still cold," she says. "Are you . . ."

"Let's not worry about that right now."

"Are you dead?"

"No," I say. "Berkley's gone, Elza. I killed him."

"How is that possible?"

"Inside the Lake. The Shrouded Lake. I unraveled him. I used one of the stars there. I can barely make sense of it myself. What happened to you?"

"I ran when you said. Berkley wasn't watching me. All he could think about was you and the Tree. He was so sure he was about to win. Then I got lost in the fog, and I've been walking, trying to find my way back to Holiday. I don't know where we are." Elza gestures at the fog, the trees, the grayness. "This still looks a lot like Deadside."

"The Barrenwhite Tree promised to let Dunbarrow go," I say, "if I got rid of Berkley. I think we should go speak to it about that."

"What if it doesn't?"

"It will," I say. "These things, their whole world is built on promises. If they promise you something, they're bound by it. That spirit will keep its word."

"And you're sure?"

I pause.

"Reasonably."

"Oh, fantastic."

"One thing at a time, OK? Berkley won't bother me again. I'm free. I really did it. Now, which way to the Devil's Footsteps?"

Elza frowns. "This way, I think. I was running really fast, and you know how easy it is to get turned around in this fog."

We move off in the direction she was pointing. The forest is mute and hueless, a dim expanse of tree trunks and roots and low bushes, all glittering with frost. The ground is white snow, heaped into drifts by the wind. Elza must be freezing cold. Flickers of blue light play through the trees ahead.

"How long have you been out here?" I ask as we walk.

"I don't know. It's hard to keep track. How long did you spend in the place you went to?"

"No idea."

The glow cast by the Barrenwhite Tree is growing stronger. The air is filled with a languid flow of light, greens and blues shimmering in waves around us. There are bodies tangled in the roots, sleeping figures with snow on their faces. I try not to think about what Berkley had me do, eat that poor drained gray spirit. *I ate your brother.* No. You're gone. I don't need to think about you anymore.

We pass a tall oak tree made from stone, and we're at the passing place again, the gateway that the Barrenwhite Tree claimed as its own. The snow is shallow here, with a circle scorched on the earth where I fought my father. The Tree hasn't changed; it's still an unearthly tangle of ice and light, its trunk glittering like a lightning strike that froze at the moment it touched the ground. I clutch Elza's hand in my four-fingered grasp and keep my other hand on my sword hilt. Margaux Hart is seated in the snow before the Tree, her legs crossed, like she's meditating. The golden swan mask is lying on the ground beside her. She looks at us as we walk toward her, and her eyes are still rolled right up in her head, so only the whites are visible. I come close enough that I can see the wet pink flesh in the corners of her eyes. She doesn't stand but looks up at us.

"*You have returned,*" Margaux says in the Tree's cold voice.

"I destroyed the Speaker of Secrets," I say. "I unmade him."

"*I know. I felt it. You did as well as I hoped.*"

"Did you know this would happen?" I ask the Tree. "Was this what you wanted?"

"*I cannot claim this was my plan, although turns of my cards hinted at this outcome. Horatio told me of his son and of the Speaker's great interest in you. I saw a chance to antagonize an old foe, and that is all. I never dreamed this night's petty drama would be his downfall.*"

"What was Berkley to you?" Elza asks the Tree.

"*A sibling. A rival. A traitor. A lover. I do not expect you to understand our ways. The passions of the first spirits are beyond anything you could imagine.*"

"There must've been something he did," Elza says.

"*The elders all agreed that the world should be split, that life and death be instituted. We felt otherwise, the Speaker and I. We swore never to harm each other, and we fought them. It was the greatest battle you can imagine, the first war, and outnumbered as we were, I was certain none could stand before us. And he surrendered. He betrayed me, betrayed what we stood for, and bowed*" to them. *And for this they made him a great spirit and made of me what you see today."*

"You said you'd release Dunbarrow," I remind the Tree. "You said you'd let go of your thralls and make it like this never happened."

"I did. I swore by the power of eight."

"So keep your bargain, Tree. Release us."

"I had hoped you might choose to ascend," the Tree replies. *"I hoped you would forget my promise."*

"I didn't."

"I need sustenance," the Tree complains. *"What am I to do?"*

"We don't care," Elza replies. "You made a promise."

"I spared you," I remind the spirit. I keep my hand on my sword. "I spared you, and you swore to let Dunbarrow go in return. Let us all go, and Margaux, too."

"She looked into the heart of the black sun," the Tree says, moving her lips, *"and she found me there. I was waiting. She embraced me."*

"We're not negotiating," I say. "Let her go, too."

"Very well," the spirit says. *"You spared me the blade, Luke Manchett, and so I keep my promise. I thank you for this, and also for destroying the Speaker, where by terms of our concord I could not."*

"Without your strength, I couldn't have done it. I thank you for that."

"*To the outworlds I return, then. To the land of exiles. I bid you farewell, Luke Manchett, Elza Moss. We will not meet again.*"

"I hope not," Elza says.

Margaux lets out a wail, and the Barrenwhite Tree starts to recede, like it's growing backward, every icy branch and tendril of light retreating back into its frozen trunk. There's a shrill chiming noise, and the trunk of the Tree, with the figure trapped inside, vanishes into the earth. With a final fountain spray of aqua-green light, the spirit is gone. Gray mist still flows through the clearing. Margaux collapses onto the snowy ground, with no strength left in her body.

"Is it really gone?" Elza asks.

"Yeah," I say. "But we need to close the gateway again. That's the last thing."

Elza opens her mouth, and I pull the stone easily from her gums. She winces.

"Did that hurt?" I ask.

"A little. You hand is really cold."

I walk over to Margaux, lying on her back in the snow, her red hair like a vivid bloodstain against the white, and I take the second stone from her mouth. I hold the two of them in my palm, and then I realize.

"The third one . . . My stone. Berkley took it."

"So?" Elza asks me. "You can't close the gateway?"

I look at the black sword in my right hand. I look

(311)

around me, at each of the oak trees of stone, and the idea comes to me again that there's a language written against the gray fog in these bare stone branches, symbols like the ones I saw swirling in the stars in the depths of the Shrouded Lake, and I hold these words in my mind, remember how it felt to be among those stars, remember that we're made from them.

"We need three," I say. "But there is a way."

I drive the black blade into the frozen ground in the middle of the circle of stone trees, push the sword into the gateway that stands between Liveside and Deadside, and I say a word I've never heard and could never write down, but the sword understands me and the gateway does, too, and the black sword becomes a stone, weathered and dark, seven feet tall, larger than my hand, even though my hand still grasps it and places it, and my head is filled with a high glassy ringing sound. I release the sword, now a standing stone that looks a little like a blade, and then I plant the other two stones, taken from Elza's mouth and Margaux's, into the soil, and as I place them, they grow to become full-size standing stones as well, completing the circle. I breathe out. The gray mist fades away. Around us, the seven stone trees are turning back into living wood.

(new year's day)

I hear the Dunbarrow clock tower chiming, church bells ringing. It's midnight, the beginning of a new year. The fog is gone, and I can see the sky again, stars fixed in their proper positions, the comet just a blue-green streak overhead. We did it. We're back in the real world, back in Liveside. I turn away from the standing stones.

The snow is still here, smothering the earth. Elza forges her way through it, stepping around Margaux.

"Is that it?" she asks.

"It's over."

Elza reaches out to hold me and stumbles straight through me, nearly tumbling into a standing stone.

"Whoa—sorry."

"I forgot you left your body back in the tent."

"With Holiday, yeah."

"So are you . . . dead?" Elza asks me. "I don't understand."

"I don't know. I don't think so."

I try to look for my lifeline, the thread of light that connects your body and spirit when you go spirit walking, but I can't find it. If it's still here, this must be the thinnest it has ever been. I don't feel scared, though. I can still read the spread of tree branches against the night sky, see sigils in the curls of Elza's black hair. I know I can fix this.

"What about her?" Elza asks, pointing to Margaux. "I'm not carrying her all the way through the forest to the school."

"She's going to get really cold if we leave her out here."

"Oh, I don't know, Luke." Elza shrugs, looks around the clearing, as if hoping someone else will back her up. "We've got to find out what happened to everyone else. We don't even know where your mum and Darren are. I'm not sure if I'm that worried about the person whose fault all of this is."

"It's not Margaux's fault," I say. "The Tree took her over."

"The Tree that we let go," Elza says. "We just let it go."

"What else could we do?"

"I don't know. Just doesn't seem right." Elza shivers, looking up at the comet in the sky. "It'll come back, won't it? Eight hundred years or so. The comet will appear in the sky again, and the Tree will get hold of another town. And they'll all be eaten, absorbed, whatever it actually does to those poor people."

"Maybe," I say. "Probably. But what can we do about that? To get rid of Berkley, I had to make promises to the Tree. I said I'd let it go. Great spirits take promises seriously. I couldn't go back on it."

"I know. I just keep thinking about all those people we saw in the forest—"

"There's nothing we can do, Elza. We rescued Dunbarrow. We'll be long gone when the Tree comes back. Eight centuries. We can't solve every problem."

She sighs. "I don't like it, is all."

"If we stopped it, other people can, too," I tell her. Do I believe what I'm saying? I'm not sure. But I gave the Barrenwhite Tree my unbreakable word, and now it's gone beyond our reach. There's nothing we can do about that.

"Look," I say, "we should get Margaux somewhere a bit more sheltered, at least."

"And by *we* you mean me," Elza grumbles. "Since you can't touch anything."

"Hey, I killed Berkley and closed the gateway, OK? Division of labor."

Elza grabs Margaux and drags her through the snow, to the edge of the clearing. There are some bushes that have a sort of hollow underneath them, somewhere sheep might shelter from a storm. I can see old scraps of yellowing wool clinging to the branches. Elza hauls Margaux into it, arranges her Apostle's robe so it covers her skin completely. That'll have to do for now.

We make our way past the oak trees, through the snow-shrouded forest, following the track down toward the high school. The people tangled up in the roots and branches are gone. The trees are no longer the twisted gray monsters we walked through to get here; instead they're birches and pine trees, the forest floor crowded with dead orange bracken. The snow crunches beneath Elza's feet. A clear night sky is visible between the trees.

We break out of the forest and are standing on the rise above the school playing fields, also blanketed in snow, with the square flat-roofed buildings of Dunbarrow High beyond them. There's a dark dome in the middle of the rugby pitch: the tent Berkley made is still here, and I can see Titus's armor glinting in the moonlight, heaped where we killed him. Elza walks and I drift, through the scruffy bushes that separate the farthest sports field from the forest, across the snowy grass, and up to the horsehide tent.

"Holiday?" I call. "Are you there?"

Bea's sleek dark head emerges from the door flap. She barks sharply and runs out to greet us, firelight leaking out onto the darkened snow through the doorway. Holiday follows, looking sickly, her hair a tangle. She holds her wyrdstone out in front of her.

"Who's that?" she asks us.

"It's us," Elza says. "Luke and Elza."

Still scowling, Holiday keeps the wyrdstone raised. "Don't move," she says. She presses the stone against my face, then Elza's. Nothing happens, and she relaxes.

"It's really us," I say. "I promise."

"I had to be sure," Holiday replies. "After that thing that looked like Alice—"

"I don't blame you," Elza says.

"Is it over?" Holiday asks. "The fog's gone."

"It's over," I say. "We're back in the real world. We closed the gateway."

"I thought you were . . ." she says. "I woke up, and your body was by the fire, and it's all torn up."

"I know," I say. "I'm sorry. It must've been scary."

"I wanted to come find you both, but I was so weak, I could barely stand. . . . Your dog's been with me, though. What happened to you?"

"Honestly," Elza says, "I don't know where to begin."

"Mr. Berkley . . . the Devil . . . he's gone," I say. "The Tree, too. Dunbarrow's safe. And, Holiday, I'm so sorry for what happened to you. I should never have bound you to the sigil. That was so dangerous."

"Did it help you close the gateway?" she asks.

I think about the Knight, Dumachus, dissolving into ash and smoke. It was a small step in the scheme of things, but it was a step forward.

"Yeah," I say. "It did."

"Then there's nothing to apologize for," Holiday says firmly.

There's a strange buzzing noise.

"Is that someone's phone?" Elza asks.

"Oh my god, it's me," Holiday says. She rummages in the pocket of her parka and pulls out her smartphone. The touch screen is lit up, displaying a call from Alice Waltham, of all people.

"We really are back," Elza says. "I suppose mine will be working as well." She takes her phone out and holds the power switch.

"Hello?" Holiday says. "Alice! Are you OK?"

Bea whines and tries to rub her head against my leg. It goes right through. I need to get my body back. I move toward the tent.

"Mum?" Elza says. "Hello! Happy New Year. How are the fireworks?"

No time seems to have passed. It's so weird. We spent days in here, trapped in Dunbarrow, and in the outside world nobody noticed we were gone.

"What do you mean you're at *Stonehenge*?" Holiday gasps. "Are you sure?"

"Yeah, Luke's just with me now," Elza says. "We're up at his mum's boyfriend's house, remember? Yeah, I didn't think there'd be reception there either—"

"Well, OK," Holiday says, "you're right, if you can see a sign saying Stonehenge, it probably is Stonehenge. You don't have to be so sarcastic with me. I've been really worried about you!"

I melt through the wall of the tent. My body is in a bad way. Eyes open, staring at the ceiling. My legs are broken, blood soaking my jacket. There are big, awful teeth marks on my shoulder, my forearm. I'm not sure if I'm breathing.

I bend down beside myself. I know I can fix this. I don't need a sigil to do magic, don't need Berkley's book either. I can read the language of the world, can see the letters the flames form as they flicker over the coals. A chapter of a book without end, being written before my eyes. I catch a flame in the palm of my hand and plunge it into my body's chest, letting the warmth spread, willing bones to knit and blood to flow. My body's eyes flicker, opening and closing rapidly. I place the flame inside my still heart and will it to beat. There's a gasp, and then a breath. I withdraw my hand and fall back into myself.

Holiday's still on the phone outside. I walk through the snow, my breath making clouds in the dark air, footsteps crunching in the snow, and grab Elza around the waist, kissing her neck. She laughs.

"You're OK?" she says. "It worked?"

"I'm fine," I say. No need to mention I brought myself back to life. "We need to get back to Mum and Darren."

"Where do you think they are?"

"Hopefully they're still at Darren's place. They'll have been outside, away from all of this. We need to get back there and check for them there first."

"How are we going to get back there? It's miles away."

"I can move us there."

"How?"

"I just can. I understand how things fit together. If we want to go there, we can go there."

Elza looks at me hard.

"What really happened to you?" she whispers. "When you closed the gateway, I've never seen anything like that. Your body was torn to shreds and now it's fine. How can you do things like this?"

"I don't know," I say. "I think I went . . . wherever magic comes from. I don't have to think about it anymore. I can change the world if I want to."

Holiday hangs up the phone. "Alice ended up at *Stonehenge*," she says. "You know, that big stone circle on Salisbury Plain? She said something took her out of the gray forest she was lost in and pushed her through the stones."

"Yeah," I say, "sorry I put her so far away. It was really hard to aim."

"You did that, too?" Elza asks.

"Like I said. It's hard to explain. Listen," I say to Holiday, "we need to get back to my mum. I don't know what happened to her. Can you find some way of getting word to Mark and Kirk? They'll need an ambulance. Maybe don't call it to the actual house, though? People would ask questions."

"Yeah," Holiday says, "of course."

"We have to go," Elza says. "But, like, maybe I'll see you later?"

"I'd like that," Holiday says. "Sure. Give me a call."

"All right. We'll do coffee or something."

They hug, and then we're walking again, back up through the snowy bank to the forest, to the standing stones. Holiday watches us go. Bea runs beside us, pushing her way through brambles.

"This really is a night of magic," I say.

"What do you mean?" Elza asks.

"You just made a friend!"

"Oh, shut up."

"I'm serious," I say. "That's cool."

"We were always friends," Elza says. "We just forgot that for a while."

The woods grow thicker, steeper. We scramble up the track, snow dampening the cuffs of my jeans, and cross into the ring of oak trees, coming again to the three standing stones, the largest a blade of dark rock stuck down into the snow. Margaux is leaning against it, red hair tumbling over her shoulders, wrapped in her dark gray robe. She looks at us blearily as we approach.

"This is a dream, isn't it?" she asks me.

"Of course," I say.

"Do you know who we are?" Elza asks Margaux. Bea runs up and sniffs at her.

"I'm supposed to be on the beach," she says.

"Luke," Elza says, "what are we going to do with her?"

"We're going to find Darren and Mum," I say.

"How? We haven't seen them since she . . . since the Tree took hold of us. How do we know where they are?"

"I can get us there," I say. "Believe me. Just hold on."

"I was looking at the eclipse," Margaux says, as if nobody had interrupted her. "And I heard a voice saying it loved me and asking if I loved it, too. And now I'm here."

"That's all right," I say. "This is going to be fine. It's just a dream."

"It's so cold—"

"Take my hand?" I ask Margaux, in a kind but insistent tone. I hold out my right hand to her, and she tentatively takes hold of me, her skin clammy and warm despite the bitter chill of the night. I lead them into the middle of the three standing stones.

"How are we going to get back?" Elza asks.

"Just keep hold of me. And grab Bea, too."

Elza does as I say, slipping her free hand underneath Bea's collar. I close my eyes and turn my mind inward, trying to see the pattern again, to read the language written below the world's skin. There are veins of power in the earth, and where they converge, they make passing places. I can feel them pulsing under our feet, shimmering like the trails the stars leave as they travel. Mum and Darren. Let us get back to them. I don't want to be here. I want us to be there. Deliver us.

Elza lets out a sharp cry, and her hand tightens around mine. There's a ringing noise and a rushing sound, like a storm wind blowing inside my head, but I keep my eyes closed, focusing on Mum's smiling face. We're coming back to her. The ground under my feet shifts and shudders, bucking like an animal's back.

The earth seems to sigh, and then it quiets. I open my eyes.

We're still standing in a forest at nighttime, but there isn't any snow underfoot. There's firelight between the trees, and I can see the side of a stone cottage covered in ivy. Darren's place. I let go of Margaux's hand.

"We're safe," I say. "It's OK."

"Luke," Elza says, "how is this possible? What did you do?"

"Mr. Berkley, when he wanted something to happen, it would happen. You don't need his Book, not if you can already speak the language it was teaching you. You don't need a sigil. I just understand it now."

"That's a little scary, Luke."

"Yeah. I suppose it is. I think the things he gave me, the rings and the Book, they open the path, but only a little way. The rest you have to find yourself."

I'm not frightened, exactly. Just surprised at how easy this was. I wanted us to travel here and we did. Could I have done this all along? Can everyone do this? Maybe as we're born we still know how, still remember the language the stars spoke as we rose from the depths of the Lake, and the moment we take our first breath we forget. Maybe that's the power necromancers really use; the strength of the first magic that's inside every spirit, whether they remember it or not.

"Luke?" I hear Mum's voice, away in the trees. I let go of Elza's hand.

"Here!" I shout. "Over here!"

Elza lets go of Bea. The dog rushes off through the forest, barking delightedly. I follow her.

Mum is standing by the bonfire, wrapped in her poncho, staring at us with confusion. I realize suddenly that me and Elza are both wearing different clothes than we had on when we vanished, but hopefully nobody will think to ask about this.

"Luke, where on earth have you been?" Mum asks. "I've been worried sick!"

"What do you mean?"

"We've been looking for you for an hour! Where did you go?"

"Where did *you* go? Last I saw you, you were walking away from me!"

Mum looks at me for a moment, then starts crying again.

"Sorry," she says. "I'm sorry."

After everything that's happened, I don't know why I'm arguing with her. What's wrong with me?

"No," I say. "I'm sorry, Mum. We saw Bea in the forest. We had to go get her."

"You saw—" Mum looks at Bea and her tears dry up. "What is she doing out here? She was locked up in our house! How did she come all the way up here?"

"I dunno. She must've gotten out."

"She was locked in! I did it myself!"

"It's a mystery."

Darren comes around the side of the house, holding a flashlight.

"There he is!" he says. "Margaux with you?"

"I'm here!" she says. "Darren!"

"All right, Sis?"

"Where are we?" she asks him. "I thought we were on the beach!"

"Sis, did you take something and not tell me?"

Margaux looks at us with wide eyes. "Who are these people? Why are we here? That boy told me this was a dream, but I think he was lying—"

Darren wraps a comforting arm around her. "How about you come lie down inside for a bit? Maybe chill out a little?"

Mum looks at me hard. "Is everything really all right, Luke?"

"Fine," I say. "It's OK. We just saw Bea in the woods. She kept running off. Darren said he'd gone to get you and talk with you. We didn't realize how long we'd been gone out there."

"We're very sorry, Persephone," Elza says. "I don't know what we were thinking."

Mum's face softens a little. "That's all right, Elza," she says. "I'm glad you got hold of Beatrice. How she escaped and got up here . . ."

"Dogs have very good homing instincts," Elza says.

"This isn't her home," I say. Elza shoots me a *stop undermining our excuses* look.

"Well," Mum says, scooping Bea up into her arms, "I'm

glad you're all safe, at least. But we all missed midnight, Luke! We've missed New Year's!"

"Well, we're here now," I say. Darren's taken Margaux indoors, and it's just me and Mum and Elza out by the bonfire. "Happy New Year."

"Do you want a drink of something, love?" Mum asks.

"Yeah," I say.

Elza closes her eyes, breathes in deeply.

"I'd like a very large drink, please," she says.

Mum brings out a bottle of champagne and pours it into some tea mugs. "We forgot the glasses," she explains, holding a mug out. "I hope this is all right."

I take a sip. It fizzes on my tongue. What'll happen tomorrow, I don't know. Will anyone in Dunbarrow remember what happened? How will they explain the blizzard that covered one town in the northeast at the exact moment the new year arrived? What's Mum going to say when she finds our window broken and the living room covered in blood? I have no idea. But somehow, after everything else we've just been through, they seem like manageable problems. The gateway is closed, and Deadside has faded away. Berkley's gone, finished, crushed in my hand until there was nothing left. The Barrenwhite Tree is banished, back to whatever void it haunts, outside the world. I'm still here, and so are the people I care about.

Elza slips her arm around my waist. She balances up on tiptoes and kisses me, and her lips fizz with champagne. The kiss tastes of victory. Stars burn in the blackness overhead, constellations, galaxies, secret alphabets.

I wake up on Darren's floor, winter sunlight falling in a razor-thin line through a gap in the curtains. Morning, January first. Bea grumbles in her sleep beside me. I sit up. Elza's on the sofa, wrapped in a sleeping bag.

After what feels like three days' worth of fog and darkness, I'm desperate to see the sun. I get up as quietly as I can and head around the side of the cottage, back to the bonfire, and find Darren and Mum sitting out there, wrapped up warm against the winter cold.

"Sleep all right?" Darren asks me as I approach.

"Yeah," I say. "My neck's a bit stiff."

He prods at the ashes with a stick. There's more heat in the remains of the fire than I first thought; I can see red embers among the white ash.

"Well," Darren says, "I'll go and see about the house."

He gets up, brushing his hands off, and walks away around the side of his cottage. I sit down next to Mum.

"He's worried about his sister," she says. "She was awfully strange last night. Did she say anything to you and Elza? That she might've . . . taken anything?"

"Not at all."

"Well, I think he's going to drive her over to Brackford today."

"Are you OK?" I ask her.

"A bit headachy," she says.

"Not like—"

"No." She smiles thinly. "Not like they used to be. Don't worry. No fireflies or flashes. I just drank too much."

"I'm really sorry about last night," I say.

"I'm sorry, too," she replies. "I got too worked up, love. I'm sorry."

"I shouldn't have said what I did. About Dad."

"It's OK, Luke. If you feel angry with him—"

"I do," I say. Then I remember him slashing the necks of the deer, letting me and Elza escape. I remember cutting into his throat with the sword, remember his warped body dissolving into fog. "But he did love us."

"He was a difficult person," Mum says. "I do wish you'd known him better. I really thought there'd be time when you were older. I know it might make you upset to see me with someone else," she continues. "But I have to have my own life."

"Darren's all right," I say. "We just have to get used to each other."

The last thing that happens is this: I'm sitting with Sunday-morning hair, wearing inside-out pajamas, reading a letter printed in ordinary black ink on white office paper. The letterhead reads UNIVERSITY OF CAULDGRAVE, and they've sent a short message congratulating me on my conditional offer to study physics. Outside, in the backyard, Bea whimpers and bats at the door. I finish my cereal and then walk over to the back door to let her in. She trots past me, alert and businesslike, shooting me an annoyed look, as if to say, *What took you so long?* I look through the open door at the backyard, our stone wall, sheep fields beyond that, spring apple trees with white blossom starting to show. A pale blue sky, striped with long, crumbly clouds. Dunbarrow, just as it always was.

My name is Luke Manchett, and I'm eighteen years old. It's been fifteen months since the mess on New Year's

Eve with the Barrenwhite Tree, more than two years since I first met Mr. Berkley and signed for Dad's Host. The Book of Eight and my sigil are long gone, and I've done my best to concentrate on school, friends, Elza. The things I'm supposed to be thinking about.

The Tree left, and the snow melted, and quite soon there was almost nothing to show it had happened at all. Nobody remembered anything, except for the six of us who lived through that whole night. The local newspaper reported on the shocking amount of vandalism during New Year's celebrations, and people wrote letters to the editor to say it was proof we should bring back hanging, but nobody was ever charged for anything, and in the end the shop windows were repaired and everyone basically decided to forget about it. Mum replaced our broken window and got a new sofa, one without bloodstains all over it. The Devil's Footsteps never had enough visitors for it to be widely realized that they've changed.

I hear Mum on the stairs, and before I really know what I'm doing, I rush across the kitchen and hide the university letter in my pocket. Of course I should tell her. It should be the first thing out of my mouth: *They offered me a place.* But I don't say it. Instead I stand examining my orange juice as she comes in, dressed in the poncho-type thing she wears every morning, and starts clattering around, looking for eggs.

"Morning," I say to Mum, as though nothing unusual were happening.

"Morning, love," she says, half turning around, giving me a sleepy grin.

"All right, mate?" Darren says, coming in with Bea trotting behind him.

"All right, Darren," I say. He proposed a few months ago now; the wedding's in the summer. They're having a multi-faith celebration of their bond in a mountain retreat. Elza says she'll help me pick out a flower headdress to wear.

Mum cracks an egg on the side of the pan. Darren loops his arm around her waist and she smiles.

"I think it looks like a pink day," she says, gazing out at the sky. "Don't you think?"

"Absolutely," I say.

My phone buzzes on the table.

It's a message from Elza: OXFORD WANTS SOME OF THIS! FULL SCHOLARSHIP :)

"Oh, wow," I say. "She got in."

"Who did?" Darren asks.

"Elza," I say. "She got an offer for English at Oxford. She got that . . . the Herbert West Scholarship."

"Oh, Luke," Mum says, beaming, "that's fantastic! I know she deserves it."

Another message: I'M COMING OVER.

"You heard anything yet?" Darren asks me.

"No," I say, "still waiting."

"Well," he says, "I never went to university and I did all right for myself. Don't worry about it."

"You live in the woods, mate," I say. Darren bursts into laughter. One thing I've come to learn is he actually has a pretty good sense of humor about himself.

"I'm sure he'll hear from them any day now," Mum says.

"Look," I say, giving Bea's head a scratch, "Elza's driving over. I'll see you both later."

"OK," Mum says, smiling. "Do good things today. You're a special person."

Elza's car is black, of course, and reminds me of a frightened horse, jolting and bolting whenever she tries to slow down or start it up. Still, she adores it, which is what matters, I suppose. We leave Dunbarrow behind us and drive through high moorland roads and then down to the coast. I can see the ocean shining in the sunlight as we crest a hill, crinkled with tiny waves, like a sheet of aluminum foil pressed flat.

"So you didn't tell them?" she asks me again.

"Not yet."

"Honestly, Luke. You and keeping your secrets. Why would you not want them to know about it?"

"I'm not sure. I suppose I feel like if I show them, that'll be it."

"What'll be it, Luke?"

"Then . . . I don't know. Then I'll be normal again. I'll head off to university. We graduate. Get a job."

"That's usually what people do."

"And then that's it. Forever."

"You make it sound like a death sentence. You can do something else if you want. I know Darren and Persephone will be happy with whatever you decide to do."

"It made me feel really weird."

"The letter did?"

"Why are we pretending like this?"

"Luke, I really don't know what you're talking about."

"We've just been . . . I don't know. Acting like nothing ever happened. Like there isn't another world. Like we didn't speak to spirits that've been around since before the earth was created."

"What's your point?" Elza asks.

"Don't you think there's something better we could be doing? Like, more important?"

Elza squints into the sun at the road ahead. We're nearly at the beach now.

"What do you mean? Charity work? Religion? Politics?"

"Not exactly."

We stop the car and get out. The wind is colder here, coming in off the ocean. We make our way across the spine of the dunes, ocean glittering on our left, marshland and then fields on our right. Seabirds circle in the clear sky. Ahead of us is a grassy crag that stands tall above the rest of the coastline, the foundations for an ancient castle, broken open and empty, nothing but low, mossy walls and the blunted remains of a tower.

"So are you actually going to congratulate me on my Oxford admission?" Elza asks me as we walk. "They're pretty difficult to come by. Or so I've heard."

"Yeah! Of course. Well done. It's amazing. Were your parents pleased?"

"Dad was crying. So yeah, I'd say so."

"I knew you'd get in," I say.

"Everyone says that. It didn't feel like that to me, I can tell you. Especially after that interview . . ."

"Elza," I say, "you're the smartest person I've ever met. It's no surprise."

"Aw," she says. She's actually blushing, something I never see. "Thanks."

We walk farther, and then we reach a path down to the base of the cliffs underneath the old castle, and I motion for Elza to follow me. It's not too steep, winding around the rocks until we're standing right underneath where the castle would've been. It's low tide, and the cliffs wear a skirt of dried seaweed. Cut into the rock face is a black cave, large enough to drive a car into. I stop in front of it. For a moment I feel strangely cold, like a cloud covered the sun. But the day is clear and bright.

"So what is this?" Elza asks me. "Why did you want to come out here?"

"I wanted to show you this," I say, pointing to the cave. "It's a passing place. A gateway to Deadside. Like the Devil's Footsteps were."

Elza scrapes a circle in the sand with her boot.

"All right. So it's another old gateway. We know they're all over Britain. Again, why did you bring me out here?"

"Because I've been thinking. We . . . I . . . ought to do something."

"Something about what, Luke?"

"About Deadside. It's mist and chaos and monsters trying to eat each other. No wonder so many ghosts want to stay here."

"An unfortunate truth," Elza says. "But aren't there other parts of it? I thought that's what you said."

"There are," I say. "But I've only seen them once, for a moment. When I was falling back out of the Shrouded Lake. I saw Elysium, Elza. The place the Oracle and the other pilgrims were hoping to reach one day."

"You never told me that," she says, scowling. "Why are you always—"

"I just didn't know how! I wasn't sure what I saw. It was so confused."

"So you saw Heaven," Elza says. "What does that mean? How can we change Deadside?"

"I saw it," I say. "That means I can find it again."

"How?"

"By thinking of it. That's how Deadside works, remember? If you know a place, hold it in your mind, you can come to it. But nobody knows what Elysium is like. So they can't."

"You want to go and find Heaven," Elza says. "That's what you meant when you said there was something more important you could be doing."

"Yes," I say. "I want to find it. And then I want to take other people there."

"Like who?"

"Anybody! Like Andy and Ryan and Jack, for starters. I don't want them hanging around Dunbarrow forever! I'd take anyone who wanted it. You shouldn't have to get stuck in Asphodel after you die."

Elza's still frowning. "How do you know it isn't meant to be like this? Maybe Asphodel exists for a reason. I'm not saying it's good, I'm just saying."

"I think it does. You're supposed to go through it, on your way somewhere better. But I don't know if it was ever meant to be as difficult as it is. So many souls must get lost, or eaten, or despair and become monsters themselves. I want to help people on the path. And I have . . . all this power. I changed when I went into the Lake. I know how to make things happen. I know I can help people."

"You want to be a shepherd," she says. "The good kind."

"I just think we've been given knowledge almost nobody else has. Berkley showed us things we weren't meant to see. My dad just used that knowledge to make himself more powerful, and look what happened to him. We can try and make both the worlds better."

"Why say this now?"

"Because it's such a huge idea, Elza. It's been in my mind since I met Larktongue and Bald Samson, but I couldn't put it into words. It's been growing . . . but I've been scared. It's such a big job. Deadside is so enormous. I don't think we've seen even a fraction of what's out there, beyond our world. It could take a lifetime, more, even to find Elysium, let alone work out how to take other spirits there. But I guess getting the university letter made me really think about what I'm going to do with myself, beyond our exams or whatever. The future's real. It's really happening. We can make a difference."

"You keep saying *we*," Elza remarks.

"Elza," I say. "I love you. I don't want to do this without you."

The ocean air moves Elza's hair in a wave, black fronds flapping across her face. She pulls it back with one hand, and her eyes are glistening.

"I love you, too," she says. "You know that. But this is insane. Where do we even start?"

"Here. Now."

"All right." Elza laughs. "This is where we begin. What should we do?"

"Come to the other side with me."

"What? Luke, come on. You're kidding."

"We go through the gate and come back. It's like learning to swim. We dip our toes in."

"Yeah, it's like learning to swim in a bottomless gray ocean full of hungry sharks. Deadside, Luke . . . I don't even want to think about going back there."

"It's a start," I say. "We go through and come back. If we're going to do this, we have to start somewhere."

"I didn't even think we could go through. I thought you needed a sigil."

"I've been into the Shrouded Lake and I came back. If I want to go through the gateway, I can."

She doesn't say anything.

"You'll be safe," I say. "We'll be there a few moments and come back. I just want you to see it."

"So how can I come with you?"

"Sit down. I'll show you."

We sit side by side, facing the ocean. There's a strong breeze, carrying the smell of sea salt, seaweed, a fresh briny tang. Elza crosses her legs under her body, like she's about to meditate.

"It's hard to step outside yourself at first," I say. "It gets easier. Just try and forget you're here."

I stare into the movement of the waves, shifting patterns of sunlight and shadow, relentless, ever changing. I listen to the tidal noise, like breathing, thinking about my own breath. I focus on the play of light over water and forget myself.

I'm standing beside my own body. I'm sitting on the flat stone, sand flecked on my shoes and jeans. Elza has her eyes closed, frowning. Her hair moves with the wind. She sighs loudly and opens her eyes again to find me standing there.

"Already?" she asks. "How?"

"I've done this more than you," I say. "It takes practice."

She scowls. "I don't even know what I'm supposed to be doing. Forget myself? How am I meant to do that?"

I reach out to her with my spirit hand.

"Let me help," I say. "Close your eyes again."

She does. I take hold of her hand, not her body's hand but the hand inside it, and pull her to her feet. Elza leaves her body without a sound, standing up out of herself, looking for a moment like a double-exposed image. Her body remains seated beside mine, cross-legged.

"Open your eyes," I say quietly.

She does and looks down to see herself sitting at her own feet. She jolts but doesn't scream.

"That's so weird," she says.

"I'm still not used to it," I say.

I turn around to face the passing place. The cave has been waiting for us this whole time, dark and patient. I imagine walking into it, imagine the moment when the seam between the worlds will become apparent.

"We'll only stay a few seconds?" Elza asks me.

"Yeah," I say. "This is a test flight."

"I must be insane," she says. "All right. Let's do it."

I take her cold hand in my own. The cave mouth yawns in front of us. Elysium. I won't find it today, maybe not for decades. But I know it's out there, somewhere. I know we can reach it.

We move from sunshine to shadow and pass through the gateway together.

ACKNOWLEDGMENTS

First, I'd like to thank my agent, Jenny Savill, who found a home for Luke's story, and my editors, Kate Fletcher and Jessica Tarrant, for their hard work and dedication, not just to this book but to the whole trilogy. I'd also like to say thank you to everyone else who works at my publishing houses, for their work bringing this series to you.

I'd like to thank my family and friends for their love and support, and I want to thank our deerhound, Ruby, for being the best footrest a writer could ask for.

Last but not least, I want to say thank you to everyone all across the world who bought copies of my books, reviewed them, or sent me messages about the story. Your support means a lot to me, and the trilogy would not exist without you.

LUKE'S STORY BEGINS WITH A LOUSY INHERITANCE:
HIS FATHER'S COLLECTION OF VENGEFUL SPIRITS.

EIGHT UNIQUE, POWERFUL, RESTLESS, *MUTINOUS* SPIRITS.

★ "Gripping. . . . With well-drawn characters,
some truly creepy ghouls, and entertaining banter,
this is a self-assured debut that's as funny as it is
terrifying." —*Publishers Weekly* **(starred review)**

★ "Dark and witty. . . . A well-constructed, truly
unique plot and perfect pacing combine to immediately
hook readers." —*School Library Journal* **(starred review)**

Available in hardcover, paperback, and audio and as an e-book

www.candlewick.com

LUKE THOUGHT BANISHING HIS FATHER'S HOST
WOULD BE THE END OF HIS TROUBLES.

THE NEW GIRL IN SCHOOL IS HERE TO PROVE HIM WRONG.

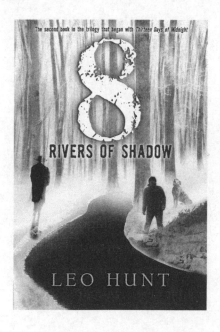

"Whopping good suspense in the netherworld." —*Kirkus Reviews*

"As dark and witty as the first work in the series, this sequel is a perfect follow-up." —*School Library Journal*

Available in hardcover and paperback and as an e-book

www.candlewick.com